DEAR TO SATURN

MERLIN SENTHIL

BONLEO BOOKS

BONLEO BOOKS™

An imprint of Senthil Studios™

La Mirada, CA

www.senthilstudios.com

First edition

ISBN: 979-8-9953290-0-8 (Paperback)

ISBN: 979-8-9953290-1-5 (Hardcover)

ISBN: 979-8-9953290-2-2 (E-book)

Library of Congress Control Number: 2026908285

Cover artwork by Sober Scorps

For Baby June.

CONTENTS

PROLOGUE

It could've been any night—with a deep blue sky sprawled out like a blanket upon the world, stars sprinkled and planets sparkling on God's canvas—but it wasn't just any night, because one star shone brighter than all the others, twinkling, even pulsating, like a heart beating, like it was speaking . . . and it grew so bright, it outshined the moon, and from this swelling light sprung forth a beam, which flew in a flash like a bullet from heaven's gun, and with godspeed, it sped toward earth—twisting and turning, swirling and swimming, and diving down, down, down—and it rolled upon the hills, then made its way to the river, where it began to run, galloping like a horse on the water's surface, bouncing along the babbling brook, making its way toward the sound of swooooooshing and clannnnking, and here, it settled—settled on a middle-aged Sri Lankan man in rags who was standing in a shallow spot of the riverbed sifting a woven basket, and his eyes lit up in the darkness as the beam lit up his hand, because lying in his palm was a rough, uncut, blue sapphire gem—and the star hit the stone like a celestial spotlight, and its facets exploded, sending blue beams in every direction, because this was the one that he chose, the one that was dear to *him* . . . dear to *Saturn*.

ONE

She was the kind of beauty that made a man's heart pound and a woman's heart sink. And she came out of nowhere. It was like a demon in denim flying in Wendy's peripherals. A blur of blue in a blink. Wendy's eyes had been narrowed in on the jaggery, which she was holding tightly—tighter now—scrutinizing it to make sure it was the right one.

Wendy needed the brand of the South Indian, caramel-tasting sugar to be the exact one her grandmother-in-law's recipe required. But when that sweet block was in her face, her eyes reading the label, and the correct label nearly confirmed, that's when *she* came whizzing by.

Kesh, Wendy's husband of three years, had been following her like a wounded puppy. He could not grocery shop to save his life. She had asked him to grab milk while she grabbed everything else, but he couldn't do it. "They don't have any. I looked everywhere," he had told her. Kesh was a great guy, a good husband, a hard worker, charming, funny, and mostly helpful—but when it came to finding things, he was completely helpless. He became blind. This is why she seldom brought him grocery shopping with her.

But this was a rare occasion.

More rare than she realized.

Hopefully . . . *very rare.*

Wendy had told him to push the cart. He was wheeling it behind her while scrolling on his phone. Some wives might loathe this. A typical husband that is a typical has-been. He *used to* be charming. He *used to* be romantic. But once the ring went on, the love ran out. *Now*, he's a leech, sucking the life right out of you, expecting everything from you while offering nothing in return. And his mistress is his phone.

Wendy's parents were the epitome of this dynamic. Exhibits A and B.

But Kesh *was* different. *Really.* He *was*. She didn't mind when he needed a mental break and went on his phone. Everybody has their flaws, and he was always trying with her. He listened to Wendy talk about her day. He watched corny rom-coms with her. He told her how beautiful she was *almost* every day. He would surprise her with picnics and flowers and weekend getaways. He would even say sorry when he was wrong. He was a good husband. He was bad at looking for things, sure . . . but he had found her, *right?* They had found each other.

That's why what happened in the baked goods aisle was very unusual.

Wendy pulled the jaggery out of view and watched a woman leap into the air and jump onto her husband. Her legs wrapped around his waist and her arms around his shoulders. It was a position Wendy did not like. *What wife would?* This was a full straddle. Like when long-lost lovers finally reunite. Or when that couple in a movie that shouldn't be together finally give into their lust for each other.

But this was *her* husband.

And . . . *who even was this woman?*

Kesh had nearly dropped his phone, admittedly looking more shocked than Wendy when he found himself catching a strange woman. Wendy couldn't blame him for catching her, but why his hands went straight to her ass—that was going to be a conversation topic for later.

The woman pulled back her face from the hug, and they studied each other while Wendy studied them. A deep study. Their faces were very close. Kesh's confusion turned to wonder and then a smile slowly grew. The woman interlocked her fingers behind his head, and Wendy, honestly, thought they were going to start making out.

But they didn't.

"Maya?" Kesh asked with a perplexed smirk.

Maya nodded with an innocent smile.

She slowly, *very* slowly slid off of him. But her arms stayed around his neck.

Wendy wanted to interrupt. She wanted to get in between them or say something. *But what would she say? What could she do?* She suddenly felt insecure, so uncomfortable in her own skin. In her own marriage. In this whole situation. *What was happening? Who was Maya and what was her problem?!*

"I'm sorry—I'm just, like, so shocked right now," Kesh said.

"I know!" replied Maya. "At first, I thought it wasn't you. But then, I was like, 'No it's totally Kesh!' Sorry for just, like, attacking you. I just—my brain processed *Kesh*, and I just couldn't help myself." Her arms dropped to her side. She smiled and touched his arm. "It's so good to see you."

Kesh rubbed his forehead, smiling shyly. It was at this moment that he must've remembered his wife—remembered that he even had a wife. His eyes jerked over to Wendy, and he tried to maintain his smile through a look of embarrassment. Wendy was worried she might burst into tears or else burst the jaggery in her hand out of pure wrath. But she kept her composure.

"This is my wife, Wendy," Kesh said finally.

Wendy now stepped into the conversation as Maya spun around —which only made things that much worse because . . .

She . . . was . . . *gorgeous.*

Literally, an Indian goddess.

Did she just step out of a Bollywood movie? A yoga billboard?

If you could make a woman from a man's mind, she was it. The perfect blend of youth and beauty. She was both the epitome of modern American female pomp yet not plain or fake in any way. Her female features were distinct and natural. She was a woman who could turn heads and touch hearts of ages present and past, in cultures near and far—a true and timeless beauty.

Her big brown eyes you could get lost in; her perfect smile was contagious; her full lips and long lashes drew you in; her skin was like butter and without blemish, and tan; and her hair was dark, long, and thick.

And while Maya would have sparkled buried in a trench coat— as it is with beautiful women—she opted for an outfit that accentuated her body and did not bury it. Her tight, high-waisted, light blue denim jeans displayed her curves. Wendy had an identical pair that she loved, but the last few times she'd put them on, for whatever reason, made her think she looked fat.

Maya did not look fat. Above her small waist and flat belly was a cropped, tight tank top, white, almost sheer, and—very visibly— without a bra underneath. Wendy fought hard to not think about how Maya had been pressed up against her husband in that outfit seconds ago.

He must've felt . . . *everything*.

"Hello," Wendy blurted out with a forced smile. She flung her hand into the air, crooked and with a jerky wave, then whipped it back to her side as quickly as she had put it up. Awkward.

"Oh," Maya turned back to Kesh, "you're married? I would not have just straddled you if I—" Maya laughed, practically falling onto him.

Wendy was trying her best to play it cool, but something was not right with this girl. The touching, the eyes, the accidental flirting—it all looked so casual and innocent but certainly was not!

"I'm Maya, by the way," replied Maya to Wendy, tilting her head and smiling, very friendly, like this *wasn't* awkward at all.

"We used to be neighbors," Kesh jumped in. "We grew up next to each other. I've told you about her, remember?"

"I haven't seen you since, what, middle school?" asked Maya.

"Yeah, probably. It's been forever."

"What are you, like, up to now? You look so good."

While Kesh stumbled through a long-winded summary of the last decade and a half of his life, Maya slid her hands along her neck, pushed her luscious locks back, then scooped them up into her hands and brought them to the crown of her head—still listening intently with her eyes ever on Kesh—and fitted a cluster of hair in one fist while she stroked strands back, tight, with the other hand. She then switched hands to repeat the motion, till plucking a hair tie from one wrist, pulling the hair through, and wrapping it all up in a high pony.

Just the way Kesh is always telling Wendy he likes it. *Seriously?*

Kesh and Maya continued to catch up while Wendy watched, occasionally chiming in when Kesh would bring her up or glance at her. But she was pretty much in her own head . . . which wasn't really a good thing.

For a while, Wendy half listened, but the rest of her brainpower went to studying Maya's every physical feature. At first, she really was in awe of such a physically flawless creature. She was merely admiring.

But was Maya really *flawless*? Nobody was.

So she began searching for flaws. Anything that would make her feel a little worse about Maya and a little better about herself—sometimes, rambling on in her mind about a found imperfection only to realize it wasn't an imperfection at all. For example, she noticed that Maya had a dimple on her right cheek and not her left. She thought about dimples for a while after that, posing the argument that they are essentially a butt-chin but on the cheek, and nobody likes butt-chins, so . . . it's basically a *butt-cheek*.

But then Wendy remembered how Kesh had dimples, and how she loved them, and how most people thought dimples were cute! —and that she had been exclusively looking at Maya's right side, and when moving two steps to the left, realized that Maya did indeed have a matching dimple on her left cheek as well.

So much for that argument.

After a while, Wendy began to feel guilty. She had gotten all worked up, objectifying and judging this stranger that she didn't even know. *Why?* While they had a very adult conversation, she was acting like a child. Even if it was all in her head, this was so unlike her! She was never the jealous type. They had a very trusting marriage. There were no fights about friendships or who was texting whom or anything like that—not since early on in their dating relationship anyway. They were loyal to each other and honest about these things.

He was a good husband, and she trusted him.

Wendy's mind kept coming back to how Maya had hopped on her husband like a hoochie, but then, she would shrug it off. Some girls are just like that: *sluts*.

Besides, to be fair, Maya didn't know they were married. You'd think she would have seen them together or noticed a ring, or maybe, just maybe, erred on the side of caution—but, to be fair, *technically* . . . she didn't know. She didn't know.

Kesh and Maya talked about jobs, family, life—and of course random stories from when they were kids that somehow Wendy had never been told. She especially didn't like the one where they and their siblings all took a bath together in elementary school.

Who was raising these kids? She knew the answer. Nannies.

Eventually, Wendy thought it'd be best to just let them catch up as old friends and trust her husband. It's what Kesh would do if he was in her situation and she knew it. Even if Maya made her feel small, she needed to be the bigger person.

"I'm just going to finish up the groceries while you two catch up," Wendy interrupted. "Still have some things to get—nice meeting you, Maya."

Wendy had decided to do the noble thing.

"You sure?" Kesh asked.

Wendy smiled and nodded. She left them. You can only stand in the same aisle of a grocery store for so long anyway. She took the cart and steered it away. The sound of the squeaking wheels eventually became louder than Kesh and Maya's conversation, and once she turned the corner, she couldn't hear them at all.

Who knows what they're talking about now?

Who knows how close Maya's standing to her husband?

Who knows if he's checking her out?

Not Wendy.

She tried to focus on the shopping—not that that was any less frustrating. Getting these ingredients was actually important, very, and she was getting distracted. Running into Maya was quite the event, but they had an even bigger one coming up, and this chain of events had become a chain around her neck, and it choked her—especially around this time of the year.

It wasn't just today, it wasn't just Maya, it was the *Muthus*.

Who were the Muthus? Well, they were Wendy's in-laws, and to her in-laws, everything she did was a crime—starting with marrying their eldest son. Why their bright and successful Indian son chose to marry a poor, mostly white girl from Michigan they could never understand. And their lack of understanding led to a lack of love—not toward Kesh, of course, just to his "feral wife," as she'd heard Kesh's grandma, Saraswathi, call her more than once.

Wendy was actually one-eighth Indian! Her great-grandfather spoke the same language as the Muthus, Tamil—which is the oldest living language today—and certainly shared many of the same roots, though Wendy never met him and wasn't the recipient of any sense of inherited culture. Sadly, it had all been lost by her grandfather who migrated to America and didn't pass down an ounce of his heritage to his children.

Kesh had seen their relationship as an opportunity for Wendy to embrace lost parts of herself, but the Muthu family didn't see things the same way. They saw a white girl and verbally argued with her about the accuracy of the fact. Like she would lie about her own heritage! But in their defense, it's not like she *felt* very Indian. If there was an ounce of minority in her somewhere, it was hiding, and she knew not where.

Wendy and Kesh did not have an arranged marriage, obviously, but, whenever the Muthus were around, they had what she called a *rearranged marriage.*

No boundaries. No rules. No autonomy.

Kesh and Wendy bent over backward and forward at their beck and call, and what that looked like was Wendy out of the picture—at the kid's table, doing chores, keeping quiet, and the like. Even three years into marriage, the Muthus were far from seeing her as part of the family. She was more like a mistress—or a pet—to them. They acted like they only heard *bark-bark* or *tweet-tweet* whenever she spoke up.

Of course, Kesh tried his best to vouch for her, to reassure her, to roll his eyes at the ridiculousness of it all. But at the end of the day, how can you really stand up to one of the most powerful Indian families in America? They were wealthy, successful, and widely respected. Ask any Indian in America—they've heard of the Muthu family. They probably came over to America because they heard their story and wanted to duplicate it!

The Muthus owned Fairest Hotels, one of the largest hotel corporations in the country. Probably worldwide. The Muthu Group had stakes in tech, business, media, real estate; they had their hands in each pot to eat from or stir at will. Every family member had their own contribution to the legacy, too.

Grandpa Ruwan transformed a few hotels into the empire it is today but passed away a while ago; Grandma Saraswathi was the CFO of a huge media corporation, which sons, Jack and Sean, now oversaw; daughter Pam and daughter-in-law Meena ran the family's philanthropic ventures; and the rest of the family—in-laws, aunts and uncles, grandchildren—all played a role in their abundant success, but words are not necessary for their importance to be known.

Even Wendy did not know much of what they all really did. All she knew was that they were important and she was just your average twenty-seven-year-old girl.

Kesh ran the Muthus' real estate affairs, which Wendy now partnered with him in. She had gotten her bachelor's in psychology only because her family was so confusingly complicated, and it had seemed interesting figuring out how and why her parents had messed her up. Definitely not worth the loans, but Kesh quickly took care of those—despite his family's advice.

Now, she was playing her part and earning her keep in the Muthu business. They were good partners, and even though her family neglected her and the Muthus micromanaged Kesh, none of their pressuring nor prying into their privacy could pull Wendy and Kesh apart—or poison the idea of family in their minds. Rather, it only furthered their thinking that maybe it was time for their family to grow. That maybe they could do a better job than their parents—and grandparents.

That maybe they were ready for a baby.

In fact, they had been trying for over a year, and it was always on Wendy's mind. Even when she had seen Maya in those high-waisted jeans, and she'd remembered how she didn't fit in her own, she'd sort of wanted to *not fit* in them. Not because she ate too many desserts or anything, but because she had a little baby growing in her. There was something cute about a little baby bump and how she'd have to wear all kinds of big, comfy, stretchy outfits for a while.

Her sister thought she was crazy. Seriously. It's not a trendy thing to get pregnant young these days. Wendy wasn't even thirty. But she and Kesh were ready, and it seemed right. Plus, she'd always been mature for her age and had older friends. Even if other twenty-seven-year-olds were clinging to their youth and hooking up with strangers, that wasn't what she wanted for herself. She could go back to school or pursue a career later if she wanted, but she'd found her man, and they had a healthy, stable life together. To them, a kid wouldn't ruin that—it was just the next chapter in their love story. And Wendy was ready to turn the page.

But she was starting to think it was never going to happen. She was losing hope with each and every false alarm. If she was a few days late, if she felt a little sick, after every time they had sex, she would think, just maybe, *this* was the time. But it never was. And she was always reminded. How could you not be? Kids were every-where. Two of her best friends—in their mid-thirties—were preg-nant. Her social media algorithm already knew what she wanted, so anytime she went online all she saw were cute babies and baby bumps. There was no escaping it.

Even the Muthus, despite their aversion to Wendy, wanted grandchildren—more grandchildren. Pam and Sean had made the Muthu family proud with their respective spouses, boasting eleven grandchildren total. But Jack's line—consisting of Kesh, Vik, and Jothi—left much to be desired. Vik was a bachelor, playboy type and Jothi was sixteen. So, Kesh and Wendy were expected to get the ball rolling.

But the ball was stuck. The ball was broken. Whatever was wrong, somehow Wendy knew it was with her. It couldn't be with Kesh and his perfect genes. It was with her, of course. She might as well believe it was her fault—that's what his whole family believed already. As if she needed to give them any more reasons to target her. Or any more weapons to target her with. Without a child, Wendy's chances of ever being accepted by the Muthus were *shot*.

Wendy had almost forgotten about Maya. Not that thinking about infertility was any better—but it kept her distracted while she grabbed the rest of the groceries and checked out.

Wendy found Kesh and Maya sitting outside the store on a bench cracking up laughing. Whatever was so funny, she didn't even want to know. They'd had their laughs, and now it was time to go—time to go far away from this homewrecker.

Maya and Kesh shared a hug. It was a long one. *Fine.*

They shared a glance afterward. It was even longer. *Weird.*

But eventually, they parted ways. *Thankfully.*

While Wendy and Kesh headed back to their car, she tried her best to mentally make peace with the situation. It was awkward, yes. No, not ideal. But it was fine. There were more important things to worry about anyway.

"Crazy running into her," Kesh said, climbing into the car.

"Yeah," Wendy replied, trying to muster up kindness. "Was it good to catch up?"

Wendy shut her door. Started the car. Backed out of the parking spot. Yes, they were one of those couples where the wife does the driving. But again, she didn't mind. Kesh had his talents, and she had hers.

"Yeah, yeah. Definitely. I haven't seen her since I was a kid, so . . . lots of memories, but we're different now, too, ya know? I barely recognized her—but she was a kid last time I saw her, so that makes sense. Anyway, yeah, it was good to catch up."

"I'm glad," Wendy said.

She started onto the street.

"Are you mad?"

"No—I said, 'I'm glad.'"

"I know, but . . . *you're not mad?*"

"No, why would I be mad?"

"I don't know why she jumped on me like that. We used to be super close. We were like siblings growing up. But that was weird."

"Yeah . . ."

"Sorry if it was uncomfortable for you."

"It's okay."

"We're okay?"

"Yeah . . ."

An *okay* silence.

"She might be the most beautiful girl I've ever seen—like in person," Wendy said.

"Really?"

"Bet you had a fat crush on her growing up."

Kesh shrugged.

"She's hot, right?"

Kesh just smiled. Shrugged again. He did not want to play this game.

"You can say she's pretty. I've, literally, never seen someone prettier," Wendy continued.

"Okay. You look in the mirror every day, don't you?"

Wendy shook her head.

"She's not prettier than you. No matter what you think. I can tell. I got an eye for that kind of thing."

"Female beauty? Every man's got an eye for that."

"But I have a special eye for it."

"Yeah, whatever."

They hit a red light.

Kesh reached out and turned her cheek toward him. Eyes on eyes. His big browns on her baby blues.

"I'm serious, baby. I'm all yours, always. I picked you—not for your brains or personality. Strictly based on looks! No one else compares!"

Wendy rolled her eyes and gave him the middle finger, but she couldn't help but smile. *The charm was working.* But that's how it always was with Kesh. He knew how to say the right things. How to set things right. How to love her. He was a good husband, and she trusted him. Besides, this flirty, hot Maya girl—it was one random, awkward encounter, and it was over. Wendy would probably never even see her again.

TWO

A deep breath.

Sometimes she would take it so deep and so long, Wendy thought she might pass out. What a relief that would be. Anything to get her out of spending time with her in-laws. But to no avail, Wendy exhaled.

"Coming?" Kesh asked.

He had already unloaded their luggage from the car. Wendy gave him a look. *Did she have a choice?* No, no, she did not. She climbed out of Kesh's BMW F-type—a car that was more expensive than the house she grew up in. One time, when she was about six, someone parked a BMW down the street. Her family spent nearly an hour guessing whose it might've been and why on earth it was there.

Wendy never forgot her mom's rant about lavish expenses. How foolish it was. How inconsiderate. How children were starving on the streets while these assholes pissed away money. Her mom and dad kept saying "BMW" and Wendy had thought they were saying BMdumbyou. So she started saying it. When her parents caught on, they got a kick out of it, so even to this day, her family says *BMdumbyou*. Kids just have a way of saying things that stick.

So, Wendy climbed out of the BMdumbyou.

Seeing the Muthus' home never got old. It was just as frightening as it was the first time Wendy saw it five years ago, just after it had been built. The previous family home was a mansion, but this place . . . It was a palace. Like an Indian king teleported his ancient residence to the future, had it redesigned with modern materials, and plopped it on the edge of the most beautiful cliff in Laguna Beach, California. No question, it was the most beautiful building Wendy had ever seen. Sure, it didn't feel like a home. It made her feel small, uncomfortable, and somehow guilty. Like every step inside this amazing manor was a step on everything she grew up knowing and loving.

But objectively, this place was *jaw-dropping*.

With two massive domes, two towers, way too many rooms, elegant balconies and patios on every floor, three stories that felt like fifteen, dozens of floral-styled archways, and beautiful gardens and sharp-shaped hedges, it was a sight to behold.

The entrance was an exposed hall, with white pillars that stretched at least forty feet high, and, like many of the patios, woven gold designs adorned the archway. The front doors looked like a gigantic wooden egg, probably twenty feet tall. A giraffe could enter this place—a literal elephant actually had. Grandma Saraswathi's seventieth birthday was something else, or so Wendy'd heard.

Butlers were already taking their things away, including the groceries. Even though private chefs prepared all the food, Wendy wanted to do *something*. After much convincing, Saraswathi had allowed her to make one dessert. It was an Indian delicacy Wendy had been practicing all year. It was a Muthu recipe called semiya payasam—the family's favorite Indian dessert. Kesh swore Wendy's attempts at it were perfect. But Wendy was almost certain each bite would come back to bite her.

But she had to try. She was always trying.

She could just stay under the radar. Not make waves. Go unnoticed. Maybe, eventually, they would all just get used to her being there. She'd be accidentally accepted into the family. It could happen that way. Or, she could just stop caring so damn much, whether they came around or not. But as much sense as those approaches might make, they were not Wendy.

Wendy was a worrier, and Wendy was a worker. Most likely, it was because of her childhood. Certainly, it was because of her dad —Mr. Griffith himself. Scrappy, scrappy, *scrappy* was his way, and his way was with Wendy. She may be a Muthu on paper, but deep down, she was and always would be a Griffith. A gritty, grabby, gutsy Griffith. Whether she liked it or not, for better or worse.

Her dad personified the mentality of getting by by getting busy. Push, run, jump, sprint, pry, plan, press, fit, shove, squeeze, think, think, think, carry, collect, measure, count, more, harder, quicker, now! Always rushing, never resting. He had kept the roof over their heads, but the roof was low, and all she ever thought about was getting out. And though she was now out, she couldn't escape the everlasting burden of making things happen that he laid upon her.

Not being a quitter can be a good thing—

But it's very annoying.

And yet, no matter how annoyed Wendy got with herself, it never seemed to bother Kesh. Of course, he tried to calm her worries and tell her she didn't have to do this and that, but when she *did* do this and that, he told her that he loved her ambition and intentionality. That's why, even if it was only for a moment, when Kesh would slip his hand into hers, the worrying would cease—the working would stop.

The grand egg-door split in two and into the palace they went.

"Azhagiya paiyaa!" Kesh's grandmother, Saraswathi, shouted.

The Muthus surrounded them. Kesh's mother, Meena, hugged Kesh first and gave him three kisses on the cheek.

"Amma," Kesh said, squeezing her tight. "Your son has arrived."

"Why is your hair so long? Are you depressed?" Meena scrutinized his face.

"No, what? I'm—"

"Where have you been, son? Come here," said his father, Jack.

Jack was a nickname, one Saraswathi detested. His birth name was Jayakumar. He went by Jack to his American friends growing up and it stuck, so much so that when he attempted to relinquish it as an adult, he couldn't. Among his friends, in business—even by his wife, Meena—everyone called him Jack. Saraswathi alone called him Jayakumar, and no matter how she said it, it always sounded like disappointment. His siblings, Sean and Pam, were caught in the same immigrant dilemma. Jack attempted to offset this by giving his own children names that honored their heritage—and appeased Saraswathi.

Father and son exchanged hugs and kisses next.

The parents hugged and kissed Wendy too, just not as tight and not as long. When it came time to greet Saraswathi, whom they called "Paatti," meaning grandmother, Kesh bowed humbly with his palms together and said, "Vanakkam."

A young man was pouring whisky into her glass—Amrut, her favorite, a drink Saraswathi considered holy. She had become acquaintances with the master blender in India and had it imported regularly. But she set down her glass to greet her grandson. With a smile, she swiped away his bow and swallowed him up in her arms.

Her cane pressed into his back.

Hand carved in India, the wood appeared as ancient and yet undying as Saraswathi herself, and on it was fastened a gold-trimmed handle that resembled the head of a peacock, with a dagger of a beak—sharp and short—that could certainly be used in combat, golden crest feathers that had been fixed in a slicked-back manner, and sapphire eyes.

It was the most expensive stick Wendy had ever seen.

"Missed you, Paatti," Kesh said.

Saraswathi was laughing for joy, hugging Kesh and kissing all over his face.

The Muthus' affection was an adjustment for Wendy when she first joined the family, especially since her own family had an aversion to touching each other. It's almost funny how contrasting their families were. Even under the strain of the most impassioned moments, the Griffiths would hardly hug. On the other hand, despite whatever tensions might exist in the present moment, the Muthus kept on kissing each other. They could've been fresh out of a screaming match or been slapping each other an hour before— but greetings were always full and physical. Even for a hard woman like Saraswathi, she wrapped herself in mush like it was a sari when she saw her relatives—especially with her grandkids. She was a powerful, temperamental, cuddly lion. It was impossible to tell if she truly was excited to see anyone because of this.

Except when she saw Wendy.

Her disinterest was obvious with Wendy. Saraswathi gave her a light hug and a single kiss—which never actually touched her cheek. Saraswathi then practically pushed Wendy aside to pick up her whisky. Greeting her granddaughter-in-law made her so miserable, she needed a drink afterward—at least that's how Wendy interpreted the gesture.

Wendy spotted Meena, her mother-in-law, with a small smirk watching them. Saraswathi's dismissal of Wendy gave her delight. If Saraswathi was the lion, Meena was the mouse. Sure, Meena was under Saraswathi's paw, like the rest of the family, but while a mouse can't maul you, it can gnaw and sneak and squeak and torment you to death just the same. That's how Meena was.

Wendy had hoped that, having also married into the family, Meena might sympathize with her daughter-in-law, maybe show her the graces she hadn't received, but it was quite the opposite—like an employee who's bullied by his boss and chooses to work out that frustration on those below him. Bullying was passed down through the Muthus like an heirloom or a gene.

The family made their way to a pavilion in the yard where drinks and appetizers were served. An outdoor TV played Indian music videos in the background. The pillars holding the pavilion led to a gorgeous fountain. It was square, with intricately designed floral tiles. Steps climbed up each layer to the top of the fountain, where two stone peacocks caressed each other. The water shot out from between them, like a liquid umbrella, covering and coating the creatures.

It was a nice fountain.

But it cost a hundred grand.

Somewhere around that, anyway.

Wendy gave it a good once-over as they found their seats. Peacocks were everywhere. She never understood why Indians—at least the ones she knew—loved peacocks so much. Even her great-grandfather, whom she never met, was standing beside a peacock in the only photo she had of him. The Muthus had to have at least a hundred paintings or sculptures of them on the property. She had tried to do research once. Allegedly, they resembled positivity and good fortune. She wasn't so sure about the positivity, but the fortune was spot-on.

Wendy did remember reading about how a Hindu goddess had a pet peacock or some kind of special connection to one. What was funny was that the goddess had a similar name to Saraswathi, maybe even the same name. She couldn't recall exactly—but the story went that this goddess rode the peacock like a horse or bull. She liked the idea of imagining Kesh's old, stubborn grandma riding a peacock. Watching her bop around with all those colors—it was a funny image kept hidden in Wendy's mind's eye.

Sometimes, when Saraswathi was being the most infuriating, the most insulting, the most insensitive—to keep from crying or else slapping her—Wendy would bring this image to mind, and it would be just enough to calm her down.

How could you hate a grandma riding a peacock?

Once everyone had sat down, the talking started. The Muthus liked to talk. It's not that they opened up their hearts to one another or were deep conversationalists, but what came to their minds came out their mouths—with no filter in between. If they had a question, they asked it. If they had a thought, they said it.

Jack was pointing at the TV, talking to Kesh about a Tollywood star on the screen. They went back and forth about how he was the biggest Indian celebrity right now, how he was a billionaire, how Jack wanted to meet him, how they could if they wanted. Wendy had seen her fair share of Indian cinema since dating Kesh, but she did not recognize him.

When their star talk was really heating up, Saraswathi interrupted.

"If I ever get grandson, maybe he will be next big star," she said.

"You have grandsons already, Paatti," Kesh replied.

"Why are you not giving me grandchild?" She looked at Wendy now.

"We are trying," Wendy reassured.

"Jack and I were already on our second child three years into marriage," Meena added.

"You break Paatti's heart, no grandchild." Saraswathi shook her head.

"Paatti—" Kesh started.

"I say this bad. No good marriage. No blessing. Nobody listen to Paatti."

"We have doctors that can fix it," Meena added.

"Most couples our age aren't even thinking about having kids, much less trying. And it takes time—it's different for everyone," Kesh explained. "Wendy and I are open to different options, but . . . yeah."

Wendy looked at the stone peacocks, watching the water spray. She held back tears, but her eyes threatened to become like the fountain.

"No adopt. Real child," Saraswathi said.

"There's nothing wrong with adoption! My best friend was adopted," Jothi, Kesh's kid sister, argued. She had joined the family unnoticed till now. She was on her phone with a mimosa in hand.

"Where did you come from?" Kesh asked.

He got up and gave her a big bear hug, almost spilling her drink.

"Not gonna say hi to your big brother, huh?"

"Hi."

This seemed to be enough of a diversion. Meena and Jack started discussing what the chef was cooking for dinner. Saraswathi fell silent and had another whisky. Wendy wiped a tear just before it slipped out.

She needed a minute, so she snuck away while everyone kept talking. No one seemed to notice for a while. Even Kesh was too distracted, teasing his little sister and chatting with her about college and future plans. Nearly twenty minutes had passed before he realized his wife was gone.

He thought of going to find her. He knew she was upset. Probably crying in the bathroom. Maybe calling her sister. *But what more could he do?* His family was a lot. He knew that. But so did she. It was an unfortunate, unchangeable truth. She probably just needed a moment alone, and he wanted her to have what she needed.

"Like, I'm excited to meet Vik's girlfriend, that's all," Jothi said. "Just because, allegedly, she's not *just* some Instagram model. She's a *real girl*. His words, not mine."

Kesh had been thinking of his wife. He was only half listening. When he processed what his sister had said, he jumped up in surprise.

"Vik's bringing a girl home!? Wait—what?!"

"Yes, and a very promising one," Meena added.

"Really?" Kesh asked.

"She's just not another booty-call babe," Jothi said.

"She's from a South Indian family and very successful," Jack said.

"So . . . *promising*. Maybe more grandkids are soon to be in the picture, Amma." Meena gestured toward Saraswathi, but it was like she didn't hear her at all. She seemed to not hear Meena talk quite often.

"Who would've thought . . . Vik before Kesh," Jack sighed.

Kesh's head fell—his way of dealing with jabs like that—then he picked it back up and tried to ignore the comment. "But you're *okay* with him bringing a woman for Kudumba Pandigai?" Kesh prodded. "*Really?*"

"Seeeeeee." Jothi gave him a look.

"Are they serious?" Kesh scrunched his face at his sister.

"She's a good Indian girl," Saraswathi stated. She gave almost a snort.

"You softened them. The bar's set real low now," Jothi whispered to her brother.

Kesh shoved her.

"Hey!" Jothi's mimosa spilled all over the couch.

The siblings laughed it off. Saraswathi shouted for the staff to clean the mess.

Kesh was right to be surprised. His brother, Vik, had never kept a girlfriend for more than a month. And he'd never, *ever* brought a woman home. Of course, the family had seen photos, maybe glimpsed a girl in a bikini on FaceTime. But Vik was the sibling the family never took too seriously, because he never took himself too seriously. He barely worked. He definitely cheated his way through college. And he blew through money faster than he blew through women.

So, this was . . . *interesting*. Maybe his little brother was finally getting big. Maybe he'd just found the right girl. Maybe he'd seen Kesh's happy marriage and caught a wave of wisdom. Kesh liked to believe it was that. But there was no way of telling—not till they showed up and Kesh saw for himself.

But he wondered about the girl. Was she actually a stand-up woman? Was she beautiful inside as well on the outside? It takes a real woman to change a boy into a man—to change Vik into a man.

So, *who was this girl?* Kesh needed to know! But little did he know . . . he already knew her.

THREE

So, where did Wendy go?

Well, she did go to the bathroom. She did cry. She did call her sister. But then, she went to the kitchen to start on her dessert.

The head chef of the family was a nice Indian man, sixties, very smiley. He didn't speak much English, but he understood that Wendy needed the kitchen. He created space for her. He brought her the groceries she had bought. He understood enough. He also told Wendy a story. She imagined it was about killing an animal, but that was only because he was holding a large knife and a chicken breast. He told it completely in Tamil, and she didn't catch a single word. But he was laughing at himself and seemed to really enjoy the memory.

It made Wendy laugh; it was nice to laugh.

She had wished Kesh would've come and found her and made her laugh. But he was spending time with his family. They were totally out of line with their comments about getting pregnant, but he needed to catch up with them, and that was fine. She needed a break from them all—even if they hadn't even been there an hour yet—and Kesh was keeping them distracted. The more they talked to him, the less they talked to her. It was better that way.

Because Wendy needed to focus.

This was Saraswathi's recipe.

It was not going to be a recipe for disaster.

It was going to be her recipe to master.

She heated the pan and added the ghee; split the cashews and fried them till plump; roasted the semiya and added the milk; brought it to boil and put in the sago; then paused.

It was time for the jaggery.

Jaggery, jaggery, why so daggery? She had to grate it, just right. She had to boil it, just light. She had to mix it in, just slight. If she made any mistakes, just fright!

She'd practiced it a dozen times. She'd watched seven different Indian grandmothers on YouTube. Most importantly, she'd stuck to Saraswathi's exact instructions. She'd followed them more meticulously than her mother-in-law's rendition. Wendy was giving it her all. And it was seemingly coming together, even if she was falling apart at the seams.

The head chef admired her effort. She hadn't given it much thought—since her focus was singular—but she had noticed him in her peripherals observing. He even brought over other cooks to take a look. She thought she caught a smile or an appetizing grunt, but again, her attention could not be broken.

The time she spent making semiya payasam didn't quite fly by, but it did make Wendy's mind did fly away. She had been almost in a trance. Like she had been holding her breath for an hour. Like she hadn't blinked. But it was a pleasant getaway. In her distracted, focused state, she was *almost* happy.

But now, she stood over the goblets. The goblets that goaded her.

They were bronze but looked like gold, and they were filled with, basically, a milk soup. A delicious, damn-near-perfect milk soup! Thin lines of vermicelli gave the silky white pattern and texture. It was a chef's abstract art—Chef Wendy! Cashews and raisins floated like little boats in this beautiful milk bay, crescent garnishes of Wendy's labor.

The dessert *looked* delicious. It *tasted* delicious. But . . . *was it?* Wendy's taste buds were not that of her Indian in-laws. All she could do was hope for the best and know that she had given her best. She really did. A wave of relief washed over her: The desserts were done. But when that wave crashed, another arose, an overwhelming wave that seemed to never come down.

The apron she'd put on was smeared and damp. Grease had soaked through to her blouse. Boiled jaggery had dripped onto her pants. Her hair stuck to her forehead. She had sweat dripping down her back, down her arms. She didn't even want to know what her makeup looked like. Needless to say, she was going to need a shower. From one recipe to another, she was off to work again.

Wendy moved quickly. So quickly, she forgot to remove her apron. She looked like one of the kitchen staff, which may have been a boost upward in the hierarchy of humans in this house, but still. She headed out of the kitchen, down the hallway, room to room to room to room and toward the staircase when—

The entire family came marching toward her.

She thought about running past them, turning round, jumping into a closet. It all may sound dramatic, but the state of beauty and form that the Muthus expected a lady to possess perpetually was unethical. Clean, proper, stunning—those were the expectations, none of which Wendy could maintain on her best day.

And it got worse.

The family wasn't marching toward *her*.

The smiles and open arms threw her off for a moment. The looks of disgust and disappointment as Saraswathi passed her made more sense. Even Kesh's eyes looked beyond her. She turned round to discover that she was sandwiched between the Muthu family and the recently arrived Vik.

Well, not just Vik.

Vik wore a confident smile. He was a handsome man, clean-shaven, disheveled hair, a half-unbuttoned dress shirt over white pants. His arms swung open as his family charged toward him. He was ready for hugs, ready for kisses, ready for everything that comes with being the favorite child—or grandchild.

And at his side was his girlfriend.

At first, Wendy thought it was Maya. But it wasn't.

It was *another* beautiful Indian girl.

She was dressed in a sari, like Saraswathi, but it was sheer and wrapped much more tightly. For a conservative covering, it did not do well to hide the size of her waist or her breasts. She was a stunning girl, maybe the most beautiful girl Wendy had ever seen. Yes, she had thought the same thing about Maya earlier that day—but now . . . she didn't know.

Wendy may not have recognized her, but everyone else, with joyful gasps, certainly did. They all began shouting, "Rini! Rini!" like she was part of the family.

Rini didn't dry hump her husband like Maya, but she did hug him pretty tight. Kesh even picked her up in his arms. This was a miss-you hug.

How could he miss someone Wendy didn't even know?

Rini put her hands all over Kesh's face, studying him.

"Wait—this is wild! I just saw—" Kesh started.

"You're so grown up, Kesh," said Rini. "So handsome!"

Kesh's hands were on her waist now.

"You too!" Kesh replied. "This is unbelievable—"

"Let me see you!" Meena shouted, grabbing Rini and checking her out.

"I love your sari!" Jothi shouted.

"Thank you," said Rini.

"You have turned into such a beautiful woman," Meena said. "Hasn't she, Jack?"

Jack nodded his head, his eyes glued to her too.

Saraswathi smothered Vik with hugs and kisses.

"Baby, you surprise Paatti!" Saraswathi said. "Good surprise, my grandchild. Rini is good Indian girl. Very beautiful. Good family."

Vik just smiled, almost like he was about to laugh, loving the attention, loving the affirmation.

"You stay together," Saraswathi ordered.

Kesh and Vik hugged. Tight love with a tight grip.

They were brothers, foe and friend, the strongest bond and the strongest competition. Kesh and Vik were opposites yet more similar to each other than anyone else. Their love could lead to a balancing act or an act of violence. They saw the best in each other yet always wanted to best each other. Kesh publicly critiqued Vik's free-spirited, youthful lifestyle, but privately wished he had it; Vik publicly laughed at Kesh's responsibility and discipline, but he'd privately hoped he'd measure up one day.

Saraswathi gave Rini a kiss. Lips touching cheek.

This was when Wendy headed upstairs.

She thought of introducing herself, of greeting Vik and Rini. But everyone seemed to have forgotten her, standing all dirty down the hall. She snuck away easily and headed speedily for the shower.

She'd meet Rini when she was decent. Not then, not like that. She was too embarrassed to even admit it to herself—so she tried hard to not think about it—but Wendy had felt water swelling in her eyes when she saw Saraswathi kiss Rini. Maybe the shower would wash away any tears, or at least cover them up.

Wendy spent a while in the shower, somewhat cleaning her body but mostly clearing her mind. Feeling a little better but not a lot, she left the bathroom and decided to get dressed. She found Kesh chilling on the sofa. Their bedroom was like a luxury suite, containing a California king, a couple of couches, and even a small kitchenette. The room had a patio with a beautiful view over the ocean that Wendy intended to enjoy later when she needed another escape.

"All clean?" Kesh asked, looking up from his phone.

"Yep," Wendy replied.

"Semiya payasam turn out alright?"

"I think so. I really tried."

"I'm sure it's perfect. If they don't like it, they're insane, like actually crazy, and we can just write off their opinions. I'm the most sane person I know, and I've determined you are a master chef, and this is your masterpiece. Seriously. "

"Uh-huh."

"*Mmhmm.* I'm telling you. You gotta trust me."

"We'll see."

"I'll eat it all, if I can. I swear I will."

"Okay."

Wendy pulled out a few dresses from the closet and laid them out.

"I cannot believe Vik is dating Rini. It's so wild."

"Oh, yeah, I wanted to meet her, but . . ." Wendy's voice fell away.

"Yeah, you will," Kesh said. "But what are the odds, running into Maya and now Kesh is dating her sister after we haven't seen either of them in, like, fifteen years?"

Maya and Rini were sisters. Sisters. *Sisters?*

"That is wild," Wendy said, sounding very unsurprised.

Wendy should've acted surprised, since, after all, she was *very* surprised. But she played it off like she had always remembered that Maya had a little sister named Rini, that Kesh had mentioned his neighbors a handful of times, how close they were, how they were this other rich Indian family that lived next door, how Kesh had his first kiss with one of them, and how they had been heartbroken when they were broken up due to their families moving to different locations—but the truth was, Wendy had very much forgotten all of that up until then.

Maya and Rini. The sisters. The neighbor girls. The ones that got away. Wendy was still processing it all. It really wasn't a big deal. It was exciting for Vik, for Kesh, getting to reunite with their old friends. Wendy didn't really know why they made her feel so insecure, so uncomfortable. She didn't even know them.

"Makes sense why Maya was in town, though," Kesh said. "She's coming over by the way—I don't know if I mentioned that. I guess Vik invited her to get the whole gang back together. She's coming after dinner."

"Oh?" Wendy squeaked.

"Yeah . . . I don't know why she didn't mention that earlier. Guess she didn't want to ruin the surprise. I dunno."

"Yeah."

"Sorry, I know you don't know them. Probably gonna be the center of attention, but they're super nice. I guess I don't really know them anymore . . . but they seem super nice still."

"Yeah, they seem nice."

"At least there's more outsiders around—takes the pressure off us, right?"

Wendy nodded. She grabbed a dress and started slipping into it, not because she had consciously picked that one, but because she needed to do something. She couldn't just stand there—feeling awkward. She walked over to the mirror, tilted her head, and forced a smile, turned back and forth, giving herself a good scan.

Wendy had a nice figure: nice legs, nice breasts, nice face.

But was *nice* enough?

Was nice sexy?

Was nice elegant?

Was nice tan and smooth and perfect?

No, it wasn't. But did it matter? Wendy didn't want to be a model. She wanted to be a mom. A baby bump would've been nice. She couldn't look in the mirror without thinking about it. She'd take a baby over a body any day, of that she was sure.

But she wasn't so sure about this dress.

She was about to slip it off when Kesh snuck up behind her, his frontside hugging her backside, his hands crawling up her, bedroom eyes looking for a bedroom prize. He began kissing her neck.

At least Kesh wanted her. She was beautiful to him. She was enough for him. It was a nice reminder, but she wasn't in the mood. How could she be right now? There was just too much going on: the Muthus, the Indian goddesses, the dessert . . . the whole getting pregnant thing.

So she pulled away.

"Sorry," Wendy said, "just too much on my mind right now."

"I know," Kesh replied, "that's why I'm trying to take your mind off it."

"Yeah, but I can't just turn it off or disconnect my mind from my body like you can. I don't know how to compartmentalize. I've tried. It doesn't work."

"I know. It's fine. Just trying to help."

Kesh's eyes turned soft and searched for Wendy's, but she dodged the warmth of his gaze. She wanted to feel cold right now. She wanted him to see how cold she felt and not just warm her up.

"Thanks," she mumbled.

"It's gonna be fine. Don't let them get to you."

Wendy took a seat on the bed and glanced up at him. One look and she was hooked—like a fish on the rod of his heart. She couldn't stay mad, stay stubborn, when she saw his eyes on her like this. The cold just fled.

"I always get like this," she said.

"I know," Kesh replied, wrapping her in his arms. "Wish I could just take all that stress off your shoulders and put it on mine. Or throw it off a cliff. That'd be better."

"Me too."

"Gotta peacock those thoughts, baby."

"Peacock?"

"Yeah, your peacock thing. Think about Paatti on a peacock."

"I told you about that?"

"Yeah, last year."

"Ope."

Kesh laughed.

"Hey, I do it sometimes too," he said through a smile.

"You do not." Wendy was almost smiling now.

"Yeah, here and there."

Wendy shook her head.

"Peacocks."

"Peacocks."

A quiet moment.

"Sorry you didn't get any."

"I know. Now I gotta go to dinner all horny."

FOUR

Dinner was less horny and more thorny, like being caught in the weeds, if the weeds had prickers that pricked you at every point. At least that's how it felt for Wendy. She dodged four more pregnancy remarks, and although she wasn't certain, she was confident that Saraswathi had said she looked fat in her dress, even if Saraswathi had said it under her breath and in Tamil.

But dinner wasn't all bad. The food was delicious. Wine made it better. And seeing Vik and Rini together, very in love and very genuine, was a breath of fresh air in a very claustrophobic environment. Rini seemed like a good person and a good influence on her brother-in-law.

They sat at an insanely large, round, wooden table. Wendy was seated next to Rini, though their seats were three feet apart. While the family was arguing, half in Tamil and half in English, about homelessness, Rini pulled Wendy into a sidebar conversation.

"Hi, I'm Rini, by the way," she said. "We haven't officially met yet."

"I'm Wendy—Kesh's wife. Yeah, sorry, I was making dessert earlier and had to clean up."

"Oh! What'd you make?"

"Semiya payasam."

"YUM. Paatti used to make the best semiya payasam when we were kids."

"Yeah, I tried my best to follow her recipe."

"Wow. That's an honor she gave you the recipe. I can't wait to try it."

Truth was, Saraswathi didn't exactly *give* it to Wendy, not directly anyway. She had given it to Kesh and Kesh had, secretly, given it to Wendy so she could try and impress her. But Wendy figured Rini didn't need all those details.

"Thanks—" Wendy started.

"Can I just say," said Rini, leaning closer in, "you are stunning. Just such a beautiful person. I love your whole look—whole vibe."

"Oh," Wendy replied with a growing smile. "Thank you. That's so nice."

Rini leaned back into her chair. She reached out and straddled her brimming wine glass with her index and middle finger. She slid it away from her and toward Wendy.

"Do you want more wine?" she asked. "I haven't touched it. I'm not drinking right now."

Wendy glanced at her own wine glass. It was completely empty. She liked the wine. She liked how the wine made her feel. But she probably shouldn't have another.

"Okay," Wendy replied, not really wanting another but not knowing what else to say.

Wendy wondered why Rini was not drinking. Was she pregnant? If so, why make it so blatantly obvious? She could be an alcoholic working to stay sober, or maybe she promised Vik she wouldn't drink, because when she drank she went wild and that's not appropriate for her first time with the family. The possibilities were endless. But Wendy couldn't shake the thought; instead, the thought had quite shaken her. If Wendy wasn't drinking herself, there would've only ever been one reason: a baby. She had even given alcohol up for a while when she and Kesh first started trying, but eventually, after six months of disappointment, she started drinking again.

Wendy considered prodding a bit, asking Rini *why*. But she waited too long and the moment passed. Rini turned back to the conversation at large, and very much like this new mystery of Rini's abstinence, the topic of homelessness had yet to be solved.

Not long afterward, the desserts were brought out, including Wendy's heart and soul: the semiya payasam. Wendy barely touched hers; she was simply too nervous. But the responses were inching toward positive. Their mouths said little but ate much. Everyone was clearing their bowls to the bottom—everyone except Saraswathi—which was more affirmation than Wendy had been expecting.

"OH MY—" exclaimed Rini, the first one to say anything about the sweet treat. "This is SO GOOD. I can't stop eating it."

After this, Saraswathi seemed to be inspired at least to taste it. She had a few spoonfuls. No remarks. No facial cues. Nothing. But nothing *was* something.

Rini smiled at Wendy while Saraswathi took a bite.

Kesh had been right. She was nice. Maybe it would be nice to have some girls in her corner. Maybe things were finally turning a corner—

Clink-clink-clankkkkk! All eyes turned round to Saraswathi. She had been fumbling with something and apparently dropped it. Her baggy eyes widened and her pursed lips hung open slightly. Everyone thought she was having a stroke.

Was she?

No.

Her face furrowed into frustration. It was almost scary to watch it scrunch. Heads began to peer downward. Meena scooted her chair backward; everyone wanted to take a look at what fell— but Saraswathi shouted, "Nagarathey!"

Wendy had been teaching herself Tamil—with Kesh helping a little. She wasn't sure exactly what *nagarathey* meant but knew Saraswathi was telling everyone to stop. Meena was halfway toward asking a young kitchen staff girl to look under the table, but she, like everyone else around the table, obeyed.

It was a discomfited scene: everyone sitting still and silent, like dogs told to lie down or children in time-out, as they watched the seventy-eight-year-old matriarch of the family climb from her chair down to the ground, disappear beneath the table, and emit only the sound of heavy breathing as her feeble knees crawled around.

Saraswathi was on all fours on the floor, circled by the feet of her descendants. Her knees and elbows were burning; she was already sweating. The lack of light only dimmed her already weak eyes. She might not have found the ring if it weren't for a stream of light squeezing between Wendy's legs highlighting it. The ring had bounced and landed between Rini's and Wendy's feet.

Saraswathi snatched it up and returned to her seat.

While still catching her breath, Saraswathi tried to fit the ring back onto her finger. She tried, tried, tried, but it would not fit. Her fingers were swollen, and her index finger had a purple line where the ring had been choking it due to the inflammation.

"Amma?" Jack asked.

Saraswathi smacked her lips and wobbled her head the way Indians do. She tried her pinky finger next. *Too loose.*

"What's wrong?" asked Rini.

"Why don't we put it on your necklace, Amma? I can help," Meena offered.

Saraswathi mumbled in Tamil, which was hard to catch even for the Tamil-speakers at the table.

"It's her arthritis acting up. Her fingers are swollen," Meena added.

"Let's put it on the necklace," Jack agreed.

"I can help you—" Meena started.

"No—not you," Saraswathi snorted.

Kesh looked at his parents, his hands slightly in the air, almost a shrug.

"I can do it," he said. "Paatti?"

Saraswathi started picking at her necklace, fingering for the clasp.

Kesh stood up and came round the table. She didn't stop him.

"Here," he said, pulling back her long, braided hair to find the clasp. He undid it and handed it to his grandmother. She slid the ring onto the golden chain, then gave the chain back to Kesh while keeping the ring in a tight fist. Kesh locked the necklace back into place around Saraswathi's neck, and only after Kesh had given her a kiss on the cheek, a sigh and a shrug to his family, and taken back his seat across the table did she let go of the ring and let it hang free.

The ring was the most precious of all the Muthus' treasures and trinkets.

It predated their wealth and success. It had been handed down from generation to generation. It was also Saraswathi's wedding ring, and it never came off. Everyone in the family knew about the ring, admired the ring—but none were permitted to touch it. It was sacred to Saraswathi, and she had given no indication of passing it on anytime soon.

Jack and Meena were denied.
Sean and his wife too.
Kesh and Wendy barely tried.
Those then left were few.
Each grandkid, each bride,
Nobody had a clue.
The recipient was mystified,
So desires only grew.
Who got it when she died?
Only Saraswathi knew—

—Wendy had written a poem about the ring while taking a poetry class with Kesh. It was, actually, really interesting. Like an object lesson everyone was always learning. The ring—even more visible on Saraswathi's neck now—was a potent reminder and emblem that all her children and grandchildren were disappointments to her. Wendy had always seen herself as unaccepted in this family, but the truth was, every member had their doubts about their own standing when it came to Saraswathi's acceptance. She hugged them, she kissed them, she provided for them, as grandmothers do, but she also never quite gave any of them the affirmation they longed for. She held them in her arms and under her thumb simultaneously; it was a warm and heavy embrace that the family had learned to live within.

Wendy wasn't very superstitious, but the family often treated the ring as a good-luck charm, like it was a holy heirloom that blessed their fortune, though they were quick to clarify that their success was *also* due to their own ruthless determination, pragmatism, and hard work. Despite this, a major deal would not be signed, a ribbon cut, or a marriage legalized without Saraswathi and her ring present. It may be that they believed these practices carried out their prayers.

The Muthus possessed many idols and worshiped many gods, but they had no one religion—not really. Even if Hinduism was the most common worldview held among the family, they were more devoted to Saraswathi than to any deity and drawn more to her ring than anything divine.

To be fair, it's natural to ascribe power to beauty. And the ring *was* beautiful. Golden branches intertwined to form the band, which came together and sprouted outward like claws, making a nest of triangular petals that circled and shined, like the points of a star or sun, and holding on display at the head, was a large, oval-cut, blue sapphire. It was as if the ocean had been swallowed up and cast into a single glass tear. Even in the darkest room, it twinkled. Even on the ugliest days, it glistened. Even for the poorest of the Muthus, before their immigration to America, before their rise to wealth and success, before the gem was cut and fastened onto a band, in the dirtiest hand that dug in the dirt, it was held dear.

Everyone inhaled and exhaled and that seemed to relieve the tension in the air—even if everyone's eyes kept bouncing on and off the ring. Saraswathi could tell, and she began covering it up with her hand like its nakedness was her own. Meena, in particular, was chewing on her lip—Wendy noticed—while she watched the ring hide behind Saraswathi's swollen fingers. It was an unsophisticated habit of Meena's that only slipped out when she was particularly upset.

Wendy had seen it before. But this time, she figured it was because of Saraswathi's rejecting her help with the ring—and she was half right. Saraswathi wouldn't let any of them get close to it, much less Meena, and maybe that was because Meena spoke most of wanting the ring. But while she frequently argued her case, deep down, Meena knew she was last on Saraswathi's list. Which was ironic because, of all members of the family, Meena most believed in the superstition of the ring.

Though she'd never told a living soul, Meena once, by accident, found herself spying on Saraswathi in the night when her kids were young, two decades ago. It was one of those instances where she had never intended on snooping in the shadows, but under cover of night, stumbled upon Saraswathi alone and proceeded to observe her out of curiosity. It's a rare and special thing to watch a person without their knowing—the job of ghosts and gods—and if you get the chance to play dead, or God, it's no easy thing to pass up.

But what Meena kept to herself was that she saw Saraswathi looking at her ring and petting it, even speaking to it. For this reason—that Saraswathi believed the ring to be special—Meena did too. But why the recollection of this memory stirred in her now and caused her to bite her lip, she did not know. It might have been a fanning of the flame of jealousy that burned within her always: that she wanted to be Saraswathi's favorite, and one day, she wanted to *be* the next Saraswathi—but Saraswathi would never let that happen.

"How about I make you more of my chai, Paatti?" Vik asked.

Saraswathi looked at her mug, now empty.

"Okay, baby. Azhagiya paiyaa," Saraswathi replied.

Vik hurried off.

He was famous in the family for his chai. Kesh had told Wendy how Vik had first made the tea at only five years old. When Meena was sick, he set himself on making her better. It was a cute and impressive gesture, which he maintained today whenever someone wasn't feeling well. Headache, flu, cramps, girl broke your heart, bad day—didn't matter. He'd make chai and that'd make it better. Wendy had tried the chai; it was good. But for the Muthus, it was more than just tasteful, it was a means of connecting with their special, favorite *azhagiya paiyaa*—or, *handsome boy.*

Vik made a few batches, so there was chai for everyone. Whether or not the tea actually relieved Saraswathi's inflammation was anybody's guess, but no guessing was needed for how it was received; the chai came with sips and sighs of relief, like it had healing power, as was to be expected. What was unexpected, however, was that, not long after dinner, Wendy began to feel sick. So sick, in fact, that she threw up.

FIVE

Throwing up is an unnatural and humbling business. Kneeling, head bowed into a toilet, performing a U-turn on a one-way street, undoing what is meant to be done—it's the human body discharging what's wrong to be alright again. Wendy had tried to fight it for a bit, to reject the growing impulse, but you cannot win a war of rejection with your own body. So Wendy headed to the bathroom and did what must be undone.

Wendy rarely threw up—rarely ever got sick. It had become a thing about her, that she didn't really *get* sick. And when she did, it was over before it ever really started. Like she'd get the sniffles or that dry itch in the back of her throat, and she'd think it was the onset of illness, but then . . . it'd just go away.

That's what Wendy had hoped was happening when she began to feel nauseous, but it seemed she was not as immune as she thought. It couldn't be food poisoning, as everyone else had had the same food, the same chai. She couldn't be pregnant; she'd just taken a test yesterday, so that seemed unlikely. This was certainly not the best time to get the flu, and it was only getting worse.

She spent about twenty minutes in the bathroom. She threw up four times. Four times! For someone who never threw up, four was a lot. Four was a lot for anyone. Her stomach was knotted, turning, queasy. Wendy did not feel good.

Knock, knock, knock. Kesh had come to check on her.

"Babe, you alright?" he asked.

She unlocked the door and let him inside.

"You throwing up?"

Wendy was sitting on the floor beside the toilet.

"Yeah—my stomach—I feel so sick."

"What kind of sick?"

"I don't know. Something I ate—I guess?"

"*Mannnnn . . .* What can I do?"

Wendy's head hung in her lap.

"Wanna go upstairs?"

Wendy nodded.

Wendy spent the rest of the night upstairs. She would throw up a total of eleven times. When she was feeling cold, she would cozy up on the bed in a blanket and with the TV on. When she was feeling warm, she would sit on the patio and stare out at the ocean. Wherever she was, she had a trash can beside her. But most of the time, she made it to the toilet. She spent a good amount of time in the bathroom.

Kesh came up to check on her periodically, but there wasn't much he could do. Wendy encouraged him to spend time with his family and not worry about her. But the truth was, she felt horrible and didn't want to be alone. She knew she couldn't blame the man for not reading her mind, and she definitely couldn't keep him cooped upstairs during the two weeks a year they spent with his family.

At exactly ten thirty-five, she felt the absolute worst. She was lying flat on her back, clutching her stomach, crying on the bathroom floor. She had nothing left in her stomach, yet her stomach was giving no signs of surrender. Should she have gone to the hospital? Maybe. Would she, knowing the embarrassment it would cause her and the inconvenience it would be for the Muthus? Not a chance.

So, at ten thirty-five, she lay on the floor, wishing she wasn't alive. Also at ten thirty-five, came a knock at the door, because Maya had arrived.

⁂

Kesh, Vik, Rini, and Jothi sat around a massive stone fire pit. It was gas-fueled but maintained rather large flames. The blocks of stones that circled the pit were two to three feet wide each. The sound of coals popping almost overcame the sound of waves crashing beyond. The siblings and friends reminisced, telling old stories; one often sparked another, so they were quickly down memory lane and into the land of nostalgia.

Jothi held her phone in her hand, but her eyes were not looking at it. Though she wasn't alive for the memories and had only met Rini as a child a few times when their parents got together, she was as involved in the conversations as anyone. It was likely due to the fact that she knew little of her brothers' upbringing before she arrived, coupled with how much Jothi admired Rini's inherent sense of fashion, style, and humor. She was everything Jothi wanted to be and more. It was safe to say that Jothi instantaneously had a friend-crush on her.

Vik and Rini divulged much about their relationship around the fire. They had rekindled a friendship messaging on Instagram about six months ago. When Rini was in town, Vik invited her to a party. They spent the entire night and into the morning talking. Just talking. They talked about life, love, about sports, family, politics, anything and everything. After an early breakfast and coffee, having not slept all night, they conked out on the couch . . . together. They shared a nap that lasted eight hours. After the nap, well, they shared other things, more parts of themselves, and that really sealed the deal, apparently. The sparks, the depth, the history—it was a no-brainer; it was the most romantic, genuine relationship Vik had ever had, and it only increased in maturity from there. Four months later, they were here, more in love than ever and bringing their families into the mix.

Kesh was happy to be mixed in. Seeing that things were serious, he was seriously happy for his little brother. He felt proud, excited, fond of their newfound relationship, and only felt a little, tiny smidgen of . . . *jealousy*.

He fought to ignore it, shove it down deep, roll his eyes at it figuratively, but there was just a twinge of resentment toward his little brother, like a pinch in his heart that hurt only when he moved a certain way—or his thoughts moved a certain way. See, Vik had lived a lustful, shallow lifestyle. He'd put himself first in everything, and it, then, only made sense that he'd be the last person to settle down like a good man. But it seemed to Kesh that Vik had gotten his cake and would now get to eat it too. He partied, wasted money, and slept with more women than Kesh could remember, and now he had to face no consequences for his actions. On the contrary, Vik only retained more of his family's affection, approval, and attention. And to top it off, now, Vik was in love with a very beautiful woman who not only was a stand-up lady but also had a background that fit his family's desires. So Vik was on course to pretty much have it all.

Meanwhile, Kesh was the one who did things honorably. He had waded through the waters of disapproval, disappointment, and criticism while maintaining a healthy relationship with the family and Wendy. He had been faithful to her and to his family simultaneously, even though it was often far from easy. Truth was, they had been through some rough patches lately. Wendy was carrying a lot of pressure and insecurity on her shoulders due to her inability to get pregnant, and their sex life had become a reminder and instigator of those feelings.

Needless to say, things were dry, dull, and rare. Very rare—besides when they were "trying." Kesh wanted to be a father. He wanted to make Wendy happy. He wanted to be patient and faithful and all the things a good husband ought to be in rough patches. But again, it wasn't easy. And seeing his little brother with, if Kesh was being honest, a stunning woman whom he was fighting hard not to compare to his wife, gave him a twinge of jealousy, of resentment. That's all.

With all these thoughts creeping into his mind and pricking his heart, Kesh was beginning to feel guilty, and he was about to pop up and check on Wendy once again as penitence. He had his hands on his knees, quite literally starting the motion of standing when Maya came into view and everyone shouted their hellos.

The patio lights backlit Maya with a white glow, highlighting her like a model strutting down a runway. She carried a shy smile, though she didn't carry herself like she was shy at all. She wore a blue two-piece outfit that was adorned with the shapes of flowers and leaves and trimmed with gold. The bottoms looked at first to be a skirt but were, as she drew closer, revealed to be wide-leg, flared pants. Her matching top was essentially a balconette bra, which didn't leave much to the imagination but also didn't keep onlookers from imagining either. She had glitter on her décolletage and on her cheeks. Her dark, wavy hair hung long and was topped off with a waterfall braid. She was a darling emerging from the darkness.

Maya, Maya, *Mayaaaaaaa.*

Kesh wanted to look away. He did after a few seconds.

Jothi now realized she had a friend-crush on two people at the same time.

"I made it," said Maya with a full and beautiful smile.

She carried in both hands a case of beer.

But it wasn't just any beer.

It was Tuborg.

Kesh, Vik, and Maya burst out laughing. Vik clapped.

"What, what—" Jothi didn't get it.

After more laughing—and during some laughing still—

"We used to sneak sips of Tuborgs," Kesh explained, "when we were kids. That was the beer Maya and Rini's parents always had in the basement fridge."

"I thought it was so nasty!" Vik shouted.

"But we thought we were *so* cool!" added Rini.

"You're awesome for bringing that." Kesh clapped approvingly.

"The reaction definitely paid off," said Maya. "So, who wants one?"

"Sure!" Kesh replied.

"Definitely," Vik agreed.

"I'm in." Rini wanted one too.

Jothi just nodded, hoping they'd let her drink with them. She drank all the time with her family, but she was only sixteen years old.

Maya took a seat on the couch between Kesh and Jothi. She unboxed the beers and handed them out—first to Kesh and Vik, then to Jothi, Rini, and herself. They all took a sip of nostalgia together.

"I can't believe you didn't mention Vik and Rini earlier," Kesh said.

"Your girl can keep a secret," replied Maya, winking at her sister. "Hey, where's your wife?"

"Oh, she's not feeling well."

"Bummer."

"I think she's just sick of us," Vik interjected. "She doesn't really vibe—"

"She's really sick. Really. Throwing up, everything," Kesh explained.

"Well, hopefully it's just a one-day thing." Maya smiled.

"Yeah."

"Jothi," said Maya, taking a good look at her, "you're so old. You're, like, a fine-ass woman. Damn."

Jothi smiled, her cheeks turning red. The crush was growing.

"Nah, nah. She's just a kid," Kesh said.

"Oh, right, right." Maya nodded, but she winked at Jothi.

The gang downed the Tuborgs and upped the conversation.

More stories.

More jokes.

More fun.

Rini had an allure and charm about her, but Maya was more intoxicating and charismatic. She seemed to make everyone else extroverted too; she brought something out of them. Or maybe that was the beer. Hard to say. Either way, soon everyone was acting like kids at a sleepover, forgetting the night and laughing like crackheads. Jothi had never laughed so hard with her brothers. It was special for her.

Around midnight, when Wendy had finally managed to fall asleep upstairs, Maya suggested they play Kaiyil Kaiyil, which was a shortened version of, *kaiyil kaiyil serkkalam*, which essentially means *hand in hand* in Tamil. It was a pool game they used to play as kids. Despite the cool of the night and the warmth by the fire, the laughter of old friends seemed to make a pool game sound very exciting. It didn't hurt that the pool was heated.

"Okay, that's warm!" said Maya, dipping her toes in.

"Alright, I'm down."

"Me too."

"Kaiyil Kaiyil!"

Everyone stood. Kesh finished his beer.

"Wait, so what's the game?" Jothi asked.

"Okay, everyone line up here."

Maya gestured toward an invisible straight line about five feet from the pool.

"Basically," she said, undoing her heels, "everyone has their eyes closed while one person," then kicking them off, "puts their hand somewhere on their body," then shimmying out of her pants, slipping them down, "and everyone has to guess where," now just in her underwear and balconette bra, "and if you get it right, you take a step forward till you get to the person to win, but if you get it wrong, you take a step back, maybe into the pool."

Maya opened her arms into a Y-shape—like that's the game: *You fall into a pool.* Jothi got the game, but . . . was she really supposed to strip down with these strangers and her brothers? It felt a bit weird. Even if she was tipsy.

"Sorry, these pants are three hundred and fifty dollars," said Maya, laying them out on the couch.

Rini also slipped out of her sari, leaving her in just her underwear and bra.

Vik flung off his shirt and unbuckled his pants.

Maya, reading Jothi's nerves, rolled her eyes and shrugged. Then she mouthed with just the subtlest voice, "It's just your brothers."

So Jothi stripped down too.

Kesh probably should've headed upstairs. The thought had crossed his mind. Wendy had crossed his mind. But . . . not for long. Maybe it was the beers. He had three. *Only three.*

But he was having trouble thinking about Wendy, thinking about anyone . . . anything . . . when Maya was standing before him, substantially undressed, smiling, shivering, sparkling. How could something so wrong feel so right, right now?

He stripped down to his boxers and fell in line.

Maya was the caller first. Everyone closed their eyes.

"Kaiyil?" she asked.

"Head."

"Head."

"Belly."

"Ear."

"It was my nose."

Everyone took a step back.

"Kaiyil?"

"Head."

"Foot."

"Belly."

"Boob."

"Not my boob, Vik. It was my foot."

Everyone but Kesh took a step back. He moved forward.

"Kaiyil?"

"Ear!"

"Rear!"

"Knee!"

"Boob!"

"KNEE! Kesh, are you cheating?! How did you get that!?"

Kesh shook his head, surprised himself.

"Did I actually get it?" he asked.

"YES!" exclaimed Maya.

"No cheating!" Vik shouted.

"I feel like we all have a major disadvantage in this game. No way is anyone gonna win," Jothi argued.

"The point is to fall in the pool, Jothi!" shouted Maya. "Okay, again. Kaiyil!"

There were five more rounds. Kesh got four of them. On the last one, he just about made it to Maya. At the same time—

SPLASH!

SPLASH!

SPLASH!

The rest fell in the pool.

"Dude!" exclaimed Maya. "You have to be cheating!"

"No, NO!" Kesh argued, opening his eyes. "I swear!"

"Well, then, you're the best damn guesser in the entire world!"

Maya put her hands on Kesh's chest and pushed him like a squat rack across the concrete. They both smiled and laughed and fell into the pool together.

The friends and siblings swam and played in the pool for a while before making their way to the nearby jacuzzi. Steam rose from the black stone tub, surrounded by rock and foliage—and, yes, more peacock statues—like it was an ancient bath, though this one was seldom bathed in and only basked in.

Kesh, Vik, Maya, and Rini slipped into the bubbling bath with sighs of relief. Jothi was on her way too, but she got distracted by her phone going off. She plucked the device up to find three missed calls and twenty-seven texts from her best friend, Eesha.

"Shit," she said, opening the texts. These messages were longgggggggggg. Paragraphs on paragraphs, littered with expletives and typos and some guy named Derek.

"I gotta go."

Jothi dashed inside with her fingers flying at her keyboard, trying to text back before the next text attack.

"Important business?" asked Rini.

"Teen drama is my guess," Vik replied.

"I wish we'd known each other in our teens."

"Me too. We'd probably be married with kids by now."

"A girl can dream."

Rini cuddled Vik, her legs over his lap and her head resting against his shoulder. She looked up at him; he looked down at her. She stuck out her tongue with a smirk; he leaned down and kissed her nose.

The excitement of the night didn't quite slow, but it did transform. From a loud festivity, the excitement adapted to quieter activities. Laughter died down and games died out, but other desires came to life. Vik and Rini began talking and whispering, just the two of them. The bubbles covered but could not conceal the touching, the rubbing, the fondling. It was about that time someone should tell them to get a room.

When Vik's hands were really getting out of hand, Rini laughed, saying, "I think we're gonna head upstairs. Getting late anyway."

"Yeah, I'm beat," Vik added.

"Mhmm," she said.

"Mhmm," he said.

The couple left Kesh and Maya alone in silence. Just the jets.

Blub-glub-lub-blub-glub.

Kesh could've said he was tired, could've said he should go, could've just gotten up . . . but he just sat there.

Blub-glub-lub-blub-glub.

He jettisoned his voice and let the jets do the talking.

Blub-glub-lub-blub-glub.

Maya spoke first.

"They were . . . getting pretty frisky," she said with half a laugh.

"True love," Kesh replied.

When he said that, there was a twinge in his heart, like the bout of jealousy earlier that day, but this time it was something of conviction, of regret, of Wendy; but at the same time—maybe it was the jet against his back, or the warmth of the water, or the warmth of Maya's gaze—but he also couldn't quite feel the twinge, not really, not much, not for long. It seemed to just vaporize.

"I'm happy for them," said Maya.

"Me too," Kesh said. "You . . . seeing anyone?"

"Nope. Honestly, it's been a while since I felt a man's touch. I'm . . . yeah."

Maya bit her lip and looked away. She shook her head with a smile. She slipped deeper into the tub.

Kesh thought he felt her foot glide up against his, but he wasn't quite sure. He didn't pull his foot away, nor did he push it forward to see if it was her. He stayed still, and the stiller he stayed, the faster his heart pounded. The potentiality of her touch touched him potently.

"Is it crazy I'm not tired, like, at all?" asked Maya.

"I'm not really tired either." Kesh finished off another beer and set it down. "Guess it's been an exciting day."

"Wanna do something crazy?"

"Like what?"

"Should we jump in the ocean?"

"Yeah? Yeah, yeah, let's—"

"It'll be SO cold. But SO fun."

"Let's do it."

"You'll go with me?"

"Yes."

Maya climbed out first, putting her body on full display.

Kesh didn't try to look away this time. His eyes lingered.

They snuck down the private steps that climbed the side of the cliff, making their way to the empty, moonlit beach. The sand was soft. The waves were loud. The Muthus had a small beach house on the shore, and Kesh entered and grabbed towels.

"I'm already cold!" shouted Maya.

She bounced and shivered with a smile.

"Ready?!"

"Yes!"

They ran and plunged into the waves.

Kesh popped up first, then Maya. She arose with her hair pulled back by the weight of the water and her beauty burst forth more than ever. There was a twinkle in her eyes from the moonlight, and it shined out of her thick, clustered eyelashes.

Kesh couldn't take his eyes off her.

He tried, and they bounced right back.

Like a magnet.

Like glue.

Like she was the thing his eyes had always been made to see.

She swam toward him as he ducked under another wave. When the wave crashed, they both emerged from the water, closer now and facing each other.

"I'm freezing!" said Maya.

She pressed up against him, allegedly to keep warm. Despite the water's grip and chill, he could only feel Maya's body touching his. Skin on skin. Her on him. She wrapped her legs and arms around him like she had earlier that day. This time soaking wet and mostly naked. She leaned in and up, putting her lips close to Kesh's ear.

"Do you want me?" she asked.

Maya pulled back, looking up at him with puppy-dog eyes and a tantalizing smile. Kesh's heart rate had been increasing, but now his heart was ready to just about explode. He held her body in his hands while she held his gaze in complete captivity. He was mesmerized by her eyes, her lips, her curves, her figure, her touch. Every inch of his body screamed to have every inch of hers. There were no thoughts of Wendy in his mind. There were no thoughts at all—his mind was mush. There was only desire.

A desire for her . . .

Mayaaaaaaaaaaaa.

Mayaaaaaaaaaaaaaaaaaaaaaa.

Mayaaaaaaaaaaaaaaaaaaaaaaaaaaaaaaaaaaaaaa.

Kesh had to have her. He needed her. Right then, right there. Or he would die. So . . . they headed toward the beach house but only made it to the beach.

And there, they made love.

SIX

It had been the worst night of Wendy's life, and she didn't even know the worst of it yet. She had somehow survived but thought she was dying. After the vomiting subsided, the pain only increased. She was experiencing convulsions, fatigue, and utter desperation. When she woke in the morning, she could barely move. Her muscles had lost their strength. Breathing was a battle. Her stomach was tormenting itself.

Her eyes crawled open. The other side of the bed was untouched. *Where was Kesh?* She needed a doctor. She needed to go to the hospital. But she couldn't even get up. It was a struggle to turn over. She tried and her body screamed.

Knock, knock. Someone was at the door. Kesh. It had to be him. She needed him. *But why would he knock?* The door opened and the knocker entered without an answer. *Kesh, Kesh, Kesh, please, oh God, please be Kesh!*—

But it was Meena.

Her mother-in-law strolled over in a fresh sari, mostly yellow and red with bits of pink, lined with jasmine flower designs; her hair was done up in a braided bun with pearl-like pins and a golden maang tikka to top it off.

Wendy felt like a zombie reaching out to Meena; all the strength she had went toward extending her arm to her mother-in-law. But Meena stared at her like it was a joke that she did not think was funny.

"No thank you," Meena said, dismissing Wendy's hand.

"Where's—Kesh?" Wendy's voice was faint. She was too weak even to care that Meena didn't. Her eyes pleaded for help, but Meena wasn't even making eye contact. She was scanning the room, the disaster of a room now, with judgmental eyes.

"You should know your own husband's whereabouts, honey. That is, in fact, why I am here—looking for him. Paatti is asking." Meena kicked a damp towel that was too close to her foot.

"I—need—Kesh—I'm sick."

"You do look pale. Paler than usual." Meena smacked her lips. "So he's not here, then? Well, he's bound to turn up. You know—Paatti does not like to be kept waiting. I'll leave you to rest—you know, Wendy, the theatrics, all the drama, it's not going to get you any sympathy here. The crybaby crap that you kids do, that may work on your parents, but it won't work here. You think Kesh can fight all your battles, and it's really embarrassing, but it's not going to win you any points with me or Jack—and certainly, certainly, not Paatti. Be a big girl, take a shower, get pretty, and pull yourself together. I don't have time to be teaching you how to be a woman. You're a wife—you ought to know already."

Meena's lecture only half registered. Before Wendy could muster up the energy for words, her mother-in-law turned and left, shutting the door behind her, and leaving Wendy, once again, alone and in pain.

Wendy could barely think. Her thoughts were whispers compared to the shouts of her hurt. That had been the first private conversation she and Meena ever shared. She'd hardly understood her words but appreciated that she was giving advice—even if it was cruel.

Wendy dragged her arm and flung it with the help of gravity toward the nightstand. It landed beside her phone. She needed her phone. She could call Kesh. Her fingers crawled to a claw and picked at the phone but couldn't quite grip it, so it slipped and shot to the floor.

Wendy cried.

Then, with whatever strength she had left, she managed to turn and roll toward the end of the bed, just close enough to the edge that gravity, once again, aided her—this time in falling straight to the floor with a *thud!*

Wendy lay still. Her phone was underneath her. There remained no strength left to move her or maneuver. This must be her end. Her death. This is how she dies: on the floor of the Muthus' home all alone. They really were a lucky bunch. Be it the ring or the peacocks, she did not know, but they had gotten what they all wished for . . .

Wendy goodbye . . .

Goodb . . .

Goo . . .

G—

GASP. A big breath. Air and life flooded her body. Like a wave washing over her, the pain subsided and shrunk, smaller and farther, till she could think again, breathe again, move again. Wendy sat up. She put the palm of her hand against her stomach, squeezing it and pressing hard. *No pain.* She shook her head like a dog. *No pain.* She breathed in deep and heavy. *No pain.*

What was happening?

Wendy's illness seemed to have left her as strangely and suddenly as it had come upon her. She climbed to her feet. Still no pain. She marched across the room to the mini fridge and plucked out two water bottles. She downed them both. Then, she headed to the bathroom and brushed her teeth. She showered, dressed, and felt refreshed, then quickly did her makeup and hair and headed downstairs.

⸎

It was nearing noon. Uncles, aunts, and cousins had arrived this morning, livening up the place and making it busy. Cooks had a brunch buffet full of Indian cuisine prepared. Wood and bronze dolls were being set up on display, as well as traditional Indian artwork. Gifts were exchanged. Candles were lit. Kudumba Pandigai had begun.

Pronounced *KOO-doom-buh Pun-DEE-guy*, the festival was not a traditional event but a modern one, which had formed over the years when the Muthus became more distant from their time in India and began merging various celebrations into one. There were evidential traces of commonly practiced festivals, such as Thiruvizha, Navratri, and Sankranti, but the life of the party was wholly its own.

Those who were out late last night had missed the morning. Jothi was the first up. Even though she had made amends with Eesha during their lengthy, laborious call last night, she later dreamt that they were trying to murder each other with butter knives. So maybe things weren't completely resolved. But after she awoke from the dream around ten, she hadn't been able to return to sleep.

She did lie there for about an hour, trying to sleep and then pivoting to her phone, but eventually, she decided to get up.

On her way to get breakfast—which had never smelled as good as it did right then—she ran into Saraswathi, who, of course, diverted her from breakfast for a task. For a family with many resources at their disposal, including butlers, maids, and kitchen staff, Jothi could never understand why her mother and grandmother were always sending her on errands and giving her work to do. It must've brought them pleasure to give her displeasure.

Saraswathi told her to find Kesh. Apparently, he wasn't in his room with Wendy. So, where was he? Maybe he was in the kitchen ... *where the food was*. It couldn't hurt to check. Jothi snatched up a few delicacies and stuffed her face while she looked for her brother. There were many relatives that gave her hugs, hellos, and smiles ... but no Kesh.

She popped in her earbuds, grabbed a mimosa, and took a walk. She went from one impressive room to another, scanning down halls and checking empty bedrooms. She tried calling him by phone, but he didn't answer. Maybe he headed into town. She checked the driveway, but his car was still there. Maybe he was outside. She walked the property. There was no sign of him.

She made her way to the pool, where they had played last night. That had been the most fun she'd ever had with her brothers. With the age gap being ten and twelve years, they hadn't really shared a childhood. Last night, it felt a bit like she had stepped into theirs and them in hers. Maya and Rini had really brought them together and brought Kesh and Vik out of themselves. Jothi had never seen Vik so stable, so serious, with such direction. On the other hand, she had never seen Kesh stay out late, let himself go, knock back beers, and just have fun.

Kesh always seemed tense, or like he was trying to hide his tension. Ever since Wendy had come around, he had become the black sheep of the family. He was always trying to appease the family or upset them. Jothi herself never judged Kesh for marrying Wendy. He should've been able to marry whoever he wanted to marry! No, Wendy wasn't Indian—well, maybe she was a sliver Indian or whatever she claimed—and she wasn't someone the family even knew before Kesh brought her around; and no, she didn't really fit in, but she was a fine person.

If Kesh was happy, Jothi didn't really see the problem. But then again, she was just a teenager. She had no voice in the matter. She knew, like the rest of her relatives, it was unwise to upset Saraswathi. It was always best to be on Paatti's side in everything. *Everybody bent the knee to Grammie.* Jothi only called Saraswathi this name in her head or to her friends outside the family. She would never allow Saraswathi to hear it.

Her grandmother was very sensitive—her whole family was. They called it "respect and values," but to Jothi, it was just another mask that covered up insecurity. Like Eesha. Like herself. The Muthus needed their formalities and rules to pretend that they had control—control of this crazy world. Jothi was honest enough to know that this insane world could not be tamed and pretending only tamed yourself. *Why not be wild and free like the world? Why not stop pretending?*

Kesh and Vik had grown up and went to college but never quite untangled themselves from their family roots. That, Jothi intended to do. She was not going to work in the family business or become financially indebted to her grandmother. She was going to escape—start her own life. She didn't have all the details worked out yet, but it was *going to happen.*

She couldn't waste her life with these uptight ants. That's what they were—ants. Little workers, like robots, falling in line according to the queen. She had a front-row seat to her parents' everlasting ass-kissing and sucking up. It was so embarrassing. It made her cringe.

Her dad, for starters, was a shell of a man. Really, he was. Some people need to get out of their shell while others are a shell of a human—what you see is what you get. Jack was the latter. Paatti had given him so much ass-whooping as a child, Jothi figured, that she'd whooped out every ounce of courage and personality.

It was sad, how bland he was.

Apparently, her dad was a spitting image of her grandfather, Ruwan, and that wasn't a good thing. Whenever Saraswathi saw Jack, she saw her dead husband. And she hated her dead husband. What's worse, Paatti and Thaatha—grandpa—both had big egos, so they were always fighting for control and would never buckle, till Thaatha had a heart attack, then Paatti came out on top. But Jack, while he looked like Thaatha, had no ambition whatsoever. Essentially, he looked like the man Saraswathi hated and lacked the one single thing she—secretly—liked about him.

Jack was double a disappointment.

Jothi's mom, Meena, on the other hand, was like a wannabe Saraswathi. She would copy her dress and speech, and maybe it would've been sweet if she was five—not fifty-five.

It wasn't cute. It was cringy.

Paatti would be trash-talking a family member and the next day so would her mom. Or, Paatti would be saying how Indians today never pray, and her mom would be out in the middle of the yard on her knees the next day for all to see. One time, not too long ago, Paatti was saying how disgusting it is that Americans just wipe and do not clean their butts after pooping, and Jothi, honestly, thought her mom was about to pull up her sari and bend over to show Saraswathi how clean her asshole was. Jothi wouldn't put it past her. She even shuffled in her seat and stood up a little, like she was about to do it.

But all this thinking about her family was only riling Jothi up and making her even more annoyed that she hadn't found Kesh yet. She hadn't seen Vik, Rini, or Maya either. She wondered what had happened after she left them last night. How much longer did they hang out? What other games did they play? *Did she miss out on anything?* And where were they all hiding?

Surveying the pool, Jothi spotted the gate cracked open near the edge of the property. She went to check it out. It sat along the cliff and opened to the stairs that led down to the beach. As she got closer, it squeaked and swayed in the wind. It seemed almost a clue for her to find. Maybe they were down there.

Jothi scanned the rocks, waves, and sand below. She didn't see anyone. But maybe they were in the beach house. She started down the steps. There were a lot of steps. She had counted them once: one hundred and fifty-six.

On step one hundred and two, though she wasn't counting this time, she spotted movement in the beach house. She hopped down a few more steps and paused. At first, Jothi wasn't sure what she was seeing. But then, even from a distance, from up above, and through a window, the image became clearer.

She saw two people having sex.

She only looked long enough to spot tan skin and carnal movements, but it looked like Vik and Rini. It *had* to be Vik and Rini. She jerked round, not wanting to see her own brother naked, and hiked back up the steps. She did not look long enough to see who it really was, nor did she look long enough to see Maya, while being kissed and caressed, spotting her right back through the window.

When Jothi reached the top, she was out of breath and ideas. *Where was Kesh hiding?* Certainly, he wasn't in the beach house if Vik and Rini were going at it! She'd looked everywhere—well, not literally everywhere, since it was a palace—but everywhere within reason. He was bound to turn up eventually.

She was still hungry. And she needed another mimosa. She did, after all, just see her brother doing the deed. She needed something to erase that memory. So, Jothi carried herself toward the cluster of relatives snacking and drinking. The glider windows had been slid open, making this an indoor, outdoor shindig now. Jothi dodged relatives with a quick smile and a quicker turn of her head, so as to not give them hopes of conversing. She was not trying to socialize right now—

"Jothi!"

They must've not taken the hint. She was hungry! No time for chatting. No time for hugs and kisses from the old mister and missus. Ugh. Whatever. Jothi turned to find out who was calling her name. It was . . .

Vik and Rini. All dressed, drinking, eating, and casually sprawled out on the patio couch. *It didn't make sense.* How did they get up here so fast? There's no way.

"Come sit with us!" said Rini.

"*Okay* . . . I gotta grab some food."

Jothi *was* going to grab food and sit with them. *She was.* But if it wasn't them in the beach house bumping bodies, who was it? Other relatives? Cousins, maybe? Strangers that had broken in? Anything was possible, but she had sworn that she saw Vik and

Rini. It looked just like them! There was a thought that fluttered like a moth in her mind, a possibility that it was Kesh and Maya, but the thought found flame and burst before she could even really think on it. It was more of an intrusive thought than a thought that could be true.

Jothi headed back to the gate. Back to the steps.

She kept reminding herself that she was not a pervert. She DID NOT want to see ANY relatives going at it. She was purely justified in needing to make sure nothing wrong was going on. That's all. She was going to check, make sure she wasn't losing her mind, and then head back fast to the feast.

Clop-clop-clop! Down the steps. Down the steps. She was headed down the—

Up the steps! Up the steps! Someone was coming up the steps!

Clip-clip-clip up, but *clop-clop-clop* down.

They were going to meet in the middle. *Who was it?*

Clip-clip-clip.

Clop-clop-clop.

Getting closer now.

Clip-clip-clip.

Clop-clop-clop.

It was a woman.

Clip-clip-clip.

Clop-clop-clop.

It was Maya.

They both slowed to a stop on the landing. Maya wore a smile. Jothi did too, but only because she felt awkward. It was an inappropriate smile that was luckily masked as appropriate because Maya was acting like nothing particularly odd was happening at all. Just normal morning smiles and normal greetings on the steps above where she and Kesh had made love. It seemed nothing was ever odd to Maya, which was its own oddity.

"Hi," said Maya, catching her breath through her smile.

"Hi."

"What're you up to?"

"Jus' going for a walk. On the beach. Too clustered up there and need a moment to vape in peace."

"Oh," nodded Maya, "fair."

"You?"

"HUNGRY. Gonna get some food. Anything good up—"

"Anyone else on the beach?"

"Oh, I don't know. I'm not sure. I was on a call. I thought, maybe, I heard someone in the beach house earlier."

"Oh, okay."

"You looking for someone?"

"No, jus' curious."

Jothi pulled out her phone. It was instinct. The Great Escape, The Wise One, The Metal Messiah. Touch it, and it will take you away; stroke it, and it will save you. She needed a distraction, a break in the awkward tension—

"Well, I'm gonna head up."

Jothi headed down. Praise be to her phone.

Jothi didn't vape anymore. She had lied. Two months ago she and Eesha had sworn to take better care of themselves, then hurled their vapes into the ocean. Maybe her old friend would wash up on the shore—the vape, not Eesha. Jothi wouldn't be complaining. This had been an overwhelming start to the day, and she could really use a hit right now.

Jothi walked casually toward the beach house, scanning the windows for any movement, but she didn't spot a thing. She knocked, but there was no answer, so she went inside. The bathroom light was on, and the shower was running.

"Hello?" Jothi asked.

"What?!" a male voice shouted from the shower.

Jothi got close to the bathroom door.

"Who's in there?"

"WHAT?!"

"WHO'S IN THERE?"

"KESH."

It was Kesh. She had found him.

Keshhhhhhhhhhhhh—the shower ran over Jothi's subsequent silence, then squeaked to a stop just as she squeaked out, "Paatti is looking for you."

Kesh opened the door, damp, dripping, and wrapped in a towel, but his sister was already long gone. She was finally free. Jothi could now eat and drink as much as she wanted, so it was unfortunate that—upon finding Kesh and Maya near the same spot where she'd seen a couple going at it—she'd had now lost her appetite.

SEVEN

While Jothi had lost her appetite, Wendy found hers. She was still ignorant of her husband's infidelity, which allowed her to eat. In fact, Wendy had never quite eaten like she did that afternoon.

It was actually embarrassing. She was sampling dish after dish, often shoving food in her mouth before she had even swallowed the previous bite. With her cheeks protruding like a grass-stuffed bunny, she washed it all down with glasses of water, eventually snatching up a pitcher so she wouldn't have to keep returning to fill her glass. She didn't even know what she was eating most of the time. But she didn't care.

She, she, she needed to eat, eat, eat. And so she did. Banana bonda—two of those, please. Uttapam—three for she. Dosa with chutney—load it up, honey. Three kinds of rice? Nice, nice, nice. Whatever it was, familiar or unfamiliar, Wendy scooped it up and shoveled it in. The amount of food she ate and the amount of time it took was uncertain, but relatives had begun to sneak looks and whisper by the time she felt any inkling of fullness.

Once her hunger pains subsided, she began to think about other things besides food again. She thought of her relatives staring at her, some smiling in a sort of pitiful way, others patting her on the back and giving her hugs, which had made her choke once and spill her pitcher of water twice. She also thought of this very strange illness that had tormented her and then disappeared so suddenly. But she mostly thought of Kesh, her handsome, honest, *missing* husband.

Where was he?

She couldn't wait to see him again. Hovering on the brink of death—or whatever brink she had hovered on—and recovering had reinvigorated her whole physical being; and not just with a desire for food but also a hunger for all fleshly desires. Escaping such a terrible nightmare must make a girl dream . . . because her mind was filled with all sorts of passion, the sort that never appeared when she was overwhelmed with the stresses, the insecurities, the pains that her life and in-laws piled on her.

But whatever had stolen away this illness had also stolen away a few other ailments with it, and for that, Wendy was beyond grateful. She felt happy. The sun was shining, and her belly was full. This feeling harkened back to an older one—because feelings can do what people cannot: time travel. The ancestor of this emotion was present in her early summers when the labor of school ended and the liberties of childhood began.

She rarely felt this way. Only sometimes. Like when it rained for a week and then the sun came out again. Like when she blasted music in the car alone right after she and Kesh decided to start trying to get pregnant. Like now, when she'd thought she was going to die—and yet, she lived.

Wendy made accidental eye contact with Saraswathi across the room. She was pouring Amrut for herself and other elders. Her aged lip quivered, flashing Wendy with a subtle smirk—maybe intentionally, maybe duper's delight. Either way, Wendy plucked up a napkin and wiped her face. It was instinctual for Wendy to feel the need to clean herself up after sharing a glance with her grandmother-in-law.

"Wendy—Wendy."

Meena had grabbed Wendy's arm just as she stuffed another ethnic delicacy into her mouth. She spun with a mouthful, chewing.

"Please slow down. You are concerning others. You took my advice earlier and cleaned up—you're welcome—now, *please*."

Wendy nodded and gulped. "Do you know where Kesh is?"

"Jothi is looking for him. The other kids are on the patio."

"Okay."

Vik and Rini were still out on the patio. Indian music permeated the place, and it was even louder outside. Rini stood and danced softly, very in sync with the girls dancing in the music video and like she knew the dance very well. All the TVs were streaming the same song, and she wasn't the only one who knew the dance, but she was the only one who managed to bend and bop in an effortless fashion without spilling her mimosa.

Rini's dancing slowed when Wendy approached.

"Hi, Wendy," said Rini. She stared and held her look.

"Hi," Wendy replied. "You guys seen Kesh?"

Vik shook his head.

"Are you . . . *okay*?" asked Rini.

"Yeah, I'm—I don't know—I feel fine now. All better."

"No kidding. That's . . . great." Rini smiled.

"Kesh said you were *really* sick," Vik added.

"Yeah, I've never been sick like that in my entire life. I thought I was dying, but this morning I just, like, healed up. I mean, I don't wanna get anyone else sick or anything, but I think it was just something I ate. I feel great now."

"Weird," Vik sighed.

"Really weird," added Rini as her lips touched her mimosa.

"So," Wendy asked again, "you haven't seen Kesh around?"

"No, not since last night," answered Rini.

"You guys have fun last night?"

"Oh, yeah. You missed out," Vik nodded.

"It was sooooo fun!" Rini perked up.

Rini and Vik weren't fully dancing anymore, but they were still partly swaying and shaking to the beat. Wendy started to move her body along with them as they spoke but felt immediately ridiculous and stopped.

"What did you guys do—"

Vik's eyes widened and his chin rose.

"There's Maya," he said. "She'll probably know where Kesh is."

"Oh?"

Wendy turned to spot Maya coming round the peacock fountain. This was the first time she had seen her since the grocery store. She still looked stunning, but Wendy wasn't going to waste any more energy analyzing her beauty. She was in a good mood and wanted to stay in it. If she could only keep cool, she could keep the mood.

As Maya pranced toward them, Wendy noticed a sphinxlike twinkle in her eye, and it seemed to be directed—through a squint —at Wendy. It could have been the sun, someone else, or nothing at all, but Wendy couldn't help but think that Maya seemed confused at her presence, like she didn't recognize her or was surprised to see her. Despite this, Wendy didn't want to continue judging a book by its cover, so she decided not to read into it. And by the time Maya had drawn nearer, the twinkle had vanished.

"Good morning," said Maya.

"Good *afternoon*," Vik replied.

"Tired?" asked Rini.

"Nah, I feel great," said Maya. "You?"

Rini shrugged; Vik just raised his glass.

"Do you know where Kesh is?" Wendy asked.

"Yeah, he was down by the beach with Jothi," said Maya. "Brother-sister time, I suppose."

"Oh, okay. That's good. I was just looking for him."

"Yeah. So, you're feeling alright, Wendy?" asked Maya.

"Mhmm. All better."

"Hmmm. I'm glad."

"Me too."

Maya's and Wendy's eyes burned into each other. For some reason, neither looked away nor said another word for an uncomfortable moment.

Then, Wendy looked away.

"Bummed you missed last night," said Maya.

"Yeah, I heard it was fun."

"It was . . . but there will be more fun today."

"More fun!" Vik downed his mimosa.

He slid behind Rini, and she began dancing on him.

Maya began dancing on her own, but then she snatched up Wendy's hand and began bouncing their shoulders and arms to the rhythm of the song, and then, stepping in close, close enough that Wendy could see the glitter sparkling on her chest, she mouthed along to the lyrics, all in Tamil, rapid like a rap, with intense eyes and theatrical expressions, like they were best friends and Wendy could understand exactly what she was saying—although she couldn't catch a word—and when the beat ramped up, Maya shimmied, dipped, twirled, with her legs, arms, and hips, performing a very choreographed, practiced Indian dance.

Her gestures encouraged Wendy to participate. Wendy tried. But Wendy did not know the dance. She barely knew how *to* dance. When she was just about done making a fool of herself and began stepping away, Maya pulled her back in, dancing more casually now, she swayed Wendy's arms, and grabbed her hips, moving them back and forth; she was both dancing on her and with her, making Wendy feel a bit more comfortable and uncomfortable simultaneously.

Maya continued mouthing words Wendy did not understand. But Wendy kept dancing with her. That is until she felt a pinch in her arm. Like she was being stung by a bee. The sting ran down her arm and into her chest, causing her to stumble backward and let go of Maya's hand.

Maya reached back out to her, but Wendy waved her away.

Something was wrong. Was it her illness? Had it returned?

Wendy made her way to the fountain and found a seat.

Maybe the peacocks could help.

Deep breaths. In and out.

The *psh-psh-psh* of the fountain seemed to lull away the sting. She focused on the sounds, focused on her breathing, and the stinging slowly subsided. That's when she got upset, which was an uncommon emotion for Wendy. It was not her disposition. Feeling sad, anxious, stressed—those were the daily diets of her amygdala. But it took a lot for her to feel *this* way. Ever since she and Kesh ran into Maya and headed for her in-laws' palace, she'd felt sad, anxious, and stressed, but now, those emotions merged into one: anger.

What the hell was wrong with her?! Did she have cancer? Was she dying? Why did pain keep coming and going? Why couldn't she just have a nice moment? Why was someone or something always stealing it away? Why did Maya and Rini seem so nice and friendly? Why did they also make her question everything about her life?

And. Where. Was. Her. HUSBAND!?

The noise of the fountain ran against the noise in her head, and it was a tight race.

Kesh was nowhere in sight. Spending time with his sister was an honorable practice—*psh-psh-psh*—one she encouraged him to do, but when his wife had been hanging on for dear life, and he knew not if she was better or dead—*psh-psh-psh*—Kesh had no excuse. His side of the bed was untouched, and apparently, wherever he crashed, when he woke—*psh-psh-psh*—he never even came back to check on her.

Wendy put her thumb against her arm and felt her way upward. *Psh-psh-psh.* There was still no more pain. She caught and released a deep breath of fresh air. *Psh-psh-psh.* The fountain seemed to win out, lulling her anger, at least to a shallow frustration, where she could think straight again. *Psh-psh-pshhhhhhhhhh.*

Wendy did not want to face any more disappointment today, and the timeline didn't really make sense, and it was very improbable, simply based on all previous evidence, but, when her anger became shallower, a thought arose: Could all this sickness, this emotional imbalance be a sign of . . . *pregnancy?*

No. Most likely not. She had avoided taking a test until now, especially when she had taken another one so recently. But . . . she had to be sure, especially when nothing else made any sense. So, she snuck away, back upstairs, to retrieve her purse and the test she always kept and replaced inside it. She went to the bathroom, peed on it, and waited.

Three minutes. She hated those three minutes. Three times the doubt, the disappointment, the denial. No, no, and no. But she white-knuckled through the waiting like she'd done dozens of times before—because she was a Griffith, because she needed an answer to this madness, because she wanted a baby.

Three minutes later, she read those same two words that were all too familiar:

NOT PREGNANT.

Wendy wept. After she cried whatever tears she had left, she cleaned herself up and headed back downstairs. She found her pitcher and finished it. Wiping a splash of water from her lips, she watched Maya and Rini dance. More cousins, aunts, and uncles had joined in. An Indian dance party.

Wendy went back to the fountain. She watched the bronze peacocks bathe and glisten under the sun and shower. She thought of how lucky, how *blessed* she was to be a Muthu, how these eye-obsessed birds were supposed to bring fortune. She was legally a Muthu, yet the family had not accepted this truth, and apparently, Fortune had not either.

Jothi came round the peacocks, peeking through the fountain's mist. She shot Wendy a flat smile and would have rushed past her if Wendy had not stepped in her path.

"Hi," Wendy said, rather upbeat and hoping it wasn't evident that she had been crying.

"Hi," Jothi replied, too distracted to notice anyway.

"Where's Kesh?"

"In the beach house—by the beach."

"Oh, okay. What's he doing?"

"Showering."

"Did you guys swim?"

"He might've. I dunno."

"Did you have a good talk?"

"Were we supposed to talk 'bout summin?"

"Oh, I don't know."

Jothi adjusted her earbud. Wendy could tell she wanted to leave the conversation, but that wasn't abnormal.

"I gotta find Paatti—"

"Okay. She's inside—"

Jothi hurried off.

Wendy thought about going down to the beach and finding Kesh, but then she sat down and stared at the peacocks. She became comfortable and decided to wait for him, since, if he were showering, it shouldn't take much longer anyway.

And she was right.

He came through the gate about ten minutes later.

Wendy tried to cloak her frustration with an elevated voice and a smile when he came round the fountain. It helped that he was looking very handsome. His hair was damp and curly, even darker from being wet. *Just how she liked it.* His loose, tan pants and short-sleeved button-up didn't hide his build but teased it instead. He was a beautiful man, and she was a lucky lady. It surprised her how much she could miss him after only one night. Since getting married, they seldom spent any nights apart. It was a real rarity. But that's because she loved him, and she always wanted to be with him.

Wendy could never really stay mad at Kesh. When she was, it always turned out to be short-lived. He would crack a joke, an apology, or just be himself and whatever feeling of frustration she had would dissipate. *Psh-psh-psh.*

This time, it wasn't her fault. It wasn't his fault either; it wasn't anybody's fault. And it didn't matter. Whether she had cancer or food poisoning or just one hell of a night—if she could just be with Kesh, she knew it would all be okay. She knew he could calm her down, tell her where he was last night, and make it all better.

He was a good husband, and she trusted him.

She just needed *him*.

"Hi," Wendy said as she hugged him. "I miss you."

He rubbed her back. Not quite a full hug.

"Hey," Kesh replied. "How you feeling?"

"Okay . . ."

Tears began to swell in her eyes. *How did she even have any left?*

"I . . . had a horrible night," she continued. "I still have weird pains. I don't know what's going on. I took a pregnancy test but . . ."

Kesh pulled Wendy out of the hug.

"No?" he asked.

Wendy shook her head and buried her face once again.

"You didn't come to bed last night?" she asked.

"We hung out super late. I had a few beers and fell asleep on the beach."

"Oh, did they just leave you down there?"

Kesh didn't answer, so Wendy pulled herself out of the hug this time to see if she could read his face, but she could not—and she felt no warmth from his eyes. Kesh looked over to the dancers—to Maya, Rini, and Vik.

"Have you seen Jothi?" he asked, without answering her question.

"She went inside to find Paatti."

"Oh, right, she wanted me for something."

"Jothi?"

"Paatti."

"Oh."

Kesh started heading indoors and Wendy went with him. She wasn't sure he wanted her to come along, but she did anyway. Wendy slid her hand into his, and she started to feel *okay* again.

She still felt like she was missing details about last night—but did she need *all* the details? Kesh was likely only being vague to keep her from feeling like she had missed out on all the fun. He was a good husband, and she could trust him.

Kesh let go of her hand to fix the gold chain that hung around his neck, as the clasp had inched its way to the front. But he did not return his hand to Wendy's when he had finished fixing it. Instead, he used the hand to wave at Maya on the dance floor, then headed inside with Wendy following beside him.

⁂

Maya and Rini were the life of this afternoon party, hopping like two hot potatoes from relative to relative—dancing with an aunt here, joking with an uncle there—and entertaining, conversing, playing with children, teenagers, the elderly. They made the rounds, stealing looks and capturing hearts, somehow interacting with more Muthus than Wendy had in five years, and they didn't seem the least bit exhausted by it.

Vik accompanied them, proudly displaying his gorgeous girlfriend to anyone and everyone he could—along with her sister, who made him feel even more worthy of praise, like an Indian king and his desirable concubines greeting the common folk, at least that's how he liked to think about it. The relatives did not think *this* way, but they were thoroughly impressed, not only by the women's beauty but by their heritage, personal success, and effortless charisma.

Vik had been with many girls in his time, some more memorable than others, but no woman had ever made him feel the way Rini did. It was as if he had never known love until he had known her. She consumed his thoughts, his feelings, and his time. Whether he was hungry, tired, or surrounded by other beautiful women—even Maya—his heart beat for Rini alone. She was a magnet of his affection and attention, and he wanted to make her happy. Even if it wasn't something he necessarily wanted, the desire grew out of his love for her. Vik had never experienced a love like this before, where his desires changed because of his love for somebody else.

He had started paying attention to all sorts of specific things that usually he ignored. Things that never concerned him—things like her allergies and skincare routine! This is why, when they had finished chasing his little cousins around the patio and were catching their breaths, Vik pulled her aside into a private conversation.

"Babe . . ." Vik started.

"What?" asked Rini, hanging her arms around his neck. "*Babe,* what?"

Rini made a pouty face, almost matching Vik's face of concern.

"You're peeling again," Vik said.

Rini put her fingers to her cheek, where there was a bit of dried skin, reddish and peeling. Vik's fingers followed hers, but she gently pushed them away.

"Thank you. You know how my skin gets. I'll reapply my cream."

Vik nodded like he very much thought that was a good idea. He looked more concerned than most at the sight of eczema, xerosis, or whatever it was; he genuinely cared about her, even the smallest things about her.

"It's okay," reassured Rini. "Thank you."

"Of course."

"You still think I'm sexy?"

"I want you *constantly*."

"I know." Rini smiled. "I'm going to head to the room," she said, gesturing to her face, "to fix this."

"Can I come?"

"Yes."

Vik and Rini snuck away to their room. Once alone, the first thing they did was make love, and the second was to broach a conversation that they had discussed only in private and many times this week already. They talked while Rini applied a cream to the patchy areas of her face. The cream was thick, an earthy color, with specks of nature in the coating, and sealed in a glass jar—very eco-friendly, organic.

There was no label on the jar. An unknown artisan.

Vik was putting his clothes back on.

"Are you planning to ask her today?" asked Rini.

"I'm working towards it. Softening her up, laying down hints. It needs to be the right timing."

Vik sat down on the bed, looking at Rini through the mirror like he was really torn up about this. He'd never been in a serious relationship before, and trying to appease a woman was all new for him—at least outside the bedroom.

"She seems to like me," said Rini.

"Yeah, yeah! You're perfect—"

"We're perfect. For each other. I think they all see that. And you're *the favorite*."

Vik smiled at her, not disagreeing but not fully on board either.

"It's not like there's anyone else," continued Rini. "She's gotta pick somebody, and *we* make sense."

"Yeah, yeah. I'm gonna ask her. Just nervous. I don't—I don't want her to reject us and disappoint you. She's a stubborn woman. Paatti, Paatti, Paatti . . ."

"So am I, and I know what I want."

Rini sealed up her jar of cream and walked over to the bed. She seemed to be letting her guard down a bit, undressing her social persona, as most couples do when alone with their significant other—although it wasn't a drastic switch; she wasn't quite upset, only serious—and even in her seriousness, there was a layer of innocence, a coating of charm, a varnish of flirtation that made her irresistible.

Rini got down on her knees and put her hand on Vik's. She looked up at him. Her face was already looking much better.

"I wanna be a Muthu," she said softly. "I want Paatti's blessing. I wanna wear her ring and build a life with you. For our future. For our child."

"I want that more than anything," Vik agreed.

She leaned in closer and rested her head against Vik's thigh.

"So you'll ask her?"

"Yes."

He sounded confident but looked otherwise. Rini looked at her hand with her head in his lap, like she was imagining Paatti's ring on her finger, and Vik watched her in distress because he wanted to make her happy but was afraid that he couldn't.

EIGHT

Jumba-cheeka jumba-cheeka jumba-cheeka-jum. Jumba-cheeka jumba-cheeka jumba-cheeka-jum-jum. Jumba-cheeka jumba-cheeka jumba-cheeka-jum-jum. Jumba . . . cheeka . . . jumba . . . cheeka . . . jum . . . jum . . . ba . . . chee . . .

The beat of drums and lick of strings rolled through the Muthus' home, loud in some rooms and faint in others, but the palace seemed to carry a constant vibration, like the beating of a heart, pulsating in its walls, floors, pillars, and peacocks. Even when Wendy's mind was elsewhere, the slowed *jumba-cheeka* pounded in her.

Music was essential to the Muthus' way of living. It was the backdrop of conversations, meals, showers, games, and every other act humans do on the face of the earth. To them, it didn't matter if you could sing or dance—though they all could—because it was as common as eating, which they also did a lot of. Just how one man's palette may be more or less developed than another, and everyone still knows how to eat—even enjoys eating, simply because it is essential to life—this is how the Muthus saw music.

Honestly, Wendy had always appreciated this element of their culture. Music had been essential to her life as well. It was her escape from the craziness of her family, the way she processed a breakup or a bad hair day in high school, the sidekick for when life kicked her in the ass and when she needed a good ass-kicking. Different genres had different effects on her in different seasons, and over time, she came to appreciate them all. Kesh had introduced her to Bollywood music, and even before she knew any of the words, she'd liked the sound of it. Maybe it was originally because *he liked it* or because it was a part of him, but she'd liked it nonetheless.

All the singing, dancing, and music thus far was only the warm-up for tonight's event: the Bollywood Bash. It was the most dedicated time of song and dance during Kudumba Pandigai. And there were many preparations being made for it.

Decor, dress, delicacies.

Kolam, kabobs, karaoke.

Mehndi, masala, masks.

Etcetera, etcetera, etcetera—

Most of the women had busied themselves with kolam or mehndi. Many female relatives, young and old, had already begun drawing kolam in the larger rooms of the palace. Made from rice flour, powders, and flower petals, the South Indian floor art transformed the floors. Heaven was on the ground, a display of gorgeous shapes and colors.

Meanwhile, Maya, Rini, and Jothi were all decorating each other with mehndi. Using a henna paste, they tattooed artwork on each other's arms, legs, hands, necks, and faces. Beautiful floral shapes and foliage forms, thick and thin, twirled their fingers, grasped their hands, and climbed up their arms.

Maya and Rini were laughing as they did it, drinking mojitos as they did it. Wendy took note of this: Rini *was* drinking. *Unless it was a mocktail.* Maybe it was a mocktail. But if it wasn't, why was she drinking now? Maybe she wasn't pregnant. That happy thought—though Wendy felt guilty for thinking it—gave her just enough confidence to go join the women.

She was starting to get hungry again. And could've gone for a mojito. But after her binge earlier, she realized that with whatever sickness was upsetting her—especially if it was stomach-related—she should probably take it easy. So no mojitos. Mojit-*Nos*, she joked in her head.

Maya drew on Rini's cheek, while Rini drew on Jothi's hand. Maya's hands were already swallowed by artwork. It amazed Wendy how naturally talented these women were. Yes, drawing, dancing, and other gifts were all part of their culture, but how perfectly they embodied the art and tradition of their people was something she could never imagine doing. Her genes were just diverse and disconnected enough that she did not carry on any notable talent or interest in the ways of her ancestors. The fact that she was one-eighth Indian seemed to be suffocated by the seven-eighths of her that were muddled and mute.

But Wendy liked mehndi. She wanted to embrace Kesh's culture, and she often tried, despite the rolling of eyes, the raising of eyebrows, and the rude remarks. The last time she took part in mehndi was for her wedding, and she held that memory close to her heart since Saraswathi was the one who had drawn on her, making it the only memory she had where she and Saraswathi had been alone together, and the only moment where, for whatever reason, the stubborn grandmother had dealt gently with her, drawing softly and tenderly upon her skin—and even if only accidentally, had given Wendy the feeling of peace between them.

Peace. *Ah*, peace. What is peace? And why did Wendy always want it, yet never have it? She had tasted it but could never swallow it; she had glimpsed it but could not see it; she had felt it brush past her but never rest upon her. She had pieces of peace, but never peace itself. Or so she felt.

It was as if all her life she had been chasing peace, while it had been running from her. And it was faster. Whenever she slowed, she would realize that she herself was being chased. But by whom? Peace's twin brother, war. And war was faster than her too.

War wore her out. War within, war without. War with the Griffiths; war with the Muthus; war with her past; war with her future; war with Maya and Rini; war with her infertility; war with her heart, her mind, and her chasing of peace.

She felt a little war with Kesh right now. He had been disappearing on and off all day, and whenever she found him, he was still . . . absent. He was running tasks for Saraswathi, talking to relatives, hanging out with Maya and Rini, and seemed to look right over Wendy. Whenever she spoke to him, he was short with her. When she sat down next to him, he would suddenly stand up. It was like Kesh was avoiding her, and she didn't know why.

What's worse, Wendy kept noticing little things that made her uncomfortable, made her mind spin, made her feel like an insecure middle schooler. She'd already experienced more jealousy in the past two days than in the last two years of their marriage, and it was not just in her head . . . she was actually seeing things now.

Wendy was an observant person. She liked to study people. But sometimes the information you gather is incorrect. She knew that. Sometimes it's influenced by your own motives, insecurities, and mental and physical health. Sometimes being deathly ill, experiencing bizarre and inconsistent pains, or standing in the presence of two of the most beautiful women you've ever seen in your life puts thoughts in your head that may or may not be accurate. Wendy knew that she might be failing to read people and just be reading into things.

She wanted to think the best of people. She wanted to trust Maya. But she hated watching the way Maya touched Kesh whenever they spoke or laughed, and how Kesh repeatedly sat next to Maya instead of his wife, and how often she caught Kesh looking at Maya, just staring at her. Wendy's hatred was not only tied to jealousy and doubts of her husband's faithfulness, but it was also rooted in the way it made her feel about other people.

She could *feel* bitterness welling up in her heart toward Kesh, Maya, and even Rini—just like the bitterness that welled up toward all the Muthus when they belittled her or excluded her. She desperately wanted to like these people, but they were making it *so hard*. And out of everyone, Kesh was always her source of comfort, of strength, of loyalty—but he hadn't been there for her today.

He hadn't even made her laugh today.

He always made her laugh. Every day.

But she could forgive him for that. She could push aside her doubts and her observations and try her best to trust him—because he was a good husband, and he loved her, and she knew that. She believed that. She had her own baggage and problems, and she thought these were now making her judge Maya and Kesh. As far as she knew, they had done nothing wrong, nothing to intentionally cause her pain, or make her uncomfortable. They were just old friends who were excited to make new memories together. And Wendy wanted that to be true. She wanted that for them. She wanted that for Kesh. That is why she needed to keep trying to get to know Maya and Rini, why she needed to join them practicing mehndi, why she smiled and said, "All three of you look so pretty."

"Thank you, Wendy," said Rini with a flattered glance. "Coming to join us?"

"If that's okay."

"Oh, yeah," said Rini, "gotta get you dolled up too."

Maya smiled and nodded. Jothi didn't react.

"Cool," Wendy said, sitting down. "I'll just pop a squat."

Wendy immediately regretted saying *pop a squat*, and the regret was visible on her face. She had no idea where the phrase came from, and she'd never even used it before in her entire life. She wasn't sure why anyone would! She didn't know what "pop a squat" really meant. And was it *pop-a-squat* or *papa's squat*? It could be pop—thought Wendy—like popping upward, but that didn't make much sense for sitting down; on the other hand, papa's squat, like a father's squat, did not sound right either. Did men in the olden days have a particular way of squatting into a sitting position before they had recliner chairs and TVs? Wendy knew this was going to be one of those awkward moments that she remembered a decade from now with the same level of cringe. *Pop-a-damn-squat.*

"Jothi," encouraged Rini, "you wanna keep the train going?"

Jothi nodded and grabbed the materials without saying a word. Wendy got comfortable, sitting in front of Jothi while the sixteen-year-old got to work on her art. She began with a thin line on the back of Wendy's hand, just above the wrist, that curved into a perfect, simple circle, then added small bell-shaped contours that swooped down to the circle and back up to be duplicated, each trimming the circle, climbing their way around.

Jothi did this almost effortlessly, but she did not seem to behold the beauty she was creating. She was very quiet and unemotive. Wendy, however, was amazed and couldn't help but smile, both from the way the mehndi cone tickled her and how pretty the drawing was slowly becoming.

"Thank you, Jothi," Wendy said.

Jothi forced a flat smile.

"You've been so quiet today," said Maya. "You *okay?*"

"Jus' tired," Jothi lied.

"How'd your call with your friend go last night?" asked Rini.

"Fine. Eesha's jus' kinda crazy."

"Crazy friends can be fun," said Rini.

"I can be kinda crazy," added Maya with a smile.

"Yeah. *I know . . .*" Rini gave her sister a look—

But Jothi's face froze as unwanted images of Maya's craziness with Kesh flashed in her mind from earlier that day—causing her hand to stray to the left and go off pattern, messing up the design on Wendy's hand.

"Shit, sorry."

Jothi grabbed a Q-tip, dipped it in water, and removed the stray line.

"All good," Wendy said. "It's looking really pretty. I love it."

Jothi gave another forced smile and got back to work.

"Rini," Wendy said, finding eye contact, "you and Vik seem really great together, and I'm super happy for you guys."

"*Awwww.* Thank you," replied Rini.

"How'd you guys start going out?"

Rini retold in shorter form the story of how she and Vik reconnected and fell in love. During the retelling, Vik made his way over, like he could sense he was being talked about, or maybe just because he *really* did love Rini and wanted to be with her all the time. He was almost always at her side, making this moment one of the few where she was alone with other girls. Until he showed up.

Kesh was with him, and they were drinking Tuborgs.

The girls were sitting around a large, low, glass table. There was a massive couch behind them, but they sat on the floor—well, on a rug, a very fluffy, cozy, colorful rug. The glass table was their place of operation and supplies. All of them sat in a row along the long layer of glass: Maya to Rini to Jothi to Wendy.

When the boys arrived, they took a seat on the couch. Kesh had flashed a smile toward Wendy—or maybe just the girls as a whole, as it was hard to tell—but his choice of seating on this large couch was closer to Maya. Yes, it was the closest end of the couch from where he stood, and maybe it didn't matter—but Wendy *did* take note of it.

Vik sat beside him, directly behind Rini, like a good significant other.

Wendy adjusted her posture with a slight rotation so that she could see Kesh and Vik. The girls were sitting with their sides to the boys, so it wasn't a massive effort to turn toward them. Wendy, however, was sitting furthest away and had to make the most effort to turn. She looked at her husband and waited for another smile, or for him to take notice of her, which he did not—and she took note of that too.

"What're you boys up to?" asked Maya.

"Just played pool," Kesh said.

"I won," Vik added. "This guy hit the eight ball in."

"Isn't that how you win?" Jothi asked.

"No, no—unless it's the last one. That's how you lose," Vik explained.

"I haven't played pool in, like, five years. Okay?" Kesh said.

"I'm pretty good at pool," Wendy jumped in. "Pretty sure the last time you played was with me, and I destroyed you so bad we never played again."

Kesh shrugged, not really offended or interested in Wendy's comment.

"Don't like to lose, huh?" said Maya, giving Kesh a look.

"Who likes to lose!" Kesh gave Maya a wide-eyed glare.

Vik took another sip of his beer. Wendy didn't recognize the beer, but she saw that Kesh was also having one. He drank a Tuborg Green while Vik drank a Tuborg Gold. She remembered that she'd seen Kesh earlier drinking a Tuborg as well but hadn't put much thought into it. She wondered if it was an Indian beer and if he liked it, though she'd never seen him drink one before.

She tried to fix the name—TUBORG—in her mind so that she wouldn't forget it. She had a file on her phone that she called *Kesh Care*, which was a list of random ideas and facts about Kesh. She'd picked up the trick from a marriage article she had read back when they were engaged. It was just to help her remember things about her husband that most wives would forget . . . if they didn't write them down.

Kesh was the type of guy who was easily pleased, but that didn't mean that Wendy didn't want to go above and beyond for him. He seemed to like all things equally, to have no preferences or opinions, but she knew that was only to put her interests before his. There were things he wanted, even if he didn't always vocalize them.

The Kesh Care List consisted of things like potential gifts, ways he liked to be encouraged, adventures he wanted to take, something he wanted to try in bed, how he only went rock climbing once as a kid but loved it and wanted to go again . . . and now, maybe

Tuborgs—if they were, in fact, a beer he really liked and Wendy never knew.

"What're you drinking?" Wendy asked.

"Beer."

"Indian beer?"

"Danish, I think," said Maya.

"Popular in India though," Vik added.

"Wherever—I'm glad you brought it," Kesh said to Maya.

"Mhmm." Maya smiled back.

"It's an inside joke," explained Rini. "Our parents used to always have them in the fridge, and we'd crack one open at night, and share it at, like, a sleepover when we were kids."

"We brought some," said Maya. "Do–do you wanna try one?"

"Oh, that's okay. I don't really like beer, and I'm still recovering physically from last night."

Wendy twisted herself to face her husband more directly.

"So, does it taste as good as when you were a kid?" Wendy asked Kesh.

"Better than I remember, honestly."

Wendy thought about adding Tuborgs to her list as a potential gift idea for Kesh, but she held off on it. Maybe it was because Kesh was being short with her, and she didn't want to get him any gifts right then. Or maybe it was because something in his voice, whether it was his tone or temper, came off as disingenuous. *Did he not like the beer?* He was drinking it. *Did he not like her question?* It was hard to tell.

The group continued to chat while the girls drew and the boys drank. It was mostly light-hearted banter, and Wendy tried her best to listen well and participate, even when her jokes didn't land and their jokes landed on her, but she couldn't shake the feeling of exclusion, of being the odd one out, of somehow being unwanted.

The only one who seemed to be having less fun than her was Jothi. The teenager, who frequented her phone, had it nowhere in sight; she was often very lively with her family members, wearing no filter and speaking her mind—but today, she was tight-lipped. She drew on Wendy and didn't look up. It was unusual.

After a while, Maya and Rini seemed to be finished, or at least pausing for a break. Their artworks dried as they reclined against the bottom of the couch. Maya got comfortable in between where Kesh and Vik sat; they were just above her, as she was still on the rug—and she was sitting closer to Kesh than Vik. Wendy noticed this because her shoulders were rubbing up against her husband's leg.

It wasn't the most sensual touch: a leg and a shoulder. But she disliked it all the same. It was just one of the many situations Wendy had witnessed that made her uncomfortable with Maya. Yes, the girl was beautiful—but so was Rini! And Rini didn't make her feel as bad as Maya did. Both had incited jealousy and insecurities, but Rini had been kind to Wendy, conversed with her, not touched her husband so many times. Those things make a difference!

Maya turned around, put her hand just above Kesh's knee, and looked up at him with a smile.

"Want another beer?" she asked.

Kesh nodded with a smile.

"I'll take one," Vik said.

"Me too," said Rini.

"Jothi?" asked Maya.

"I'm good."

Wendy shook her head lightly. She was good too—well, not that good: Her eyes were fixed on Maya's fingers, Maya's teal and glitter nails, still resting on her husband's thigh. This woman had no boundaries, no respect, no heart. *Right?*

Wendy didn't want to be controlling. She didn't want to be jealous. And she tried to justify and explain away a woman's hand on her husband's thigh—but the action was not right. If it was accidental, it was careless. If it was intentional, it was heinous. If it was moral in her mind, her morals were malign!

"Kesh," Wendy said, rather normal, even though she wanted to shout.

His eyes crawled their way to her.

"Hmmm?" he purred, almost inaudibly.

Wendy stared him down, her eyes shouting the words she could not say: *Do you not notice the woman's hand on your thigh? What are you doing? What is wrong with you?* This wasn't telepathy—the words were written all over her face, but Kesh wasn't reading them. He was always *so good* at reading her, at knowing what she needed and what she wanted. But right then, he didn't seem to care; he didn't seem to see.

Wendy did not say another word and Kesh's eyes drifted off her.

"Gonna grab the beers," said Maya, slipping her hand higher up Kesh's thigh and using him to climb to her feet.

"I'll come with you," Kesh said. He popped up off the couch.

"Kesh . . ." Wendy said in a stupor, "can we . . . talk for a minute?"

"Yeah, yeah, sure. Just, um," Kesh said, while his eyes drifted toward Maya as she started walking away, "wait till I get back with beers. I'll be back in a few. We can chat or whatever."

"Okay . . ."

Wendy watched him hurry off with Maya. *What was happening?!* She felt like a kid whose crush didn't like her back. BUT THIS WAS HER HUSBAND! And she had to wait to talk with him so he could . . . *what exactly?* Grab beers with Maya?!

No, no, no, no, *no.*

Maybe Wendy was losing her mind or being a crazy wife or whatever—but if Kesh was the husband she thought he was, a man who loved her and could be trusted, he would understand. He would understand that what he was doing—or not doing—was making her very uncomfortable, and he'd been neglecting her, and it was not okay.

Jothi had stopped drawing on Wendy and was watching her intently: watching her eyes hold back tears, her lips hold back curses, her mind—though invisible—spinning and spiraling. Jothi saw all these things very clearly, things Vik and Rini would have seen too if they had been looking at Wendy.

Jothi thought about confessing what she had seen earlier, but thoughts of doubt, unanswered questions, and unavoidable awkwardness flooded her mind, drowned her heart, drowned out the part of her heart that wanted to tell Wendy, and before she could decide one way or another—

Wendy sprang up! She was off to find her husband. It was time to talk.

Not when he got back. Not in a few minutes.

NOW!

NINE

The Tuborgs seemed to be hiding, as did Maya and Kesh. Wendy walked quickly to the nearest four fridges and mini fridges that she knew about, but she didn't see them anywhere. She checked the kitchen, the patio, and tried to find Maya's room—though she didn't actually know where Maya was staying. She spent twenty minutes looking for them and returned to Vik, Rini, and Jothi twice with no luck.

Unbeknownst to her, she came close to finding them once. She hurried down a hallway—at this point holding back a waterfall of tears—toward the front entrance. Maybe the drinks were in Maya's car, she thought. They had to be in the garage or outside somewhere. Wendy was running out of explanations. That *had to* be it.

On her way down the hall, she passed a closet door, which was seldom opened. It contained only an assortment of extra blankets and pillows. As Wendy rushed by, the loudness of her spiraling thoughts, her anxious heart, and her impatient footsteps veiled the sounds of Maya's moaning from inside the closet.

Wendy had been five feet from the adulterers. An arm span from the disaster of blankets and pillows that swallowed up their bodies. A stone's kick from the cascade of kisses Kesh showered over Maya's body. So very close to seeing how very far from trustworthy Kesh had proven himself.

And no surprise, the cars were another dead end. So Wendy gave up and found a seat back with the others. It was obvious that she had been crying, but no one said anything. She sat there and waited, trying to rationalize Kesh's disappearance while simultaneously considering the fact that maybe, just maybe, he was . . . *up to something.*

But what? Was he really cheating on her with Maya?

This thought had crossed her mind, but it had also cross-dissolved into a rationalization. *There was just no way.* Even after all the distance he'd put between them that day—between the vanishing acts and the acts of apathy—Kesh was still her husband. He had loved her well for five years. He was a good man and a faithful one. *She could trust him.*

So she sat with her doubt, her questions, her anger. She was going to let him have it, but she wasn't going to jump to any conclusions just yet.

Ten minutes later Kesh and Maya returned with more beers. He drank a Tuborg Green again and brought a Tuborg Gold for Vik while the others drank Tuborg classics. Kesh and Maya were very smiley, a bit disheveled, and unfazed by their half-hour absence. Like it always takes thirty minutes to grab beers. No, *no*, it does not.

Wendy stood up upon their arrival. As soon as the beers had been passed out, she climbed over the others and pulled Kesh aside.

"Can we talk?"

"Oh, you wanna . . ."

Tears were filling her eyes.

"Please—" If she spoke anymore she would start crying.

Kesh made eye contact with Maya, and she didn't quite nod, but the look she gave him was one of affirmation, like her eyes said *it's okay.* It was the kind of look a parent gives a child who is holding a piece of candy wondering if they're allowed to eat it. So Kesh was *allowed* to speak with his wife. Good.

"Yeah, yeah, okay," mumbled Kesh. "We can—we can talk."

Wendy and Kesh walked in silence to an even more silent room. Once they were alone, really alone, Wendy began to cry. Tears slipped out of both eyes and wiggled down her trembling cheeks. Kesh slowly wrapped his arms around her and hugged her. *So he wasn't a complete monster.* He rubbed her back.

"Are you mad at me?" she said, face buried in his chest.

"No, no, I'm not mad at you."

"I feel like you're ignoring me," Wendy said, pulling herself from the hug, "and you're acting weird, like not yourself," she added while wiping her own tears. "And I'm happy for you to reconnect with your friends, and I want that for you, but spending so much time with Maya, just disappearing with her . . . I feel like you are avoiding me because of it, and she's always touching you—you have to know that makes me uncomfortable, and I'm not trying to be all jealous or anything, but I don't know this woman at all—and I know you do, but it's been like a decade since you've even seen her, so you don't really know her. I mean, like, you have to see what I'm saying, right?"

Kesh nodded lightly, like he understood. *But did he?* He did not say.

"And I thought I was gonna die last night! And I feel like you don't care. I still don't even know what's wrong with me. I thought maybe I was pregnant or miscarrying or—but, but, but I don't even know."

Wendy wiped a few more tears. She caught her breath.

"I'm sorry that I, um," Kesh started, "hurt your feelings. I don't . . . wanna . . . do that."

Wendy would have continued ranting, but she remained silent because she wanted to give Kesh space to talk, to explain himself. She bit her tongue and hoped Kesh would use his . . . certainly more than he was.

"I understand, um, why you're confused, um, but it's a bit complicated of a situation, and I can't share it all right now, um, because . . . she doesn't want me to get into it."

Huh? Wendy was not following. It wasn't quite that Kesh was derailing the conversation as he'd done before that day but that his train of thought simply had no tracks to begin with.

"What does that even mean?" she probed.

"I can't really get into it . . . right now. Ummmmmm . . ."

"Who is *she?* Maya?"

"Yeah, um, but, you know, it's just not the right timing."

"Kesh. I need more context than that. Don't you see how this looks?"

"Yeah, but it's not gonna help worrying about it, ya know?"

"What? WHAT? Kesh! What is wrong with you?"

Kesh took a long sip of his beer.

"Honey, I'm trying to trust you," Wendy pleaded, "but you're making it very hard right now."

"I'm sorry."

"Can't you just set some more boundaries with her? I just—I don't even understand why there's any hesitation at all, but, look, I need you. Whatever's going on, I get some priority here. I'm your wife."

"Honestly . . . I am setting a lot of boundaries, believe me . . . even if it doesn't seem so from your vantage point."

"What is wrong with her?!"

"Nothing! Nothing is wrong with her."

"Something! Something is very wrong with—"

"Just leave it! We need to stop talking about this."

Wendy was far from being ready to leave it. If anything, she was more confused than before! She felt like she was playing some sort of social deduction game where she didn't know if she could trust the person she trusted the most, and where everything she was being told was either a lie concealed by truth or a truth concealed by a lie. But this wasn't a game. This was her life. And each mixed message only further mixed her up.

Why was Kesh playing these games?

"I'm being very reasonable here," Wendy said, "but you're hurting me, Kesh."

Kesh lifted his hands and his beer and held them there; he wasn't gonna lay a hand on her, nor was he gonna give her a hand. He just silently stood there . . . like his hands were tied.

"Kesh. *Kesh.* Kesh?" Wendy said. What more could she say?

"Wendy, Wendy, Wendy," Kesh said. What less could he say?!

Kesh slowly backed out of the room, turned his back on his wife, and left. Wendy tried to rationalize Kesh's responses and his lack thereof, but nothing he had said made any sense to her. She imagined slapping him, screaming in his face, even withholding sex for weeks—but that only made her feel guilty. Being angry wasn't going to fix anything. And she wanted to fix this.

She grabbed a drink and went up to her room. She went onto the balcony, sat, and thought. She could see the patio below, displaying various relatives—many she barely knew—mingling, dancing, chatting. She felt safe up here away from them, sort of relieved because she could watch them socialize without feeling ostracized.

Wendy turned over the vague and short phrases Kesh had said to her: *It's a bit complicated . . . Just not the right timing . . . I am setting a lot of boundaries . . . I can't really explain . . . She doesn't want me to . . .* It wasn't much to go off.

Wendy wondered what sort of boundaries he had set. Was Maya just not respecting them? Did she have no control over herself? Was she mentally ill? *Yes—maybe that was it*, thought Wendy. Maybe Maya was mad. There was something so horribly wrong with her that Kesh pitied her and had to be sensitive.

But Maya didn't seem insane. And what sort of mental illness makes you touch another woman's husband uncontrollably?

Maybe there was Muthu drama at play, some business with the Muthus that Maya was involved in. It didn't make sense why Wendy had to be kept out of the loop, but Saraswathi *was* very particular about family business.

When the sun was starting to sink into the ocean, Wendy checked the time. She had been sitting up here for over an hour. The time had escaped her, just like her husband and this whole situation. She felt a little better only because of how little she knew. Clearly, there was something going on, and whatever it was, she did not possess enough information to make any true judgments.

At least not any major judgments. She definitely knew that Kesh had handled the situation poorly, that he had hurt her feelings, that he was going to have some explaining to do once he did start doing some explaining. She also knew that she hated Maya. Maybe *hate* is a strong word, but her feelings were stronger than a dislike. Maya had stirred up trouble, whether in her marriage or in the Muthu business—she did not know which—but she knew that Maya had done something. She was still *doing* something.

Wendy tried to tell herself that she just needed to be patient and that everything would become clear in time. Even if there were problems to be discussed and dealt with in her marriage, she and Kesh would sort them out later. Sure, getting through the evening might be challenging if she caught Maya getting handsy or flirting with her husband, but she could try her best to intervene and also to just let it go. Getting worked up wasn't going to work this out. *And Wendy was going to work this out.* One way or another, before or after Kudumba Pandigai, Wendy would solve this mystery, and she would reconcile with Kesh, and everything would be okay. Kesh would explain; he would make her laugh; he would tell her he was sorry; and they would be okay!

Wendy watched the sun slip behind the rippling horizon and bequeath a pleasing, purple permutation in the sky. In her heart, she felt that this was a sign of hope, that even when the sun has gone to sleep, it is still only around the corner and is generous enough to leave behind other lights and little bits of its beauty so that its return will not be forgotten; but while the sky gave her hope, it did not give her help, which is what Wendy needed. Because while the sunset may be pretty, it would be brief, and soon after it would come the darkest and longest night of Wendy's life, so much so that she would forget the beauty of this sunset, maybe even the sun itself—for the daylight had sent the worst of her worries to the shadows, but in the night, the worst would be free to wander and breed with truth, birthing worries unimaginable.

TEN

The Bollywood Bash was about to begin. Guests were being ushered into the biggest room in the Muthu palace—which already had high pillars reaching up to a high ceiling, marble floors, and walls displaying humongous paintings and tapestries—but it was completely transformed every year into a beautiful ballroom for this event.

Staff offered appetizers and cocktails.

The DJ was already pumping rhythm into the ready room and ready bodies.

The majesty and decor of the room were eclipsed only by the diverse colors and designs of everyone's outfits. The detail of patterns, the varying of colors, and the unique style of each man, woman, and child's clothing could be studied singularly for hours. Some were more traditional while others were more modern—but everybody wore their own beauty proudly. The makeup and jewelry—all shapes and colors of jewels and varying gold—only accentuated the importance of the night.

The bash was anything but bashful, and that was especially clear when Maya and Rini entered the ballroom. Unsurprisingly, the sisters stood out even among other outstanding outfits. Like moths to flames, or magnets to metal, or dry throats to fresh water were everyone's eyes to these girls.

Rini wore a peach sari ensemble with a deep V-neck choli. Draped over her shoulders was a cape-style jacket with slit sleeves, complimented by gold floral embroidery and contrasted by mint-green lining. Her bell-shaped earrings were like dresses themselves, with three levels dangling down in an hourglass formation, mostly made of gold but with a green gem centered in each bell. Three golden necklaces, also with green gems—clearly a matching set—adorned her neck. Her hair, threaded with jasmine flowers, was pulled back and braided.

Maya wore a similarly styled sari ensemble with a choli, but hers was turquoise with a magenta trim and the gold embroidery was wavier than the floral designs and coated in thousands of sequins. The choli was really only a strapless bra, which would've left her neck very bare, if it were not for the chunky gold choker and golden chains carrying blue gems adorning her. Glitter glazed her chest and cheeks, and her hair was pulled back tight into a bun, also with jasmine flowers, and a maang tikka.

A cocktail server lost balance of the tray in his hand and dropped a few glasses when he saw them enter the room—and barely anyone even noticed because there were more shocking views to be looking at—yes, Maya and Rini.

While the glass was promptly cleaned up, Kesh and Vik greeted Maya and Rini. They wore traditional clothes that happened to match the women in color, Kesh with a light blue and Vik a light green, both wearing silk dhotis and kurtas with gold trim and designs. Both men had curly hair, but Vik's was cut short and styled so that you couldn't quite tell how curly it was while Kesh's hair was longer and wild. They were both clean-shaven, and their smiles, upon greeting the girls, were full and perfect, revealing both their attraction and their attractiveness.

Kesh and Vik could've been twins, but Kesh's face had a fullness, an age that Vik's did not. It didn't quite make him any less attractive, but it gave him a less youthful appeal and more of a mature charm.

The four of them really did look like Bollywood movie stars.

Jothi watched them from the balcony above. She was looking very beautiful herself . . . but she sure did not feel it. There was a knot in her stomach that seemed impossible to untie. Somehow, she felt worse than Wendy whenever Kesh and Maya touched because she knew . . . she knew *the truth*.

But she didn't want to believe it! How could she? Her own brother . . . She always looked up to him. He was the *good* one. No matter what her parents or Paatti thought, she knew he was the best of them—

Or *was* the best of them.

Why would he ruin a perfectly good marriage? Or, even if it wasn't perfect—a *good* marriage. Jothi couldn't understand it! If anyone was going to stick it out in a world where couples often stuck it to each other, she had been confident in them! Why would he throw all that away?

Yes—Maya was hot. HOT. Probably the sexiest woman Jothi had ever seen in her life.

And boys can only handle so much, *sure.*

But cheating? Lying? Being so blatantly obvious that he couldn't care any less about his wife!?

That was not Kesh. It just wasn't!

Jothi would never admit it, but she was thinking about jumping over the balcony railing—maybe landing right on top of Maya and Kesh. She could take them all out of their misery at once. But *no* . . . she was just left to sit with her thoughts and the mystery of this misery.

And was she supposed to get involved? She literally hated drama. Even with her friends, she tried to avoid it at all costs—which was pretty damn difficult when you have a best friend like Eesha. But she did her best! Jothi did not want to be at the center of Muthu infidelity. It wasn't her job to clean up her big brother's mess or to comfort her sister-in-law whom she barely ever spoke to.

But she couldn't just stay silent either. The guilt was eating her away from the inside, and she could barely keep her outside from showing it. In fact, she'd been dodging *Are you okay?* questions all day.

Jothi watched Kesh hand Maya a cocktail with his right hand while his left hand gently grabbed her ass. They were crazy! Literally, anyone could've seen that! She was seeing it. And it was disturbing.

So she jerked her head away from them and scanned the fifty or more other family members below, most of whom were already on the dance floor loosening their joints and losing their pride. Sometimes, Jothi couldn't believe she was one of them.

She looked for Wendy. It shouldn't be that hard to find a white girl in a sea of Indians . . . *Ah*, there she was! Poor Wendy, cooped up in the corner, sitting on her phone. It made Jothi want to cry. Her sister-in-law looked very beautiful. She was wearing a magenta sari with a choli, not too different from Maya and Rini, with a sheer pallu draped over her shoulder. Her complexion didn't quite match the outfit, but Jothi admired her for trying.

She was always trying . . . *trying* to fit in.

And she was pretty—very pretty actually!—especially if you could take away the stress and constant sadness that seemed to always linger upon her face. Kesh had no good reason for being unhappy with her. *Wendy was hot too.*

Jothi watched her for a while, trying to reason herself out of going down there to keep Wendy company, but in the end, she couldn't do it, and her guilty conscience won out. She did take her time getting to her sister-in-law though: grabbing a snack here, a drink there, chatting with a boy that was kind of cute but maybe her cousin—distant cousin!—definitely distant cousin.

But eventually, she walked her way to Wendy.

"At a party and you're on your phone. You're no better than me—" Jothi almost got cut off by the sound of a little boy cracking up at the table next to them, headphones on and watching his iPad. "Or that kid," she added.

Jothi had decided to start out with a joke. Hopefully, that was a good idea.

"I think he's having more fun than I am," Wendy said.

"Brought you a drink."

Jothi handed her a glass.

"Really?"

"Yeah."

"Thanks."

Wendy took the drink. Jothi sat down beside her.

"Ready to dance?" Jothi said after a bit of silence.

"Not really . . . but maybe."

"You gotta—"

"Is something going on with your family?"

"What do you mean?"

"Kesh has been kinda off."

"Oh . . . not that I know 'bout."

"Does he seem off to you?"

"Kesh?"

"Yeah."

"Maybe."

Wendy stared at Jothi like she wanted to know more.

Her eyes burned straight to Jothi's soul, but Jothi tried to keep cool.

"Vik, too, though," Jothi added. "Not used to seeing him with a real girlfriend—but he seems *off* in a good way."

"Kesh's off in a bad way . . . you feel like?"

Damn!—hot damn! Jothi was saying too much. She wasn't used to needing to filter her words. She tried to backpedal.

"Oh—uh—don't—know—uh—maybe, but—what do you think?"

Wendy shrugged, but clearly, she was onto something. Jothi wanted to know what Wendy knew, but she also did not want to get any deeper into this conversation, because who knew what slipup she might slip in next! She decided to tread carefully . . . very carefully.

"Can I ask you a question?" Wendy asked.

"Mhmm."

"Are you close with Maya and Rini?"

"Close with Maya and Rini? No—literally, hung out with 'em more the last few days than I ever have . . . in total."

"Has Maya, like, said anything or done anything . . . *weird*?"

"Weird? Like how?"

"I just don't really get her."

"Oh?"

"Maybe it's just our personalities—"

"Personalities, yeah—"

"But I don't know. She and Kesh . . ."

Jothi was in too deep now. She needed to get out of this conversation. But she was stuck. She just kept involuntarily backchanneling verbal cues to Wendy, literally, repeating her words back to her! Why was she doing that? Jothi had no idea. All she knew was that she was very uncomfortable in this situation and that she had no control over where this conversation was going.

"She and Kesh . . .?" Jothi asked—still doing it!

"They're pretty close?"

Suddenly, every possible doubt flooded Jothi's mind. *Did she really see Kesh and Maya having sex?* Maybe it was someone else. *Would Kesh do such a thing?* Maybe Kesh just happened to shower down there right after. *Did Jothi really know what she was talking about?* Maybe they were just walking on the beach. *Shouldn't she talk with Kesh and Maya before saying anything?* Maybe Maya only lied about not seeing someone down there because people would get the wrong idea. *What if Jothi ruined their marriage?* Maybe she would start a rumor that would ruin it all!

"I don't know!" Jothi snapped.

"Okay, sorry . . . just getting in my head lately."

Jothi's earbud had flown out of her ear when she snapped. She picked it up and fidgeted with it for a moment. The DJ cranked up the music, and it seemed that the conversation had fizzled out.

But Jothi leaned in, though avoiding eye contact, and spoke up so that Wendy could hear her over the music.

"Maya jus' kinda the wild, flirty type," Jothi said. "But maybe she's . . . I dunno . . ."

"Yeah."

"I dunno how to say this kinda thing . . . but . . . you're cool, you're beautiful, you're a good wife—Kesh's lucky to have ya.

Don't let anyone take your stage. You should have some fun, take a load off."

Wendy almost smiled. It made Jothi *almost* feel better—although deep down, she still felt as guilty as ever, especially because she was putting a Band-Aid on a bullet wound. A little hope would not stop all hell from breaking loose. But she had tried . . . tried to do *something*.

Jothi stood up and left Wendy, and before she could decide where to head next, her mother, Meena, pulled her onto the dance floor. She might not have felt like dancing, but she'd practiced this one all year. Her whole family did. So she danced with her body, while her head and her heart did other things: like reassuring herself that she said a nice word to Wendy and should feel proud of that, like reminding her that while she did have information and was responsible for that, she also did not know the full story, and like refocusing her next best course of action, which was talking with her brother to find out what the hell was going on.

⸭

The dancing continued for hours. There was a blend of traditional and modern numbers, and somehow everyone there knew them all. Wendy mostly watched, but she did join in for a couple that she and Kesh had practiced. She didn't mind dancing in a crowd of others, mostly all doing the same movements. There was something wonderful about it: the unity, the synchrony, feeling like she was just one cog in an enormous family wheel.

She kept forcing her way to Kesh, trying to dance beside and with him. But somehow, he kept disappearing. As soon as she would get close to him, he'd jump or spin or shimmy away. It didn't *look* intentional, but it sure felt it. He would vanish from her side and appear by Maya's.

Into the night, Kesh, Maya, Vik, and Rini remained on the dance floor only ever leaving to down a cocktail or glass of water or a Tuborg. It was like they were all best friends who spent every moment together. They sang with all the breath in their lungs, danced with every part of their bodies, and smiled without ceasing. Even amid Wendy's growing bitterness, she had to admit that she thought that this was what true friendship must be like. Somehow, despite the years of distance, this group of four hadn't separated their hearts for one another one bit.

Kesh was generally a happy guy, but the smile on his face now, Wendy seldom saw. And when she did see it, *she always remembered*. It was the kind of smile that conveyed unhindered happiness, a completely uncontrollable feeling, the result of a focused and present joy that only comes from souls bonding to one another.

Kesh had smiled with her this way.

She remembered seeing it first on their honeymoon, when they had cracked up laughing—what they were laughing at originally she actually could not remember—but what made them laugh harder still was that Kesh had taken a sip of his mojito and spit it all over a random old man in a burst of laughter; the man just got up and walked away, and Wendy would've felt bad, but she was also laughing—*dying laughing*—so hard that her belly was like a rock, and she couldn't breathe. And deep inside her, in that moment, when Kesh had looked at her and smiled with spit and mint hanging from his chin, she knew that her soul was mingling with his— and that she *loved* him, and that he *loved* her, and that marrying Kesh had been the best decision of her entire life.

Wendy wanted so desperately to be happy for Kesh, to smile at his smiling. But she couldn't. She couldn't smile at his hurting her, at his vague and confusing excuses, at his hands touching and twirling . . . *Maya.*

When it was too upsetting to watch them, Wendy watched Saraswathi. It amazed her how this seventy-eight-year-old lady could kick and shake and spin the way she did. There was one dance where she had one hand on her hip while she popped it, her other hand in the air shaking her peacock cane, and her foot kicking out in the air, swinging back and forth. Her sapphire ring bounced on her chest, doing its own dance. It emitted a brighter and deeper sparkle than any other jewel in the room, and when it leapt it lapped even Maya's and Rini's captivating beauty. It was a beauty that only increased with age and yet never grew old. Both the ring and the ring bearer were doing a dance that seemed to last forever.

But eventually, Saraswathi did sit down. Most of the elderly did. And the kids got bored or got sent to bed, some of the elderly, too, leaving just the young adults dancing. There was a shift in the atmosphere, one the DJ, the lights, and the very humidity of the room seemed to be in on. It was as if the hours of physical exertion had removed all sense of self-consciousness, social restraint, and veils covering nightly desires.

The boundaries—*whatever they were*—that Kesh had set up between himself and Maya were slowly melting away in the heat of passion, and Wendy—*poor Wendy*—was sitting front row to the show. They took the stage, and she took the cage—involuntarily forced to watch her husband and his mistress's show of affection.

The rhythm in the entire room took a turn toward sensuality, and the able bodies followed the beat. Every young couple on the dance floor went along. The shaking was more unashamed, the popping more proud, the twirling more torrid; each movement was mischievous, and every touch was titillating, like each dancer was an expert in the art of temptation. The faces of the elderly still in the room were judgmental, but still nobody interrupted because the gestures weren't too explicit . . . *yet.*

Maya and Kesh were center stage.

They were leading the number—a couple to count on.

It was as if they had practiced this dance their entire lives. Their bodies moved like waves upon the water, like leaves upon the trees—from lips to hips and down below, each thrust and twirl had perfect flow.

The other men and women, including Vik and Rini, encircled them. The men were on Kesh's side, the women on Maya's. It really looked like a dance-off in a Bollywood movie. Many of the dances that night did, but this one was more carnal than any Bollywood movie Wendy had ever seen.

Kesh was a good dancer, and he was putting out moves Wendy had never seen, but it was evident that Maya was outdancing him. After a few minutes of ping-pong, her movements eclipsed his, and he became another one of the backup dancers—like Vik and the other men—while Maya put on a show for all.

It was a fusion dance that combined strong footwork, sharp hand motions, belly dancing, hip thrusts, popping, locking, and some gestures Wendy imagined only strippers perform. Everyone was watching her. Men and women. Meena and Jack. Saraswathi and Jothi. Everyone except Wendy . . .

She was watching Kesh.

She had seen enough of Maya's movements, but what she could not take her eyes off of was her husband—the man she loved more than anything in the world. She watched his eyes like magnets on Maya, his smile so smitten, his body bent toward hers. Maya was dancing in front of everyone but *only* for him.

It did not make sense. Wendy wanted to look away to keep her heart from breaking, but in his look, she could see *that* smile, and she knew what it meant! She could see not only that his soul was bonding to Maya's . . . but that he *loved* her.

ELEVEN

Wendy wept.

In a room full of people, under the chandelier lights, beside some child who should've been sent to bed but was still watching YouTube on his iPad, Wendy's lips quivered, her eyes ran red, and her sari collected tears. She cried and no one seemed to care. No one seemed to notice. *Especially not Kesh.*

When the final number finished, the crescendo of the Bollywood Bash, Maya and Kesh embraced each other and ran up the spiral steps that led to the balcony. Wendy and Jothi watched from two separate ends of the room, their fears being realized.

But Wendy's tears didn't go fully unnoticed. In fact, Jothi saw her, and Vik and Rini, and Saraswathi and Meena too. They all watched Wendy not only cry, but stand up, and climb those spiral steps. From down below, they could see Maya and Kesh run along the inner balcony and outside onto a third-story patio.

And yes, Wendy followed them.

It wasn't just her vision that was blurry from the waterworks. Her steps and thoughts were foggy too; her whole being was in a dull state. She didn't know what she was doing; her mind was mush. She didn't know what she was feeling; she somehow felt everything and nothing simultaneously.

But she was walking . . . walking up the steps . . . stepping along the inner balcony. . . . And she could hear the DJ playing a familiar beat below, as everyone cleaned up and said their good nights . . .

Jumba-cheeka jumba-cheeka jumba-cheeka-jum.

She headed for the outdoor patio.

Jumba-cheeka jumba-cheeka jumba-cheeka-jum.

She turned the corner and stepped outside.

Jumba-cheeka jumba-cheeka—

The cold breeze hit her.

Jumba-cheeka-jum—

She saw warm, orange flames. A gas-lit fire pit.

Jum . . . jum . . . ba—

And Kesh on the patio sofa.

Cheek . . . a—

And Maya on his lap.

Jum.

Wendy's heart sank. And the image drowned out all music, all sound. There was absolute silence. The sound of quiet reigned until her ears honed in on the subtle sounds of sin. It was as if Wendy wore headphones that directly connected to microphones on their chests. The connection was clear, and the feed was direct.

The smacking of lips.

The breaths of pleasure.

The rubbing of Maya's thighs on Kesh's pants.

Wendy watched and heard *every* detail of depravity. Her eyes were glued—like magnets to their malice. She wanted to look away, but she couldn't. She tried, and her eyes drifted right back. Her steps crawled toward them, and they continued unnoticed. Lips on lips. Skin on skin. *Her* on *him.*

"Kesh . . .?" Wendy's voice was neither quiet nor loud, neither harsh nor soft.

Maya turned around before Kesh, then he peeked from around her. She wore a wily smile, while he looked at his wife almost dazed. Wendy didn't realize, but tears were streaming down her face again. She only noticed when a drop leaped from her chin to her hand.

Maya slowly, *very* slowly climbed off Kesh . . . only to lie on the sofa on her belly and rest her head in his lap, with one hand on his knee and the other sprawled out.

Kesh looked down at Maya and flashed a smirk.

"Kesh!" Wendy had no other words.

This was *her* husband—the man she trusted, the man she loved!

"Wendy, look . . ." Kesh started but then looked down at Maya.

"Go ahead," said Maya, turning onto her back and looking up at him from his lap.

"Why?" Wendy asked. Why would he do this to her? Why would he hurt her? Why would he break her heart? Why? Why! WHY!?

"I didn't want to hurt you, Wendy," Kesh said. "But there's no easy way to do this . . . I loved you, I did, but I don't anymore—I just *don't*. And if you love *me*, you'll want me to be happy. The truth is, *I love Maya*. I love her like I've never loved anyone before. Even if that's hard to hear, I'm sorry—but it's the truth."

"You're breaking my . . . my heart. I love *you* more than any-thing."

"I'm sorry."

"Can we talk? Maybe just—alone—without her—"

"I really don't know what else to say! I love Maya, and she loves me, and that's—that's how it's gonna be. Don't make this any harder . . . for you. This is what's best for you, too, trust me."

Wendy wasn't crying anymore, but her body began shaking, like her eyes had run out of tears so other parts of her body were crying instead. She was suddenly nauseous, like she might throw up —or maybe faint.

Maya slipped off the sofa and stood. She gave Wendy an annoyed glare and then turned to Kesh. She bent over and put her hands on his knees.

"Come on," Maya pulled him off the couch, "hard to get any privacy around here."

"Kesh, she's a monster! You can't be with someone like that."

Kesh did not respond. Instead, he and Maya strutted past her and headed indoors. Wendy did not move.

"Maybe I'm a monster," said Maya, just out of Wendy's earshot, "but I'm *your* monster, *right*?"

"Mhmm," Kesh replied with an honest smile.

They hurried along the inner balcony of the ballroom.

⚇

Jothi watched them from below—holding hands, running off. It was primarily only staff left in the ballroom now. The rest of the guests were heading out the doors. Jothi spotted Vik and Rini exiting with the crowd. She hurried over to them.

"Hey—" Jothi started, grabbing her brother's arm.

"Hey! Jothi. Wanna jump in the pool?" Vik asked.

"YESSSS," inserted Rini. "Let's do it!"

"What's going on with Kesh?"

Vik looked to Rini, both not confused, not worried.

"Didn't you see—?"

"I dunno," Vik exhaled.

"They don't even have a good marriage, right?" asked Rini.

"I don't think so," Vik added.

"Yeah, yeah, yeah, they do! Pretty sure."

"Doesn't—*really*—seem like it," said Rini through her teeth.

"You guys don't care?"

"I dunno." Vik shrugged. "Wendy's never really fit in with our family. I dunno why they're even together. She just—she's—she's—she's—"

"She's not . . . *Maya*." Rini shrugged.

"Saraswathi's gonna be pissed! She hates divorce." Jothi could not understand how they could be so dismissive. Sure, Vik's never taken relationships that seriously, but he finally was! What if this was them? Wouldn't they care?

"It happens," Vik said.

Guess not. Jothi rolled her eyes. They were no help. How was she the most mature person in this family? She'd never even been in a serious relationship!

"Whatever." Jothi walked away.

"So, no pool?" Vik shouted.

"Come on, Jothi! Jump in the pool!"

Jothi ignored them. She needed to find her other brother.

⚇

Wham! Wham! Ziiiiiiiiiiiiiiiiiiiiiiiiiiiiiiiip! Wendy packed her bags in a fit of many emotions. *Rage!*—she flung her suitcase open. *Despair!*—she sobbed as she jammed clothes inside. *Confusion!*—

she grabbed things that were not hers and left things that were behind.

Wendy had no idea where she was going. She had no idea what
she was doing. This was the single worst moment of her entire life!
Worse than the night before when she had been lying on the floor
dying, crying, and throwing up. Last night she had been physically
sick, and yes, she felt physically sick at this moment too—but she
also felt sick in the depths of her soul.

It was her soul that needed to throw up now. She needed to
vomit up her entire life because she had been poisoned—the one
good thing that she had ever had, poisoned!—because the love of
her life was a lie!

And it still didn't make any sense. Like a puzzle piece being
jammed into someone else's puzzle. The absurdity of it all only
made Wendy feel even more humiliated. How stupid was she? How
could she not see this coming? What was wrong with her? How
could she love and trust someone who tossed her aside like—*like
chopped liver!*—as her mother would've said. That was her mother's
favorite phrase. She said it quite often about Wendy's father. Divorce wasn't taboo in Wendy's family, nor were an unhappy marriage and infidelity. This would only confirm that Wendy was no
better than them . . . even though she'd tried so hard—SO HARD
—to be a good wife, to pick a good husband, to do it right.

How did it all go so wrong?

Wendy tore off her sari. She slipped on sweatpants and a hoodie—hood up.

She hauled her luggage through the palace, avoiding eye contact
with any and everyone she passed, not that she could've made eye
contact through her swollen and glossy eyes. At one point, she

thought she heard Saraswathi's thumping peacock cane behind her, but she didn't look back. She continued to the garage.

She found the BMdumbyou and climbed in.

As Wendy rolled down the driveway, she started hyperventilating. The Indian palace still towered over her. The night's shadows could not hide its majesty. Lanterns lit up various sections with a golden glow while the moon backlit the building with a blue hue. This place had never felt like home until now.

This, too, was absurd. Wendy always felt uncomfortable in the palace, like it was someone else's house, someone else's family. She never felt like a *Muthu*. But as she drove away, she felt like her own identity was being stripped from her. She wasn't a Muthu, but . . . *she was*. The last five years of kissing Saraswathi's ass, of learning Tamil, of learning to be okay with nice things and rich friends—was it all for nothing?

Despite all the things she complained about and dreaded, she had absorbed Kesh's family and life into her own. It was part of her. He was part of her. With each short, quick breath she took, she couldn't imagine a life without Kesh Muthu.

She exited the security gate and entered the neighboring area of cliffside houses that were only around ten to fifteen million in listing price. The Muthus' palace was closer to forty. The road wiggled along, parallel to the beach, till ascending up to the main street.

It was pretty quiet at this time of night, and Wendy rolled down the windows to get some fresh air. She tried to catch her breath, to slow it. But every time her face turned calm, her lungs inhaled, and she looked composed, her face would contort, the air would fly from her mouth, and she would cry. Again and again.

Eventually, she slammed on the brakes, swerved to the curb, and parked. She buried her face in her hands as if they were a grave she could lie down and die in, but then her fingers crawled to her scalp and scratched their way out of her hair, and she let herself cry some more. For about two minutes straight she cried.

Then she slowed to a stop. Her head was throbbing.

She climbed into the backseat and found a half-empty bottle of water.

She guzzled it and lay down like a runner after a marathon—it was an emotional marathon.

What now?

Wendy needed to think. She *needed* to talk to someone. She could not go through this alone. She knew that. She felt that. But who to call? She could call her mother—but she did not want to do that. She could call her sister. They weren't the closest, but she would take her side, and she would want to cut Kesh's balls off. She was a feisty one, and maybe Wendy needed someone feisty in her corner.

The most reasonable person to call would be Wendy's friend Erin. She was Wendy's closest friend. They hadn't spent that much time together lately because Erin had two kids and one on the way, but they tried to keep in touch. Erin was a good friend; she was just busy.

But Erin lived in Indiana. What time was it in Indiana?

Like two in the morning.

Would Erin even answer? Probably not. But Wendy needed to talk to somebody! So she decided she would call her. If there was ever a time to wake up a pregnant lady in the middle of the night, it was when your life was ending, right? Wendy reassured herself and looked for her phone.

Her phone . . . *where was it?*

Wendy searched her pockets, and the car, and then her suitcases and bags, but could not find it. She must've left it in her room or somewhere in the palace. She couldn't even remember the last time she used it that day. Maybe when Kesh disappeared with Maya to get beers? The thought made Wendy punch the back of his chair—the passenger seat—five times. That ass! Was he really cheating on her this whole time?

Wendy shook her head and tried to shake the thought. She needed to focus. When was the last time she even used it? Getting ready for the bash? At the bash? At the bash—yes! She had used it at the bash because Jothi made fun of her for it. So it was on some table, or cleaned up by kitchen staff, or, maybe, she grabbed it and took it to her room unknowingly.

It could be anywhere. Just not here, not with her.

So she couldn't call Erin. She couldn't call anyone. She was alone.

How was she supposed to do anything without her phone?

She couldn't book a hotel.

She couldn't buy a flight home.

She couldn't even look up directions.

Okay, okay, *okayyyyyy*. She would do things old school. Just drive till she found a random hotel, figure out the flight and phone problems tomorrow, and—

A BURST OF LAUGHTER shot out from Wendy's mouth. Her face fell against the back of the chair, squishing an ironic smile till it was only half the irony.

She wasn't going to find a hotel. She wasn't going anywhere . . . besides *back* to the Muthus. Why? Because an image had popped into her head, an image of her wallet sitting on the table in the corner of the room, where she had set it right after they arrived at the palace and not touched it since—especially not in her state of despair when she loaded her things into the car and drove off.

So she had no phone, no wallet, and thus no way of going anywhere but back.

⁂

Jothi was tired of being the mature one. It didn't suit her. It was like an unflattering dress that was tight in places it should be loose and loose in places it should be tight. She was just a kid! She liked not caring about things, not caring about people. She liked sitting on her phone while drama played out and she just watched. But here she was, huffing and puffing, speedwalking around the palace looking for her older brother. If she was ever going to be playing cat and mouse, she wanted it to be with a hot college boy—and she would be the mouse! But instead, she was the cat, and she was looking for two adult mice that couldn't keep their whiskers off each other.

She saw Saraswathi and Jack talking in the kitchen. She had the feeling it was about Wendy . . . maybe about Kesh and Maya. She watched them hug, say good night, and head to bed. Jothi thought about asking them if they'd seen Kesh, but she didn't want to talk to them. So she didn't.

She just wanted find Kesh. Her brother was a reasonable guy—probably the most sane person she knew. Even if he had got his heart hooked on Maya, she figured he would come to his senses soon . . . and maybe he just needed a nudge in the right direction. *What was she now, a moral GPS?* This whole thing was way out of her territory.

Jothi was starting to talk herself out of it when she walked past the pool and saw, out of the corner of her eye, movement around the peacock fountain. Her head jerked toward the motion and she followed it. She passed the peacocks and could clearly see two people across the lawn, heading out the gate and down the steps to the beach.

Even in the night, she knew it was them. It was Kesh and Maya. Headed back to their lovemaking spot. Nympho freaks.

"What am I doing? What am I doing? What am I doing?" Jothi mumbled to herself while she hurried after them.

The familiar *clip-clip-clip* echoed into the night. As she descended, the waves slowly masked the sound more and more. She was gaining on them, and by the last landing, she was about caught up—and they heard her.

Maya and Kesh turned with squinted eyes to spot the follower. Jothi met them on the landing. She was sweaty, though she knew not if it was from hurrying down a hundred steps or from nerves.

"Jothi?" Kesh said with a smile.

"Vape time?" asked Maya.

Jothi tried to swallow her nerves, but it didn't work. It was just a swallow. Less spit and even more nerves now.

"What—what're you guys doin'?

"Hmmm?" Kesh replied.

"Bro—like, you're not all discreet, so don't pretend."

Jothi was trying to keep cool, but she was freaking out. What was she doing here? This was none of her business. Why was she trying to save her brother's marriage if he wanted to kill it? Was it her job to save it?

"Thought we were chill, Jothi," said Maya.

"We are. I like you. But-but-but he's married." Jothi looked at Kesh. "Paatti is not gonna be happy about this. I saw her talking to Dad."

"Okay?" Kesh shrugged.

"They saw you guys dancing. And Wendy crying."

"We're in love," said Maya, putting her arm in Kesh's and leaning her head on him.

"What about Wendy? Kesh, *come on*—"

"You don't know what you're talking about," Kesh interrupted. "I love Maya more than anything. Me and Wendy are done. It's over. You should be happy for us."

"But like . . . you guys *just met* . . . like, for the first time in, like, a decade? Right? I just feel like this is not the *right way* to go about it."

"Love transcends all that shit!" shouted Maya, then she kissed Kesh, and Kesh kissed her back. A wet, long, tongue-filled kiss.

Jothi watched and was, quite literally, shocked.

"You guys are crazy!"

Maya pulled out of the kiss but kept her arms wrapped around Kesh. "Love makes ya crazy!" she said and then tilted her head with a flirty smile and gave a nonchalant shrug. "We'll tell everyone when the time's right."

"Alright, we're gonna head to . . . *bed*," Kesh said, sliding his hand around Maya's waist. "You should too."

"Look, I don't wanna be here. This is awkward for me. But you gotta treat Wendy better than this. I mean, girl to girl—you just gotta go make this right. Even if you're gonna ruin your marriage—she don't deserve this."

Kesh raised an eyebrow and looked like he was about to laugh.

"Or I'll tell Paatti—*before the time's right*. She's gonna disown you, bro."

Kesh shook his head like it wasn't a big deal, but Jothi knew very well that every relative, no matter how much Saraswathi loved them, ran the risk of getting booted if they pissed her off enough.

"You're, like, a little, whiny spy," said Maya. "Watching like a perv this morning, snooping around, telling your adult brother how to run his love life—"

"How'd you know I—?"

"And . . . *threatening us*?"

"*Keshhhhhh* . . . you know I'm right. I'm only doing what you would want me to do if you were thinking straight."

Kesh looked at Maya. She smacked her lips and nodded through a fake smile. She grabbed Kesh's hand and pulled him forward, shoving past Jothi.

"Alright, alright, let's go *back upstairs*," she said like it was the worst place in the world.

"Cool, cool, cool. Good." Jothi turned around. She couldn't believe that they were actually going to listen to her. But they were! Probably the most honorable thing she's ever done. And Kesh—whenever he came to his senses—was going to owe her big time.

But for now, she felt a wave of relief washing over her. She had stepped out of her comfort zone, used wisdom beyond her years, and done the right thing! Even when it was very, very, very, very, *very* awkward, she had held her ground—

The *ground*. It seemed to slip right from under her feet.

Maya had spun, in a flash, grabbed Jothi with a grip that dug into her skin, and shoved her backward. The stars were under her. The beach house lights above her. The waves everywhere. Her vision became a blur of shadows, and Jothi was so, *so* confused until—

WHAM!
WHAMMM!
WHAMMMMMM!

Her body hit step after step after step, tumbling down three flights of stairs into a clump of a silhouette on the sand.

"*Ooof*," said Maya with a cheeky smile.

"Oh shit! What did you—" Kesh put his hands on his head.

"I had to do it, baby," said Maya. "Go get Rini."

TWELVE

"I can't let you in, miss," the security guard said.

"I'm Wendy Muthu. Okay? I left my ID and phone, but I, literally, just drove out of here a few minutes ago. I mean, this is Kesh Muthu's car. I can show you the . . ."

She dug in the glove box for the registration.

"I'm sorry—I can't."

"Look!" Wendy handed him the registration.

"I understand, but—"

"But what? I'm going in there. I need my phone, my wallet. And I have every right to go in there! Please, please, *please*. I have had a horrible night, and you don't need to hear about it, but I need to get in there."

"Miss, I can't."

"Okay, look. My husband is cheating on me. I left because I'm losing my mind and my world is, literally, crumbling down, but—but I can't even go to a hotel or call anyone if I don't grab my phone and my wallet. *Okay?*"

Wendy caught her breath.

"I'll let you use my phone to call someone."

"No! Let me in! LET ME IN!"

"I've been specifically told *not to* let you back onto the premises."

"What? By who?"

The guard shrugged. Either he couldn't say or he wouldn't. Wendy hugged the steering wheel and pushed her face up against it. She was stuck.

The guard, a mid-forties Asian man, watched her with conflicted eyes. He looked like he wanted to let her in, but he also seemed to want to keep his job. Clearly, he was the stickler-for-the-rules type and not the stick-it-to-the-man type.

Then, without really thinking beyond the thought of impulse, Wendy laid her hands on the horn. *BEEEEEEEEEEEEEEEEEP. BEEEEP. BEEEEEEEEEEEE—*

"Stop, please stop. Miss! You're gonna get the cops called on you!"

Wendy removed her hands and flung them in the air hopelessly. The guard snatched up his phone and stretched his hand out the window, offering it to her.

"Call someone. Anyone. Someone inside," he said, pointing to the palace. "Maybe they'll let you back in."

"It's late, and I-I-I—I don't even have anyone's number memorized."

Besides Kesh's number, of course. But Wendy figured he'd been the one that locked her out. Who else? There was no way—no way in hell!—she was calling him to let her back in.

The guard's arm was going limp a little bit like he was getting tired of holding it out. Poor guy was trying to help her. But his offer wasn't really helpful!

Wendy bounced her head on the steering wheel while his offer bounced around in her head. *She had no other options.*

She snatched the phone out of his hand but had to hand it right back to him so that he could unlock it. Then she called Kesh. Her heart was in her throat—her broken, shattered heart.

Brrrrrrrrrring. Brrrrrrrrrrring. Brrrrrrrrrring.

The call went to voicemail.

She tried once more.

Brrrrrrrrrring. Brrrrrrrrrrring. Brrrrrrrrrring.

Voicemail.

Wendy had married a monster. She had slept with a beast! This deceitful, grotesque creature that had promised to give her his everything had taken everything from her. And left her trapped with nothing and no one.

She fought her desire to chuck the phone into the windshield.

She passed it back to the security guard as an idea popped into her mind.

"I'm sorry." He frowned.

"Night."

Wendy put the car in reverse, whipped it around, and sped away. She flew down the wiggly road, and just before ascending to the main street, she parked. It was an open street spot outside of an Italian-styled house. Like many on this street, it appeared humble and tiny, like a suburban ranch, while in actuality, this house kept eighty percent of itself hidden from street view, with three floors that descended down the cliff toward the beach. The true size of these houses could only be seen from the sand. Or Google Maps.

Wendy loved Italy. It was the first place Kesh took her on vacation. It had been her first vacation, and her first time out of the country. She loved the food, the people, the buildings. Even before the trip, she'd loved the exterior of stones and low roofs and greenery that wrapped around the modern Italian-styled homes.

She would've stopped to admire this house too, if she hadn't been seething with anger and on a mission to get her phone and wallet.

Wendy climbed out of the BMdumbyou and started walking. At first it looked like she was heading for a random house, but she wasn't. She walked the line right in between two houses, where the sidewalk transformed into short steps down a tight alley. The pathway was blanketed by branches and greenery, with fences that were swallowed up by bushes on either side.

This was a little-known accessway down to the beach. It was technically open to the public, but it was usually only used by people who lived nearby and were in the know.

Wendy was going to get back into the Muthus' palace.

She was going to get her wallet and phone.

Even if she had to hike there at midnight.

She descended about eighty steps to reach the beach. She thought about taking off her shoes, but it would've been a short-lived action, so she kept them on. At least she was comfy in her sweats and sneakers. She trudged beneath mansions until reaching the rocky part of the journey.

This is why she had kept her shoes on. The jagged rock formations and clusters of barnacles and mussels were worse than LEGO bricks—worse than broken glass. The waves had worked the rock to perfection. It was unmoving and yet sharp as daggers. The beautiful tide pools welcomed you to study the detail and beauty and the little life it sustained, but only if you were patient and careful.

And if you wore shoes. Wendy had learned that the hard way last year.

Even with the shoes, this wasn't an easy climb. She hopped from rock to rock, sometimes slipping; she tried to avoid puddles but still got splashed, completely sinking her foot at one point; she even cut her hand on the face of a rock when she caught herself from falling. The waves were teasing her, crawling toward her and dipping away, keeping their distance and then flooding her feet, like they wanted to pull her out to the deep but wouldn't.

Wendy was tempted to let them take her away.

Eventually, she reached the remnants of a rusty barbed wire fence, which meant that she was close to the Muthus' property. Technically, every beach in Laguna is public, and when the Muthus attempted to block off access to the beach beneath their property, they were legally obligated to remove it. Hence the traces of a fence, bolts, and concrete pressed into the mesh by wind, waves, and time.

She had to do a bit of bouldering around the main bend, which conveniently created an even greater unlikeliness that anyone would venture into the Muthus' domain.

The thing about sweatpants is that, despite their comfy and nonchalant appeal, they are not very protective. So when she pivoted with her right foot and swung her left onto a higher crevice, her shin made contact with a protruding piece of rock and cut right through the soft material and drew blood.

But Wendy kept climbing, and soon she made her way around, first spotting the lights from the beach house, which appeared like warm, blurred orbs in the fog of night but signaled she'd made it. Wendy hopped onto a flat piece of rock, her hands finally free but quite cut up, and paused to catch her breath.

She was surprised how her own adrenaline supplied her with a feeling of empowerment—like scaling rocks at midnight and losing a little blood had somehow manifested itself as revenge on Kesh, even if in a minor manner. She was, quite literally, at her lowest point: hitting rock bottom in her heart, her world, her own view of herself—but that pure and simple fact, that she was persistently relentless, a woman who didn't give up easily, was a slight uptick.

When her breath slowed and quieted, Wendy thought she heard voices. But it was difficult to pick up over the shouts of the waves. So she fixed her eyes ahead. From the beach house's porch light, she could see a figure standing on the sand.

It was *Rini*. Wendy recognized her peach sari, which looked a grayish brown in the dim lighting. But it was definitely her.

Wendy stepped from rock to rock, getting a few feet closer.

Maya came out from the shadows, too, stepping into the light with Rini. Just the sight of her, even from over one hundred feet away and at night, yanked a knot so tight in Wendy's stomach, that her whole body became as stiff as the rocks beneath her, like she was using all her strength to try and untie it.

After all the excuses Wendy had made for her, all the times she gave her the benefit of the doubt, Maya was everything Wendy feared . . . and more. Wendy wondered when Maya had hatched her plan to steal Kesh away. Was it in the grocery store? The moment she heard that Vik and Rini were together? Or maybe she never planned it out! She just spontaneously decided to slaughter a happy marriage.

Maya and Rini took a step further into the light, and another figure gradually shifted out of the shadows. It was Kesh. His back was to them, and he was shimmying in the sand, his arms stretched out, as he pulled . . . *arms?*

Yes, arms.

The arms of a body out of the shadows.

Huhhhhhhhhhhhhh?

Wendy climbed down from the rocks and hit the sand. She crouched and moved toward them under the cover of darkness.

Getting nearer, she could instantly tell whom the body belonged to: Jothi.

The teenager's hair was mangled, her body coated in sand, and she was completely limp. Maybe dead.

Wendy's head spun, and she felt dizzy—like there were a hundred hands being raised to ask her questions, and they were swirling around her: a blur of palms and arms. But Wendy's mind couldn't even form words at this point; all her thoughts were jumbled, fragmented, only question marks and expletives. Her thoughts were loud but unintelligible—and they all fell silent when Wendy saw Maya's mouth move.

"...her up..."

Wendy only caught two words from the distance. Kesh dropped Jothi's hands to the sand. Then, he got down to his knees, scooped Jothi up, awkwardly rolled her onto his shoulder, and stood back on his feet.

Wendy guessed that Maya must've told him to pick Jothi up. That was about all her mind could process. She could observe what she saw even though she didn't understand it. Wendy watched the image ahead, lit up in the night like a movie in theaters, and she was the audience: silent and watching and detached from reality.

Maya and Rini led the way. Kesh followed, with his little sister slung over his shoulder. Wendy stayed near the waves so that she didn't become visible by the beach house lights and so that her footsteps would be masked. But she followed them.

They walked toward the opposite end of the beach, leaving the Muthus' property behind and continuing on. Wendy's mind was stunned silent, but one thought slipped through the fog: *Where are they going?*

The further they walked, the more afraid she felt. The knot in her stomach had only tightened and now wrenched in her throat. Wendy had never been so aware of her own heartbeat.

Another thought had slipped through: Was she following not only adulterers but ... *murderers?*

She crept quietly in the sand, the waves, at times, swallowing her ankles. She paid no mind to the cold or the wet—as long as she was hidden. There weren't many lights anymore, and she could barely see the others, so Wendy took that as a good sign. But she remained vigilant, hoping the darkness *did* cover her.

They passed two more properties before slowing. They stood at the base of a wooden staircase and seemed to be conversing, but Wendy couldn't catch any words. She didn't even consider drawing nearer. *Way too risky.*

Wendy watched them climb the stairs. After the second flight, they become invisible in the night, only appearing again briefly about two flights higher, due to a light or two emanating from the house above. It was too dark to gather a full image of the house they were headed toward, but Wendy did spot a handful of details.

The staircase looked wooden and was overgrown with weeds and shrubbery. There was an excavator and mounds of dirt up the hill. There were horizontal and vertical lines silhouetted by lights above that looked like the outline of a building in progress. Also, the lights, which shone from the house, were harsh and white, like construction lights.

Wendy had driven past this house before. It was a mansion that was being almost entirely rebuilt, and it had been taking quite some time, as she remembered seeing it under construction last year.

Kesh, Maya, Rini, and Jothi's body reappeared again as dark shapes at the top of the staircase and then exited Wendy's view.

What now?

Wendy needed to think.

Now that they were gone, she *could* think. But how long did she have? She needed to think quickly.

Wendy made her way up the beach so that she was no longer in reach of the waves. She veered left about fifty feet, away from the staircase and opposite the route to the Muthus' mansion. She hid behind a barrel, which she guessed was a trash can. The spot provided her a view of the top and bottom of the staircase for if and when they returned.

In and out. Wendy took a deep breath. But the fog in her mind wasn't clearing and comprehension was far from nearing. Nothing made sense. She was living a nightmare. *But she wasn't.* This wasn't a dream even though it should've been. Her sense of reality was too crisp, and she was too aware for it all to be made up by her mind.

But maybe she was just insane—that could be it. That was easier to comprehend than the reality before her!

Wendy was truly open to that. Maybe she was just *crazy*, and she didn't even know it. Maybe she was secretly a drug addict on the street and her whole life was one big trip, or she was mentally unstable, maybe from drugs or genes—who knows!—and this was all an episode.

If that was true—Wendy inhaled deep—she needed to be humble and agreeable enough to accept help. Say, everyone else— friends, family, co-workers—told her that she needed to enter a psychiatric facility, she needed to be willing to go. If—if!—it was everyone's word against hers, she would listen to them. She would have to.

But . . . *was she crazy?*

Wendy had no way of telling. How could she trust her unfaithful husband and his horrid family, who never once even treated her like a human being? And would a crazy person really be so understanding of their craziness? That sounds like a sane person . . . right?

Even if she was crazy, Wendy couldn't assume that! She had no prior history of mental illness, drug abuse, or any reason to believe so.

Wendy exhaled! She almost forgot to breathe. She tried to control her breathing. She was going to need oxygen to think straight, that's for sure.

Innnn . . . and . . . ouuuut.

Innnnn . . . and . . . ouuuuuuut.

Innnnnnn . . . and . . . ouuuuuuut.

Wendy thought about praying. God, praying? She hadn't prayed since she was a kid. And to what god, exactly? If there was a god—or gods—why did she need to pray for help in a situation like this? Any normal human, seeing her circumstances, would step into it! So where was God? Then again, nothing about this was normal! Maybe there were no normal people—no gods, either! And what could come from talking to God? Didn't he know everything already? It didn't even make sense. It's a waste of time! And time was a thing Wendy did not have right now.

It was just her. And she needed to act.

Wendy decided that she needed to do what she thought was right based on the information she had, as long as she was open and willing to listen if this reality didn't match up with what she typically knew to be true.

There was still so much she didn't know. She couldn't jump to any conclusions just yet. But she also had an obligation to help Jothi. If her sister-in-law wasn't dead, she needed help or rescuing.

So . . . *what now?*

Wendy thought about calling the police. But she had no phone. She could try and get it, but then she would lose sight of the suspects. And what if they caught her? What if she couldn't find her phone? What if other people were in on whatever this was?

Wendy considered her options: She could follow them up the steps. She could try to wake a neighbor. She could run back to the Muthus'. Or she could wait for them to return. Each option had so many variables and unknowns.

Wendy didn't really decide to wait, but by not making a decision, her waiting decided for her. In her peripherals, she saw a tiny blur of black at the top of the cliff—and the knot that had loosened a little while she thought was wrenched tight once more. Hiding behind a trash can in the middle of the night, her marriage in shambles, playing murder detective, Wendy had never felt more alone.

She heard faint feet on steps and whispers in the wind while her eyes inspected the dark, looking for any motion. She followed the pace of their descent—much faster than their way up—and caught glimpses of them in the moonlight, eventually seeing Kesh, Maya, and Rini hit the sand.

Jothi's body was not with them.

They headed right, in the opposite direction of where Wendy hid and back toward the Muthus' property. Wendy didn't follow them. She waited till they turned the bend, till she couldn't see them anymore, and then waited a few minutes longer. Just to be safe.

Then, in a dash, Wendy ran to the steps. She sprinted up, but after the first flight, decided it was better to be quiet, remembering that she had no idea what was waiting for her upstairs.

She flipped her hood back up—it had fallen off at some point during her bouldering—and took the steps with stealth. She further regretted ever sprinting up the steps when her body realized how many there were. Suddenly, her exhaustion, sleep deprivation, and growing thirst sounded like alarms with each step.

But she made it to the top.

It was quiet, and Wendy wasn't sure that she would be able to locate Jothi's body in the daylight much less the night. The yard was an unlevel mess of holes and mounds, black tarps covered God knows what, and there were piles of stones, wood, and pipes everywhere. If they buried Jothi's body here, Wendy wasn't going to find it.

Dread began to press heavily upon her. While she was sitting on the beach waiting for them, what were they doing up here? Were they burying Jothi? Finishing her off? Had Wendy just sat still while an innocent teenager was murdered? Wendy felt like faceplanting into one of these holes. She even leaned forward, tempted to do it—

A shadow flickered on the wall!

She simultaneously crouched and perked up. And a little bit of pee slipped out. Not that it mattered, since she was already all wet and her shoes completely soaked. But, but, but this was terrifying! And, to add to it, an uncontrollable sweat began to tingle over her whole body—even though it was freezing outside!

Wendy wanted to rip her hoodie right off.

But she was not making any sudden movements. Not now.

The construction lights were coming from inside the half-torn-down and half-rebuilt mansion. It could be Jothi inside. She could've been the shadow. Wendy crept across the yard, avoiding ditches and various hazards, made her way onto a platform, and peered around wooden beams, where she saw work lights on a yellow stand in a more constructed part of the house. A large shadow shifted across the floor and wall.

She wiped sweat from her forehead.

A bag of tools leaned against a stack of two-by-fours. Wendy gingerly plucked up a hammer. *Protection*—just in case. She took measured steps, the kind where the heel precedes the rest in a wave-like motion, soft and intent on the concrete floor.

Wendy made her way down the structure of a hallway, tightly gripping the hammer, and peeked around the corner. Her eyes followed the shadow to . . .

A construction worker.

He was sitting against a wall, earbuds in, scrolling on his phone. His screen lit up a middle-aged Hispanic face. There were more work lights to his left, and Wendy leaned further around the bend to see them—

BUT HE SPOTTED HER.

He sprang up and flicked out his earbuds.

Wendy hid the hammer behind her back and stepped round the corner.

"Who—who are you?" he asked.

"Hi, um . . ."

Wendy's eyes drifted toward the other work light, which illuminated Jothi's body, bound to a steel beam.

"Hey! Who are you?!" he shouted.

"They . . . sent me," Wendy said, coming up with the quickest lie she could think of, "to check on her. Sorry to spook you."

Wendy tried to shove the hammer into the back of her sweatpants.

"*Who* sent you?" He studied her.

"You know who," Wendy lied. She flung off her hood and flashed a smile, hoping she didn't look as ugly as she felt right now.

"They didn't say—"

"Sorry to spook you," Wendy repeated. She still had her hand on the head of the hammer. On second thought, she realized it was not going to hold in her waistband—and maybe she was going to need it.

"Who sent you?"

"Maya—that's what I call her, anyway, if, maybe, you know her by another name, I dunno."

The man nervously bit his nail.

Wendy watched his eyes look at a chisel on a stool beside him.

Why did he look at the chisel?! Was he going to kill her?

"We're cool, man. We're cool." Wendy was pleading for her life in the voice of a surfer.

"I'm gonna call Maya and verify—"

"Do you know if she has a pulse?" Wendy said, taking a few steps toward him and looking over at Jothi's limp body. She could not let him call Maya.

"Hey! You stay." He lifted his phone. "Lemme confirm with her."

His thumb ran across the screen of his phone, *and Wendy ran at him!*

The hammer slipped from her grip, plummeting down her backside, and her hands flung ahead of her, as the construction worker looked up, and she swatted the phone from his fingers!

It flew across the room. Hit the floor with a *crack!*

Sliddddddddddddddddddddd across the concrete.

Wendy jerked her head to see where the phone landed, and she was thrown backward; she felt the construction worker's hands pressed hard against her, one just above her heart and the other on her neck. It was a shove of rage and mess. The force flung her so strongly that the fall felt like flying and time seemed to slow until her ass *slammed!* on the cement and her back against a wood pile.

A cloud of black filled Wendy's vision and slowly dissolved as she watched the construction worker sprint in a fit for his phone toward an area of the room that had been obscured from Wendy's view by a stack of crates . . . and where two women were bound to another steel beam.

The women squealed with muffled voices!—shaking and shifting in their restraints—as the construction worker ran across a gray line that curved round the room. The line appeared soft to the touch, almost like powder or ash, but when the construction worker's foot stepped on it, the materials did not sink or scatter but remained firm.

The man reached for his phone and froze. He looked over at the bound women, his eyes shedding thick, red tears.

"No, no, no, no, no—" he muttered, spinning and dashing back toward the gray line!

But his eyes filled with red.

His movements became stiff.

Blood ran out of his nose, his ears, every orifice of his body.

He opened his mouth to speak, and a thick, sludgy, crimson substance leaked out. His facial features began to shrivel and sink into his face—like the very blood in his body was being sucked from his skin and forced out his frame. He contorted, twitched, and collapsed just beyond the gray line, gasping and choking on the concrete before abating.

The black fully subsided from Wendy's vision, and she focused her eyes on the lifeless body before her, which looked more like a monster than a man now, and then on the two women, who were bound in vines and had smothered whines, because *their mouths were hidden.* It was as if their lips had been folded inward and roots had been sewn through their skin to shut their jaws, and despite this deranged arrangement of their faces, and even the adornment of bruises, dried blood, and ash upon their skin, Wendy immediately recognized them.

Even in this ugly display of horror, she recognized the two most beautiful women she had ever seen: Maya and Rini.

The real Maya and Rini.

THIRTEEN

Dragging a dead or near-dead teenage body along the beach seemed to have been no hindrance for Maya, Rini, and Kesh, as they strolled like it was just any night under the stars. Kesh and Maya held hands the entire walk back. His eyes were so often on her that he tripped multiple times on the sand. The moon and stars revealed only a glimmer of Maya's beauty, but the mysterious contours of her body and the faded hue of her skin were plenty to excite him.

Kesh was eyeing Maya, but she was eyeing Rini, who had been rather quiet on their walk back, taking wide strides and keeping in front of them—maybe the crime had affected one of them, at least.

"I need you," Kesh whispered, gliding his hand around Maya's body.

"When we get back," said Maya, her eyes still on Rini.

"Or here. Now. In the dark."

"Not now. I'll give you a treat when we get back."

Kesh whined like a puppy.

Maya let go of Kesh's hand and stole a few hurried steps to catch up to Rini.

"What?" probed Maya.

"You're being sloppy," replied Rini.

"Oh, please." Maya wrapped her arm around Rini. "Things remain unchanged. I was cautious. Besides, we needed a bit of excitement. Least I did."

"You've had plenty." Rini shook her head. "We need to stick to the plan. It is sure—"

"*Your* plan. I'm not interfering with that, but I'm going to do things my way, because if your plan falters, which I think it is likely to do, and which is the reason I'm here—*to help*, to make sure we get what we came for—we need to cover all the angles."

"If we overstep—" started Rini.

"Don't be silly," said Maya. "The rice is washed."

The beach house lights illuminated the three as they drew near to the Muthus' property. The light also revealed that Maya's and Rini's faces were swelling slightly and peeling, with some splotches dry and flaky.

"You need to reapply," said Maya.

"You too," said Rini. "I need to find Vik. Shouldn't have left him for this long. He'll be going crazy—"

"Should I have another Tuborg before . . .?" Kesh interrupted.

"Yes," answered Maya.

Kesh ran into the beach house.

"You can make it up to him," said Maya to Rini with a smile. "Don't forget to have *funnnnn*."

Rini nodded like she was thinking it over, then her nod turned into a smile, and she hurried up the steps to the Muthus' palace. Maya plucked a flake of skin from her face and rubbed it between her fingertips. She released it and the wind snatched it up. Staring at her hand, she noticed a streak of Jothi's dried blood twirling around her finger. She brought the finger to her mouth and sucked it clean.

Her eyes flickered with felicity, then drifted to the doorway of the beach house, where Kesh stood in his boxers, chin up, with a can against his lips, guzzling down a Tuborg. From one delight to another, Maya withdrew her finger from her mouth and strutted toward him with a smile.

∞

Smiles were absent in the unfinished mansion. Wendy was about as capable of donning a smile as the mouthless women and the corpse. She had just watched a man die, and what she saw in front of her bent reality, twisted truth, shifted the paradigm of the circumstances that had led to so much pain and confusion. Wendy had convinced herself on the beach to be open and willing to accept that her perception of reality was untrue, but now she was confronted not with her own madness but the world's.

And she definitely peed herself again.

But Wendy inhaled. Wendy exhaled. And Wendy prevailed. She prevailed over the disturbing sight of the man's blood-swallowed eyeballs protruding from his head. She prevailed over the disturbing sight of the women's sewn-up faces. She prevailed over the despair that her husband had left her and abandoned her. She prevailed over the fact that the nature of things was supernatural.

And how she prevailed was by . . . crawling.

Because even in her bravery, she was still petrified, and if she were to stand, her knees would buckle, so she dragged herself forward with her hands. Immediately, she felt weighed down—not only by fear but by the hammer, which had sunken down her pant leg to her ankle. She pulled it out of her sweatpants.

Wendy looked at the faces of the women. This Maya and Rini were not confident, oozing with charm, masters of seduction, adored by all. No. They were thin—not hot and skinny *thin* but sickly. They wore long white gowns, which were splattered with dirt and blood. Their eyes pleaded with her for help. They were desperate, alone, hurting.

Quickly, their trapped lips became less nightmarish and more heartbreaking. Wendy couldn't take her eyes off them. They spoke murmurs through their cheeks, their eyes fiercely pointing to the gray line, warning her to not cross it. The closer Wendy got to the line, the more it did look like ash. It was a line of ashes that ran in a circle around the real Maya and Rini. When she was two feet away, Real Maya shook her head and yelled in her closed mouth.

Even muffled, Wendy heard her words clearly: *"STOP! STOP! STOP!"*

There was a smaller, separate circle that enclosed Jothi's body. Wendy swore she could see her sister-in-law's chest rising and falling, even if slightly, but maybe it was just a gimmick of the wind or shadows. She crawled as close as she could to the line of ash. It was much thinner than the larger circle. She made her way around Jothi's crumpled body, searching for her face, which was half hidden behind her arm—

Her arm! It was folded inward, covered in blood, and the bone was snapped, poking out of the skin. Jothi's lip was split and bleeding, and a fat, purple welt was swelling just above her left brow. A blend of sand, dirt, and blood blanketed her whole body, *but she was definitely breathing.*

Wendy was inching dangerously close to the ash line, but she could confidently see Jothi's chest rising, falling. Even the blood on her lip trembled from her breath.

So she was alive!

"Jothi. Jothi." Wendy tried to rouse her, but she did not budge.

Wendy slowly climbed to her feet. Her knees trembled but didn't tumble. The harsh work lights created a strong contrast between the visible and invisible. Everything beyond this room was black; shadows surrounded her.

Wendy walked the outer line of the ash boundary. From above, she could see dark symbols drawn in the ash. She did not recognize the symbols intellectually—but emotionally, her body had a visceral reaction, a feeling of claustrophobia, like the black of the letters was wrapping around her simply by looking at them.

She noticed hundreds of tiny dark spots just inside the boundary too, but upon closer inspection, she realized they were dead bugs. But not *just* dead bugs. They were squished of their guts and blood, much like the construction worker. *Hmmm . . .* must've flown or crawled inside and perished swiftly. Just like him. There was even a dead bird, sprawled out the same bloody way.

Wendy concluded that anything with life in it could not pass the ash.

Whatever boundary this was, it was invisible. Wendy was certain of that. She cocked her head and attempted to see the veil from any possible angle. But there was no shimmering light or lined shadow that gave shape or form to a barrier. It was imperceptible.

Real Maya and Real Rini were bound by the wrists and hands with vines, a thicker, darker, and furrier matter than those binding their lips. But a normal rope tied them to the steel beam. They fidgeted for freedom, extending their legs as far as possible, reaching for the construction worker's body.

Wendy spotted the utility knife on his belt and understood what they needed. The women reached his feet with theirs and struggled with the floor to pull his body toward themselves. But he was just too heavy and their grip too weak.

Yet they kept at it. Real Maya and Real Rini used their bound feet together to grip one of the man's feet by the ankle. He shifted an inch.

Wendy needed to help them. She thought of shoving the body from her end with a piece of wood. She saw a two-by-four against the wall and went to grab it but spotted another utility knife on the ground beside it. *Perfect!* Wendy snatched up the knife.

"Hey, hey," Wendy said. "I got another one."

The women mumbled affirmation. Wendy tossed the knife forward so that it hopped over the boundary and skidded the rest of the way to them. Real Maya covered the knife with her feet and dragged it to where Real Rini's hands could reach it. It took a few minutes to get a grasp on it, and then she gradually began to cut away at the rope.

All Wendy could do was watch. She didn't like *just watching*. While she stood there, she suddenly began to become very afraid. What if Maya and Rini returned? What if they were on their way back up right now? Would Wendy be bound in one of these things next?

Wendy turned around to peer into the darkness.

Should she go out and check?

She turned back to the women to ask them, but they were focused on the task at hand. So she stepped slowly backward, went around the bend, and looked from the hallway structure out at the dug-up yard.

She could hear the waves. She could see the top of the staircase.

Wendy thought about heading across the yard and peering down the steps to see if they were returning, but fear pressed heavy on her. She doubted whether she would be able to see much from the top of the cliff anyway and decided to rush back inside.

The women were still working on the rope.

Wendy checked on Jothi, who appeared to still be breathing, so she studied the rest of the room. There was a corner scattered with bones, some skin and fat still attached, very fresh. There was dried blood everywhere. Wendy put her fist to her mouth to hold back a gag. There was a steel worktable with clumps of hair, finger- or toe-nails, and small jars of murky, red liquid. Beside the table was a pile of cinder blocks, upon which stood a dozen or so other jars, which were slightly larger, containing different shades of liquid and la-beled with tape and marker.

The letters looked like an Indian language, but Wendy could not conclude whether or not it was Tamil.

She inspected a few of them. Some were a paste composition while others were a drinkable liquid. Looking closely, short hairs and flecks of God knows what floated in the substance. Another gag. Wendy set down a jar.

A hint of gold caught her eye from behind the cinder blocks. She circled round to find that it was a can of Tuborg Gold. Dozens of Tuborg Golds, and Tuborg Greens too, were stacked, cases and cases of them. Wendy plucked up the can and noticed instantly that the weight felt off, like the can had been sipped from already; it even sloshed slightly when rotated, but the can was sealed, un-opened.

She studied the lid, the rim, the circumference of the can, and eventually flipped it upside down. On the bottom was a small metallic bubble of epoxy. Wendy didn't blink. She didn't breathe. Even her heart seemed to take pause. It was a trance of truth, where the fog that continually clouded her heart and her mind didn't lift but began to take shape and form, and though she couldn't see through it, she could see *it*.

Clack! Wendy spun. The knife hit the ground. The women flung off the rope from their bodies and shimmied away from the center of the circle, though their feet and hands were still bound.

Wendy met them on the other side of the ash. She squatted down to their level, a safe two feet from the line. "I'm Wendy," she said. "Kesh's . . . *wife*." She lifted the beer bottle, her eyes swelling with tears. "Do you know," she asked, "what they're doing with these?"

Real Maya's eyes rang with compassion. She nodded. Then, using her bound hands, drew two words in the thick layer of dust on the concrete floor:

LOVE SPELL

Wendy's voice cracked with an abrupt cry. Her head fell in her hands. Real Rini mumbled a muffled condolence, and Wendy wiped her tears and tried to pull herself together. She had no time to think, to process. She stared at the women's hands and feet, only pushing the truth to the side temporarily by submitting to the deception of denial, thinking it couldn't possibly be true!—though she knew it was.

"You can't cut those?" Wendy asked, wiping more tears.

Real Maya wrote in the dust:

SPELL WE CANT CUT

"What are they? Witches?" Wendy asked.

Real Maya half nodded, but Real Rini shook her head. She scooted forward and put her fingers to the dust:

RAKSHASAS

"What is that?" Wendy felt the word silently over her tongue. *Rakshasas.*
Real Rini wrote:

DEMONESS

"Demons!?" Wendy ran her hands through her hair like she was going to rip it out and began talking to herself more than to the women. "What—what—what? This is insane. What can we do? Demons?"

Real Maya and Real Rini looked at her with eyes empty of hope. Wendy had a hundred questions but knew she needed to rank and prioritize, especially because the women could only answer at the rate at which they could write.

"How do we free you? Your mouths? The boundary?" she asked.

The women began to cry. Maya put out her finger and drew in the dust as a teardrop splashed onto her letters:

NO HOPE

Wendy took a deep breath. They were all going to die.
Death. Torture. Enslaved. Those were the outcomes.
Wendy exhaled. Hope . . . *was there any?*
Think, think, think. She needed to think!

But her brain was mush. No time.

The fog. It was so thick now. It was all she saw. This gruesome gray—and Kesh. She saw him vividly in her mind: climbing, crawling, clawing at these clouds of confusion but caught in them. He was just as bound as these women with vines around their wrists, and the dark magic that kept them trapped in a ring of ash was no different than the evil that kept Kesh wrapped like a ring around Maya's finger. Every break of her heart was not by his hands; every stab in the back was not by his knife; his words, his actions, his feelings were not his own.

Maya's man was a lie.

But her husband was faithful, was trustworthy—was the real Kesh.

Wendy took another breath. Innnnnnn and ouuuuuuuut.

She had to do something. Anything. Even if she couldn't stop them. Even if she was only delaying the inevitable. Maybe it was hopeless, maybe it was naive, but Wendy needed to believe there was hope—even an ounce! Giving up? It wasn't the Griffith way. It was not her way. It was not the way she might save Kesh. It was not the way she might see him again. It was not the way to die.

No, no, no, no, no! NO!

Damn these demons.

Make them burn.

Send them back to hell.

If there was a way. *If* there was a way. If, if, *if*.

Out of the fog appeared one *if*-inspired fact: *The demonesses had no knowledge of her whereabouts.*

And another one: *She was in their lair with their resources.*

Real Maya and Real Rini were watching Wendy spiral into madness then reason her way out. Her eyes flickered, turning over the circumstances in her mind, processing but not necessarily despairing. If there was any sliver of hope to be found, maybe it was in her, the sand-covered, water-soaked, white girl in sweats. Wendy's eyes were red from crying, swollen and glazed, but the blue shone through, and it was because of the glisten in her sapphire eyes that Real Rini put her fingers to the dust once more, writing:

THE RING

"The ring?" Wendy asked. "What ring?"
Real Rini continued:

SARASWA

—Real Rini paused and looked at Real Maya. They exchanged furrowed brows and blinks while Wendy waited impatiently. Then, Real Rini put her finger to the dust, starting a new word. Facing her sister, she wrote:

REMEMBER CODE?

Real Rini scooted over to the construction worker's phone and plucked it up. It was cracked but functional. Real Maya's sewn lips twitched as she summoned the numbers from the recesses of her mind. Maya had ordered the construction worker to tell her, and Real Maya had listened closely—suddenly, she nodded.

Real Rini passed the phone, and Real Maya unlocked it and passed it back. While it was being transferred from hands to hands, Wendy caught a flash of the phone's wallpaper. It was of the construction worker and his family.

Wife. Kids. *Ugh.*

Wendy turned to look at the spot where she had first seen him sitting against the wall. She didn't even notice until now, but there were a handful of empty cans of Tuborg Greens. Poor guy was compelled to obey them with the same spell of infatuation. Just like Kesh and Vik.

Tap!—tap!—tap!—tap!—tap!—tap!—tap! Real Rini's finger flew at the phone. So much faster than writing in the dust. Any small positive was a blessing on this cursed day. She flipped the phone for Wendy to read: "Saraswathi's ring. It's what they want. A powerful being is bound to the gem and forced to grant boons. Muthus' wealth and success is all the ring."

"What!" Wendy shrieked. It was so loud that the mouthless women flinched.

Wendy had entered the construction site only to have her own sight deconstructed. She had known that she knew little of what was going on, but now she knew how little.

Little. She felt so little in this big mess of madness. Yet, somehow, her size didn't hinder her from believing. Instead, it helped. All the madness made sense in this mad world. The truth was beyond her, but it wasn't beneath her. She wasn't too proud or too afraid to believe. In her heart, demons and a magic ring made more sense than her husband's unfaithfulness.

Wendy continued to ask questions, soaking up everything she could about the rakshasas' plan and process. Real Maya and Real Rini took turns typing out responses about everything they knew. Wendy didn't waste any time. While their fingertips hit the screen, she would run to check on Jothi and make sure she was breathing—continually trying to wake her by speaking, throwing small pebbles, and even splashing water on her from the construction worker's water bottle that Wendy found. She would also peek into the yard, looking and listening for any voices or movement. Real Maya and Real Rini divulged more information than Wendy had anticipated, making her further grateful for the ingenious idea of using the phone instead of the dust to communicate.

Wendy learned that Real Maya and Real Rini had been tricked and captured by the rakshasas almost six months ago, which aligned with the timeline of when she was told Vik and Rini started dating. The rakshasas threatened to kill and eat them if they did not cooperate, claiming to only have kept them alive for information. The women had seen the demonesses feast on animals and a human, shapeshift, concoct potions, fly, and cast various spells. But Maya and Rini were wary of how they display their power because of the risk of drawing the attention of other powerful beings.

How the rakshasas discovered the ring's whereabouts was never spoken about in front of the women, but even the demonesses seem to know little about its history—besides that the sapphire gem binds a powerful being much greater than themselves who has been forced to grant boons as a punishment by a god. Infiltrating the Muthu family was a game for them—but it was also because they needed to know the name of the being to summon it, and Saraswathi was most likely the only person who held that knowledge.

Wendy felt like she was drinking from a waterfall, but the waters settled when Real Maya explained that the rakshasas seemed to be in a rush when they brought Jothi and—seeing that she was already in such poor physical condition—used a relatively weaker spell to bind her. While the spell that bound them seemed to be strenuous and lengthy, they had seen the rakshasas perform simpler boundary spells before, like the one Jothi had been set in. They even memorized the mantra, gestures, and process of casting and breaking the spell. Maya added that the women's mouths were sewn shut to keep them quiet, but also to keep them from meddling in any enchantments placed on them, and that they were put to sleep during the casting and breaking of the spell that held their own ash boundary.

Hmmm...

Could someone besides a rakshasa dissolve the spell with the knowledge of how to perform it? Did you have to be a demon? A demoness? Indian? *Was one-eighth close enough?* God knows ... but Real Maya and Real Rini did not.

But! *But*—it was worth a try!

"Tell me. Show me," Wendy said.

Real Maya began with gestures and Real Rini typed out the mantra and other instructions while Wendy lost all confidence in the idea almost immediately. She simultaneously felt silly and terrified, as she mimicked the signs of demons. But Real Maya took it seriously and patiently, so Wendy tried her best to mimic that too. The mouthless beauty would even wiggle which hand she was referencing to before making the motion to avoid confusion.

Her hand formed a downward claw that rose and rotated outward, then went around in a circle while pulsating with quick jerks. Wendy copied—*well*, she thought she copied. But Real Maya shook her head. This happened many, many times. Apparently, Wendy's claw was not correct. One finger curled too much, the other not enough. Too much wrist but not enough twist. It took several attempts till Real Maya gave an optimistic shrug.

Wendy didn't even finish reading aloud the mantra once before Real Rini flipped the phone back to herself and began rewriting. She turned it back with the pronunciations sounded out beside each word. Wendy read out loud the mantra about a dozen times before feeling remotely confident in her pronunciation of a language she did not understand and words she did not know. Eventually, Real Rini gave a nod about as confident as Real Maya's shrug.

Real Rini tossed Wendy the phone.

"Is this stupid?" Wendy asked. "Like, am I going to be cursing myself or selling my soul to the devil if this works?"

The mouthless women's eyebrows flexed, and for a moment, the roots sewn through their skin gave the shape of smiles. She could almost hear a nervous laugh sound through their silence. Wendy and her shadow walked over to Jothi's boundary. She couldn't help but almost nervously laugh herself. Wendy was terrified, unqualified, and taking a shot in the dark, but, at least, she wasn't alone. She had the once-captivating-and-now-held-captive sisters, and—if she could save her—she had Jothi. Even if they were all going to die, maybe she could get Jothi to safety, to a hospital, or delay the demons for a little.

If Wendy thought too hard, her confidence would go soft. She felt that she needed to believe this could work. That she could save Jothi. And just as she readied her tongue to recite the words, her eyes snagged on the bottles of potions, and they tore open an idea in her mind's eye. There was a flutter in her heart that felt less like wings flapping and more like wings flattening: a simple soar of relief. She pushed the thought to the side, knowing truly it had no merit yet, but held onto the feeling, onto the ounce of hope!

The light flutter made her words like butter, smoothing over Wendy's tongue. She hoped her confidence would make up for whatever was lacking in her pronunciation. Her claw crawled and twitched, just like she'd practiced. And while Wendy didn't understand the meaning behind each word, she could somehow feel the meaning behind the sound of them. Maybe it was all in her heart, but she felt that she was invoking the power of a higher being, asking it to relinquish its hold on this barrier.

When the fourth line ran off her lips, she blew.

The air warmed her lips as it left, and the heat spread across her nose, cheeks, eyes, ears, and scalp. It was so warm that it gave her chills—like the breath was both coming from her and coming upon her. The gust flowed through her hair like the mouth of a giant had its lips pressed behind her. Her little breath and this big breath merged into one and unfurled the ash line so that the circle was no more and diffused into the gray and dust of the concrete floor.

Instead of rushing to Jothi's side, Wendy charged to the potions. *This was her idea!* She snatched up three and brought them to Real Maya and Real Rini.

"Can you read these?" Wendy held one up at a time.

"Poison," Real Maya typed.

Wendy held up another.

"Inflammation?" she typed this time.

The third one read மருந்து. Rini pointed excitedly with both hands the moment Wendy turned the bottle so that they could read it.

"Medicine!" typed Real Rini.

Wendy unscrewed the lid while hurrying to Jothi's side. She slid the broken arm from Jothi's face, scooped her head up in her own arm, and put the potion to Jothi's split lip. She tilted back the bottle, watching the yellow sludge slide into her mouth. Wendy hadn't hesitated till now, but it was too late. The liquid was sinking into Jothi's mouth.

"Please, please, Jothi." Wendy stroked her cheek and kissed her forehead. If this elixir was even going to help, how much would it heal her, and how long would it—?

SNAP!

Wendy flinched at the sound that rang in her ears and shot blood onto her face. She cocked her head toward Jothi's arm, where the broken bone was sinking back into the arm while flesh closed around it. Jothi's arm—as well as her entire face—began to shed flakes of damaged skin. The lump on her forehead transformed into a thin bubble of skin, which crumbled like ash. Jothi's chest rose, her lungs filling with fresh air, and then expelled a hard and healthy sigh.

And then she awoke.

FOURTEEN

Orange fought the black. It was like the sun had breathed its fire into the heavens. A smudge became a streak and streaks became the sky. Color was coming; night was fleeing. After surviving the shadows with only the LED bulbs of the construction site, a true blaze of natural light had never seemed so pure and so needed. Wendy hoped that it would not only cast away the visible darkness but the invisible darkness as well, which had buried itself inside the Muthu family.

Wendy stepped on a root. She felt guilty leaving Real Maya and Real Rini bound and silent. It was an unusual circumstance for feelings of friendship to be born, but with birth often comes both fear and pain. At this point, for Wendy, if someone wasn't a demon or infatuated with a demon, they were a friend. But if the mouthless women were her friends, she felt even more responsible to free them.

"Should we send it?" Jothi asked. She paused in the brush.

Wendy pulled out the construction worker's phone from a bag at her side. The battery was low, but it wasn't dead yet. This was the first step in their plan . . . if it could be called that. Wendy thought of halves. Her mother had always harped on halves. Half-hearted. Half-assed. Half-baked. Wendy's heart was in it—her ass too. But she felt about as confident as someone with their ass half wiped, and that's why her mother's words echoed in her head.

But there was no more time to be spent outlining any plan or tossing out ideas. Wendy already questioned whether or not squandering the night while Maya and Rini may have been sleeping was the right idea. No one knew if rakshasas really did sleep. Allegedly, they could, but it may not be as necessary as it is for humans. Real Maya and Real Rini had seen them rest, *but sleep?* There was no way of knowing. Despite the urge to rush into any sort of plan, Wendy and Jothi had agreed it was better to wait and strategize.

And that's what they did—after, of course, Jothi had a mental breakdown, processed the reality of the situation, and was caught up to speed on everything Wendy knew. Jothi remembered nothing after Maya threw her down the steps, but she was completely healed after drinking the potion. It was a miracle. Without her, Wendy would've never even known where to start. Yet here they were, hiking along a hidden path onto the Muthus' property, one only Jothi and her friends knew about. Apparently, this is how they snuck out at night.

Wendy felt like Jothi was her friend too now. Her sister-in-law was the only person she could trust out here. Jothi had seen Maya and Rini for what they really were. She had even stood up to Maya and Kesh for *her*, for Wendy. A tear had slipped down Wendy's cheek the moment Jothi told her. She almost died—would have died!—because of it. The teenager whom everyone thought cared so little was the only person who cared enough to do something. And now, they were doing something *together*—something risky and stupid . . . but *something*.

Wendy typed out a text on the construction worker's phone to Maya, which read:

"They are escapinf somehow help sh"

It was Jothi's idea to leave typos and take out any punctuation to ensure there was no suspicion. If Maya and Rini weren't sleeping, this would draw them away, hopefully long enough for Wendy and Jothi to reach Saraswathi. If the rakshasas were asleep, maybe there was still time to reach the matriarch unnoticed.

Wendy sent the message.

Now . . . it was time to wait. But how long should they wait before concluding that Maya and Rini were asleep? What if they were awake but not by Maya's phone? If they were to spot Wendy, it might be surprising, but if they spotted Jothi—healthy, alive, free —it was all over. So the timing needed to be right, and there were just so many factors that could go wrong.

"Nothin' yet?" Jothi asked.

Wendy shook her head.

The girls sat down in the bushes. Sunbeams were shooting and ricocheting off the leaves, painting the shape of an orange pretzel on Jothi's cheek, and with the assistance of the wind, the shadows would dance so that the pretzel rearranged into the shape of a bird's head, like a peacock. *Ah, peacocks.* Wendy could use the blessing of peacocks right now . . . some good fortune, some positivity . . . yeah, yeah . . . she could . . . she wondered what that sound was. *Why did it keep repeating?*

BZZZZZZ . . . BZZZZZZ . . . BZZZZZZ.

Wendy's eyes flung open. Jothi's too.

BZZZZZZ . . . BZZZZZZ . . . BZZZZZZ.

They had dozed off. Shit!

Maya was calling. It went to voicemail. There were two missed calls.

"What time is it?" Jothi asked, jumping to her feet as panic pumped in her.

"Almost eight. She called twice. Just now. We need to go. I'm sure they're on their way over."

"You think they'll be okay? The real Maya and Rini?"

"I don't know. But this is it."

Jothi nodded like she understood. Wendy had admired the sisters' bravery, openly and willingly using themselves as distractions. It was about all they could do since there was no way to free them, but no doubt the rakshasas would torture them to find out the truth. That's why Wendy and Jothi needed to haul ass to Saraswathi. *Now!*

⁂

While Wendy and Jothi were napping, Vik awoke both excited nervous and *nervous* nervous. Today was a big day for him. Last night, as Rini demanded, he had a very intense conversation with Paatti. His grandmother had a soft spot for him, but that didn't prevent her from pushing back hard. It felt like they had reached a good compromise, and he only hoped Rini would see it the same way. If she loved him as much as he loved her, everything would work itself out. Making love last night and this morning had only solidified that feeling.

He shoved his wallet in his front pocket beside the ring box to mask the bulge. Vik was never big on waiting. If something needed done, he was going to do it then or not at all—unless, of course,

Rini asked him to wait. He would wait for her. He would do any-thing for her. Even things he didn't like to do. But as far as he knew, she wanted to make this happen as much as him—not to mention, they were on the clock with the new baby coming and all. Father-hood—*was he ready for that?* No, certainly not. Not even Kesh had kids. Nobody could have predicted Vik becoming a dad before his big brother!

But Rini had changed things. She had changed Vik. For the better. Whatever the future held, he was ready if it meant that they would be together.

⚬

While Wendy and Jothi were napping, Maya climbed out of bed, neither feeling tired nor rested. She cracked open a Tuborg and fed Kesh sips in his sleep. She had to do this multiple times in the nights to avoid the spell wearing off. The first night, she had been less stringent, and he'd almost come out of it. As fun as it was watching guilt and horror flood his face, she preferred it sucking on hers. She could not wait to keep this body. She could not wait to keep *him*.

She fed him like a baby, nursing him to hell. *Drink up, little one.* She mounted him, knowing he would awaken in seconds charged with a fresh surge of passion. And she was right. Kesh's eyes slid open, his hands found her body, and desire flooded him, a desire she alone could drink up.

After sex, they got dressed and headed up for breakfast.

The sand warmed Maya's feet. The sun warmed her face. Kesh's hand warmed her ass. It was a perfect California day for a cold-blooded creature like her. The only thing was . . . *she couldn't find her phone.* It must've gotten lost in the shuffle of sex and shoving that teenager down the steps. It was the perfect task for her new boyfriend—Maya was always trying to keep him busy, preoccupied. She only had so much time to train his tongue.

"Baby, I really need you to do me a favor," said Maya, all concerned. It was so fun to play with her pet.

"Of course," Kesh replied. "What can I do, baby?"

"I can't find my phone. Can you locate it? Probably lost it messin' around with you yesterday. I really need it."

"Oh, I'm on it. Don't worry."

"Don't be gone too long, of course."

Maya strutted across the Muthus' lawn toward the patio, looking back at him with her lip between her teeth. That look inspired Kesh to be absolutely determined. He would find this phone, whether it was buried in a couch or the depths of the earth, he would retrieve it—for her. He would do anything for her. Because he loved her.

Fortunately, it was an easy find. He hurried up the outside staircase to the outdoor patio, where Wendy had caught them in the act. Kesh hoped that she was doing alright, that she would move on one day and understand. The phone was on a table, just where Maya had set it after dancing last night, and where he guessed she'd left it when they left Wendy to find a comfier, less busy place to make love.

It was a good feeling to be right, but it was a great feeling to know he would be making Maya happy so quickly. He snatched up the phone.

৪

While Wendy and Jothi were napping, Meena and Jack, alone, discussed the most pressing matters on their minds: the current state of their children and how each child might reflect poorly on them as parents—if not now, soon. Perceptions of parenthood were *their* demons. As far as they knew, the fire of hell was the burning look of disappointment in Saraswathi's eyes.

Like all of their talks, Meena was the hydrant and Jack was the hose—the hose that her flood of words ran right through. Not that her words put out any fires. If anything, she only got more fired up. Jack, though he tried to engage, simply did not have the level of passion to be heard by Meena.

"Why is it the moment we have one son finally looking for a stable relationship, the other's implodes? I don't doubt Kesh is jealous that Vik found a beautiful Indian woman, but it's his own damn fault for marrying that bat-boo."

"Bat-boo?" Jack's lips turned upward, and he turned toward his wife with furrowed brows. She'd come up with many derogatory terms for Wendy—but that was a new one.

"Bat-bat-bob—" Meena's hand reached out and fingered the air, grasping for the word. "That disgusting monkey with the-the red ass hanging out. Bat—something."

"Baboon? Buh-*boon*."

"Baboon—whatever—"

"Or did you mean buffoon?"

"What's a buffoon?"

"I don't know. An idiot?" Jack shrugged and laughed.

"Well, you're a buffoon! And a baboon—just like Wendy. Now, will you please let me finish what I was saying, Jack, dammit —buh-buh-buh-boo-boo—" Meena was just mocking him now. "Such an ass you are."

"Sorry, what were you saying?"

Meena held her hand in the air, shaking her head. She began plucking a few pieces of fuzz that had clung to her sari, then brushed along the silk for good measure, eventually working up the courage to speak again. She was even more heated now.

"What I was trying to say is—it's not like I even like Wendy, and I'm not trying to defend her or anything, but are we really going to let our son blow up his marriage—get divorced? We'll never hear the end of it. I don't know why he can't just marry a proper person and stay married. Kesh should have thought about this before he went against his family's advice. And what sort of example is he setting for Jothi? She's a wild one—next thing we know, she'll be a lesbian or single for the rest of her life. How she spends her time with that *Eeeeesha*—it makes me uncomfortable. How they hold hands and cuddle on the couch. It's not right. And I like Maya and Rini. I always have, since they were little girls. Very pretty, very polite. I just don't see how it's all going to work out, and I just know, I know, it's going to get put on us—*on me*. Your mother's going to say it's *my* fault. Kesh will be forgiven, and I'll get the chastisement. And just at the time!—the very time that, you know, Amma can't wear her ring anymore. Maybe—maybe it's time she'll think of passing it on, and all this has to happen to me. It's not going to be me now! I know it's not going to be me now."

"Maybe they'll work it out. You never know." Jack lifted his hands behind his head, interlocked his fingers, and leaned back.

"Shouldn't we do something? I don't understand—don't you care?"

"What do you mean?"

"'What do I mean?' I don't even know why I talk to you! You're absolutely no help. I raised the kids entirely on my own, of course—of course, I'm the one who's got to take care of them as adults too. I shouldn't expect you to do anything—I don't expect you to do anything."

"You want me to do something? I'll do something."

"What—what are you going to do?"

"What do you want me to do?"

"You're a buffoon and a baboon, Jack. Buh-buh-buh!"

Jack stared at her, genuinely confused, then shook it off with a sigh. He really did care, and he really would've done something if she had asked him to do something specific. But Jack didn't like to get involved in complex situations, especially if it required words. He was a simple man and complexity overwhelmed him to the point where he avoided it. He had a fear of making things worse and that kept him from trying to make anything better.

There was only one reason—one motive—that could rouse him to courageous or impassioned action, and that was his mother. He didn't know why, but if Saraswathi needed defending, which she rarely did, or someone to leap to her aid, Jack was ready. Anything for Amma. Unlike Meena's obsession with Saraswathi—which was completely selfish—Jack truly loved his mother. He looked past her comments and criticisms, the way a young lover looks past a significant other's flaws. They were nearly oblivious to him.

Meena hated this. First of all, she could never compete with genuine affection. Second, Jack had never given her the same unconditional love or immediate attention that he gave his mother. He was a mama's boy through and through—even if his mama didn't love him back. To Saraswathi, he was like a fly that continually sits upon you, despite swatting it away a billion times.

"I think I'm going to check up on Amma," Jack said.

"Great, thanks—I'm glad you feel resolved on all this," Meena scoffed.

Jack stood, scratched the back of his head, and started away.

⚇

While Wendy and Jothi were napping, Saraswathi fought her fingers with her sapphire ring. Her arthritis had caused inflammation before but never to such a degree. Fat fingers. She hated fat fingers. They were like her husband's—pudgy, disproportionate sausages. His hands were the things she missed least about Ruwan.

She slid the ring onto her chain and secured it around her neck. She did not like it being so exposed, so snatchable—not that anyone had ever tried to steal it, but they certainly tried to touch it! And it was her job alone to protect the ring, to steward its beauty, its power, and its privacy. She was already forming a habit of rubbing the area above her chest to make a quick inspection of the ring's condition. She had found her eyes drifting to mirrors too. Without the gem on her hand, she couldn't see it. But her eyes were finding ways.

To think!—Vik had the nerve to ask for it with one day's notice. Even if she preferred to give it to him over the rest of her homebred embarrassments, it wasn't time. Not yet. Not till she was on her deathbed would she part with the ring. And not—not, not, not!—until one of her descendants proved him or herself at least an inkling worthy of wielding the Muthus' greatest treasure.

In years to come, Saraswathi could imagine passing the ring down to a well-rounded contender like Rini, but it was simply too soon. Time would tell what sort of woman she truly was. Like Meena, who had seemed like a nice girl of good heritage and stable emotions at first—clearly had been faking it. Decades of impressions later revealed the truth. That chubby shadow of hers—it was only fitting that her witless son, Jack, was paired with such an embarrassment for a daughter.

Jothi, on the other hand, was a possibility. She was a smart girl but certainly not disciplined enough. If she was anything like her generation, there was little hope for her.

So . . . slim pickings.

Saraswathi made her way to the kitchen, alerting them to prepare champagne for breakfast. Her relatives looked tired after the Bollywood Bash, typical, but not a valid excuse for underdressing. That was not tiredness but laziness. She seemed to be the only person dressed for the occasion. Certainly, their heavy eyes and slouched bodies would perk up when they heard the news.

"Amma."

Saraswathi turned to see Jack approaching.

"You doing okay, Amma? You need anything? How's your arthritis?"

Jack tried to touch her arm, but—upon getting too close to the ring—she swatted him away.

"I, okay—no touch."

"You need anything?"

She spoke in Tamil, slightly annoyed, and asked him to gather everyone. Jack smiled and obeyed. Her son had a good heart, but to Saraswathi, that meant he had a *soft* heart. He lacked the conviction required to honor the Muthu name. Despite her husband's best efforts—and even hers after Ruwan's death—Jack had changed little. If anything, he'd only gotten softer.

Jack gathered stuffed faces while Saraswathi scanned the room for Vik. He sat with his arm around Rini. The matriarch gave a nod, and he stood, helping Rini to her feet. He nervously fingered the bulge in his pocket. As soon as Saraswathi opened her mouth to speak, everyone else fell silent.

"*Azhagiya paiyaa*. Baby, baby," Saraswathi said, smiling at Vik. "So good you here with Paatti, and you bring amazing woman, Rini. Kudumba Pandigai is good family time. Bring together. But this time special. Very special."

Light gasps filled the room. Heads turned to the young couple.

Meena joined Jack at Saraswathi's side.

Saraswathi fingered the ring on her neck as tears filled her eyes.

Rini eyed the ring, then shot a confused glare at Vik.

"I love you, baby," Saraswathi continued. "You share big news now."

Maya stood as one of the onlookers, watching and ready for this big announcement. She had a clear view of Vik and Rini, but Saraswathi was obscured by other heads. While Vik cleared his throat and began rambling on about his love for Rini, Maya observed Rini's face, noted the look of genuine surprise, and squeezed through an aunt and uncle toward Saraswathi to see if she still had the ring when—

Kesh grabbed her arm, distracting her. She rotated with a scowl but quickly morphed it into a friendly smile.

"What's happening?" he whispered.

Maya put her finger to her lips and gestured with her eyes.

Kesh looked to his brother, picking up a few of Vik's words now: ". . . Rini, you make me feel so alive. I've never met anyone like you . . ."

Kesh's jaw dropped and then closed on a proud smile. "I found your phone," he said, handing it over to Maya. He swallowed her in his arms so that they both could watch the proposal. Maya glanced down at her phone, the black screen filling with color as the text from the construction worker's phone sent nearly two hours ago unveiled itself.

Maya peeled Kesh's body off her. "Stay here," she commanded.

"Where you going?"

"Stay."

"Okay, baby."

Maya sank into the back of the room and called the construction worker's phone. Her eyeballs bounced, dodging panic, but fury built when the call went to voicemail.

She eyed Rini, Vik's hand on his pocket.

They were so close to the sapphire! *Finally*. She was so hungry, so thirsty, so famished. She could almost taste it! Roll its blue against her tongue. Her throat throbbed. Her skin tingled at the thought of its power surging in her, its beauty against her skin. But she needed to wait, just a little longer, to resolve this kink—

A little kink for a kinky girl.

And maybe, a light snack before a feast.

Yummmm.

⚇

Maya left Rini and the ring. She slipped out of the palace and ran across the lawn to the stairs that led down to the beach. She called the construction worker's phone once more while descending the steps—the call that awoke Wendy.

Wendy and Jothi booked it through the brush, slid through a crack in the fence, and sprinted across the lawn toward the palace within the same minute that Maya had! A sliver of seconds that saved their lives. Though they knew death was near and even likely, they did not know that they had rubbed shoulders with it. If Maya had called while crossing the lawn or if they had awoken when she first called, they certainly would have been killed, and all hope lost. But because of those seconds, they were given a second chance to dance with the devils.

Jothi knew that she couldn't be seen by the rakshasas, so she dashed along the side of the palace and climbed the lattice to her grandmother's bedroom—not knowing, of course, that Paatti was downstairs watching the proposal. Wendy ran to the back patio, trying to calm her breath, fix her hair, and appear somewhat presentable—not that she cared what the Muthus thought of her right now, but because she didn't want to rouse any suspicion if she ran into Maya or Rini.

Wendy entered the house, and it was surprisingly empty. There was a cluster of staff leaning against the wall listening to Vik's words one room over. Wendy crept toward an arched doorway that led into a massive dining room, which functioned more like a sit-down restaurant. She walked up three steps, which were tiled with peacock artwork, into the room.

Everyone was clustered, and she weaved through folks to get a better look. She was close enough to hear Vik's words clearly now.

". . . I'm so thankful for how my family has quickly welcomed Rini this week—not that that is any surprise, because she is just so lovable. I have never been so happy."

Wendy peeked between shoulders. She could see Vik getting down on his knee. Was he about to give her the ring?! *No, no, no, no, no*—what should she do? What could she do? Did Saraswathi already tell them about the being? The name?

Wendy's eyes flew through the crowd looking for her grandmother-in-law. She had to stand on her tiptoes to catch sight of her.

The old lady had her fingers on her neck, completely covering the ring so that Wendy couldn't tell if she still had it or not. Wendy's eyes jerked back and forth at—

Vik digging in his pocket and Saraswathi's swollen fingers—

Rini looking at Saraswathi and not her future fiancé—

Saraswathi's fingers rubbing, separating—

Vik opening up the ring box—

A dazzle of blue—

It caught the light, piercing even the shadows of Saraswathi's fingers, telling Wendy her grandmother-in-law STILL HAD THE RING! Relieved, Wendy's eyes rested on her brother-in-law. He opened the ring box, revealing a beautiful sapphire engagement ring, five-carat, surrounded by diamonds, but . . . *not Saraswathi's ring*.

"Rini, you are my life, my breath, the reason my heart beats every day." Vik's eyes floated to Rini, a shy smile on his face. "I want to be with you forever. Will you marry me?"

Rini's finger rose to her forehead, and she scratched an itch. She cocked her head toward Saraswathi's neck, then back at the lover boy below her. Her head gradually fell and rose into a nod, and a plastic smile crawled across her face, a murmur barely escaping her lips.

"Yes, yes, yes."

Cheers! Clapping! The family erupted in joy. Vik jumped up and forced a kiss on Rini, then squeezed her into his arms. Saraswathi wiped a few tears.

"Do you like it?" Vik asked in a whisper. "The gem's actually bigger. And it's Paatti's. A twin she had custom-made."

"This is not what we agreed."

"Oh, I know, but she said in time, ya know, we're on the list, but she needs to see us live out our marriage. That makes sense, right? Is that okay?"

"No. You have failed me."

Vik's eyes grew wide, his eyebrows furrowed, and he shook his head in shame. The celebratory noises were quieting. Wendy hid behind relatives as Rini glanced her way.

"You're not happy?" Vik pouted.

"We'll talk. Come."

Rini scanned the room for Maya, then seeing she was gone, snatched Vik's hand and led him out of the room. When they were out of sight, Wendy, too, looked for Maya. The coast seemed clear, but there was no time to spare. She made her way to Saraswathi . . . *but she had vanished.* Where did she go?!

Wendy's head spun, and so did her body.

So many faces. Heads. Shoulders. Bodies.

Young, old. Men, women.

Faces she knew. Faces she didn't.

It was a sea of skin and saris. So Wendy escaped the cluster of people, stepping out to get a wider view, and then Wendy spotted her! Saraswathi was down the long hallway, hobbling away with . . . Jothi! *Thank God.* Wendy hurried to catch up with them when she saw Kesh cracking open a Tuborg.

Pssssst! The sound of poison. The poisoning of her marriage, of her husband. Tears filled her eyes at the sight of him. The man had shattered her heart, but he had no control over his. She couldn't leave him like this! She needed him—the good husband, the man who could be trusted, the man she loved.

She needed Kesh.

"What are you doing here, Wendy?" he asked, seeing her abruptly.

"No hard feelings," Wendy said. "I just wanted to apologize. I see how good you and Maya are together, and I'm happy for you."

Kesh brought the Tuborg to his lips—

"Wait—wait! Maya said not to drink it."

"What?" He lowered the can.

"Yes, I just spoke with her to say I'm sorry and you two belong together. She told me to tell you not to drink any Tuborgs because she has a better drink for you. Something more powerful. I dunno. Her words, not mine. She told me to bring you to her."

"She always wants me drinking my Tuborgs."

"I know, Kesh." Wendy grabbed him by the hand. "But she's produced a better drink, special for you. She wants to meet you at your spot—whatever that means." Wendy pulled him into the hallway and started walking, keeping an eye out for Maya's return. She could barely hear her own voice over the pounding of her heart in her throat.

Kesh set down the Tuborg. He followed Wendy.

"She wants me to meet her in the closet?"

"Yeah, yeah. The closet. Don't worry—I'm not going in there with you, just wanna show that we're all good by bringing you to her. But don't wanna keep her waiting. She's got a really, *really* good surprise for you."

"Oh?"

Kesh began breathing out his mouth. Wendy swore she could see drops of sweat forming on his temples. Kesh began to speed ahead of her, and she followed him all the way to the comfy closet of blankets and pillows. Wendy opened her bag, revealing a nest of stolen goods. Before they left the construction site, she collected whatever demonic concoctions she could reasonably carry—just in case they came in handy!

She removed a jar labeled மருந்து. Another healing potion. She didn't know if this would even work, if it could even reverse the spell he was under, but Wendy figured it was worth a try.

"Here," Wendy said. "She told me to tell you to drink this before going in."

"What the heck is this? It looks disgusting! Are you sure?"

"Yes. Hey—don't criticize Maya. She made it for you."

A look of guilt flashed across his face. Kesh snatched the jar and downed the yellow sludge.

He started for the closet doors.

"Wait. How do you feel?"

"Good. Great."

"Crazy about Maya?"

"Well, yeah, *I love her.*" Kesh rolled his eyes.

The words hurt, but only because she hurt *for him*. He had no autonomy over his own thoughts, emotions, body. He was enslaved to a demoness.

It was because of this hurt, the pain of a loved one, that she let him open the closet doors, and why—upon him stepping into the doorway—she shoved him with the full force of her strength! She slammed the doors shut and bound the handles with a rope from her bag. The doors shook as Kesh fought to pry them open, but Wendy put her full weight against the door, tying knot after knot. She sprinted over to a botanically embroidered chair, and dragged it to the doors, tilting and locking it under the handles for extra security.

"Hey! Hey! Hey!" Kesh shouted.

"Calm down, Kesh! This is—this is what Maya wants. She'll be here soon. Just relax."

She could hear him huffing and puffing, but he stopped shouting. Wendy took out a marker from her bag and wrote in black letters on the door:

DO NOT OPEN TEENAGER ON DRUGS

(WITHDRAWALS)

It was the best and quickest lie that came to mind. She couldn't have anyone setting him free before the potion wore off. *Not that this would stop Maya.* God knows if anything could stop her when she returned. So every second counted, yet Wendy couldn't spend time counting the seconds. There was only time to act. She charged up the steps to find Jothi and Saraswathi.

⁰₀

"How else, Paatti, would I know 'bout the ring?" Jothi pleaded.

Saraswathi clutched the ring in a fist. Her eyes were firm and unblinking on her granddaughter. Her head wobbled, and she kept smacking her lips.

"I know you're scared, but you have to trust me. They are *rakshasas*, and they want the ring. You can summon the being to ask for help. They will know I escaped soon and come for us. We cannot stop them any other—"

Wendy sprinted into the bedroom out of breath and shut the door behind her.

"Out, out, out!" Saraswathi shouted while shooing her away with her hand.

"Wendy saved me!" Jothi put her hands on her grandmother's shoulders. "I was dying. We can trust her—pretty much only her." Tears swelled in Jothi's eyes. "We are running out of time. You have to summon it! *Please.*"

Saraswathi let her cane fall so that she could use her other hand to undo the clasp on her necklace without letting go of the ring.

"Here." Jothi went behind her to help with the clasp, but Saraswathi swatted her hands away. She undid the clasp herself and lowered her fist with the gem.

"You not hear name. You go."

"You can trust *us.*"

"No one trust. No one know name but Paatti."

Wendy and Jothi shared a look, then a desperate shrug.

"Okay, okay. But you need to summon it right now, Paatti. We'll go into your bathroom and shut the door." Wendy snapped her fingers with both hands. "But you gotta do this now, or we're all going to die."

"You cover sound." Saraswathi cupped her ear with her hand.

"Summon it," Jothi ordered.

"Tell us after you've said it," Wendy added.

"Okay, baby, okay." Saraswathi's grip crawled open so that the beauty of the blue shone out. It was as if every light in this bedroom reflected in it. It really did catch every light and every eye.

Wendy and Jothi went into the bathroom, shut the door, and put their hands over their ears, blind and silent to what was about to take place.

Saraswathi petted the sapphire with her swollen finger, kissed it gently, and parted her lips to whisper the word, the *name*—

KNOCK, KNOCK, KNOCK.

Saraswathi's tongue was left in suspension. She looked at the door.

"Go now, come later!" she shouted.

"It's me, Paatti." It was Vik's voice. "Rini and I need to talk with you about something important." He cleared his throat. "It can't wait."

"Soon! Soon! Paatti busy! Just give—"

THE BEDROOM DOOR FLEW OPEN.

Vik and Rini marched in.

Saraswathi closed her fist tight around the ring and brought it to her side. She fought to mask her fear, but her elderly knees trembled, and she looked like she might fall. Vik scooped up her cane and handed it to her.

"You alright, Paatti?" he asked.

"Yes, yes. But you go. Come in ten minute. I not feel good."

"Well, I'll make you some chai. That'll help. But Rini and I, we need to speak with you again about the ring. We are very grateful for the gift, but, you know, I love her, and she wants to honor our family by wearing your ring for our engagement. So, will you give it to us?"

"No, baby." She tried to connect with their eyes, but hers kept falling away.

"Paatti, please."

Rini studied the old woman, watched her shy eyes and clenched fist. She bit her lip and smiled. "Why are you afraid, Paatti?" asked Rini. "*Hmmm?*"

"Afraid? You not demand such thing. You wait—"

"I have waited *sooooo* long for this. I have tried not to *force* anything."

Rini snatched Paatti's hand with a grip like iron.

"Hey, what are you—" Vik started.

"Vik, babe, this is the only way for us to be *together*. You love me, don't you? More than this old lady. More than anything, right?"

"Of course." Vik nodded, very understanding.

"Baby! Help me!" Saraswathi shouted. "Help! Help! HELP!"

⁂

Kesh thought Maya would never return. Good thing he loved her, because she liked to make a man wait. Maybe there was something about the buildup, the tension, the longing; she wanted to stretch their hearts like elastic so that when they yanked back together, there would be an untamed hurricane of passion. But that's how it always was with her: a storm. Their love was a storm, and she was the eye of it, the focal point of everything he wanted and needed.

The simple and honest act of waiting for her aroused him. He *got* to *wait* on *her*. The most beautiful, charming, perfect creature on the planet. He could barely contain himself. Thoughts of her made him want to shred pillows—tear his clothes—scream from the rooftops—and drink more Tuborgs! His belly never grew full of them. Sure, his bladder did, and he urinated a lot more, but it was worth every piss.

Kesh couldn't believe Maya would want him to stop drinking them! Maybe Wendy did just lock him in here because she was jealous, because she was mean. Maya had told him she couldn't be trusted, that it was better if she was out of the picture. *Why did she even come back?* How did she even get on the property? He knew Wendy wasn't the type to give up easily, but now she was just being selfish! Rude! Lying and locking him in here was a waste of her energy and his time . . . *if* her intentions were impure.

He wasn't pointing any fingers or anything. Maybe Maya *was* coming to surprise him. Yet he couldn't help but feel this twinge in his heart, that he had been tricked and wronged in some way. His mouth began to grow dry. He was sweating all over. He no longer wanted to rip open the pillows in passion but instead hugged one close for comfort. He sunk back into a pile of blankets and pillows, hoping to normalize the tiny feeling of sinking inside of himself.

That twinge!—like a slight pinch in his chest. It felt fuzzy and faint, but it was growing, spreading, multiplying across his body, and his palms began to drip while his limbs trembled, and he clutched his stomach before vomiting everywhere!—and then, while catching his breath, everything he'd done and everything that had been done to him, swelled from that twinge, that pinch. Each image, each thought, each feeling pressed on him like a heavy hand —and he saw every touch and every breath he shared with Maya and felt every comment and gesture of dismissal toward Wendy. And how he had left his little sister to die on a concrete floor! And how he had shattered his wife's heart!—time!—and time!—and time again!

This was a storm. This was a hurricane. It swept him up. It consumed him. He shook and convulsed as his body, heart, and mind filled with the truth. He had to force in gasps of air because even his own lungs seemed too ashamed to keep him breathing. His sobriety broke the dams in his eyes and tears fled in fury. The love spell shattered and the shards cut him to the bone.

But in these fragmented pieces of pain, Kesh caught flashes of Wendy's investigative nature, how she had locked him in the closet till this spell wore off, and of Saraswathi's ring, which he knew held the power to save them all. The storm of his guilt brought wind of his wife sizing up against two monsters. A surge of passion that had once been lust and then shame was now rage, and it channeled through him with a heat hotter than Maya's touch—and impassioned in such a way, he *RAMMED!* the closet doors with the full force of his body.

⁂

Every shadow that flickered under the doorway and every muffled resonance of sound that crept under the muff of Wendy's hands was a tug of temptation. She and Jothi felt like children placed in time-out. They remained silent with their ears covered, awaiting Saraswathi's word, or knock, or opening of the bathroom door. Anything, something to signal that it was *okay* to come out.

But it was taking too long. It seemed to be taking too long. Wendy knew she could hear another voice—a louder voice. She could see multiple shadows moving in the crack of the doorway. But Saraswathi had not brought them out. *Why?*

Wendy and Jothi spoke only with their eyes. Questions. Impatience. Hemming and hawing. Their eyes said the same things, but Jothi was the first to lower her hands from her ears—not that it mattered much, because Saraswathi cried out so loud and desperately at that same moment that it pealed through the door and Wendy's hands.

The women's feet took action before their minds could prepare them for what lay beyond the bathroom door. Their bodies flung out the doorway only to be abruptly halted at the sight of Vik and Rini towering over Saraswathi. Wendy felt as if she had become a statue the way her body firmed and froze, locking into place in the presence of the rakshasa. Tingles reverberated across her body. A wave of harried heat fell over her. Her body told her that she was going to die.

But Rini's eyes looked surprised, and while struggling to grasp how Wendy and Jothi were here and healthy, she loosened her grip on Saraswathi's arm. The old woman hobbled toward the balcony screaming in Tamil, and Rini, still perplexed and almost amused, shook her head and followed the Muthu matriarch.

Rini began shouting in Tamil through a smile.

Saraswathi spun, swinging her peacock cane at Rini. "Po di thevidiya!" she shouted, spitting at the demoness.

Rin's smile dropped. Then, she looked back with a lip bite at Vik. "Make them hurt and squeal, babe . . . *if you love me.*" Rini reached in her pocket, retrieving a cluster of ashes. She flung the powder at Saraswathi. The old woman hacked. Rini's hand contorted to a claw, and she began to speak in Tamil, twisting her hand and cursing Saraswathi.

"Summon it, Paatti!" Jothi screamed.

"No, baby. She cannot know name."

Saraswathi's skin began to boil, her face swelling and blistering.

"You will tell me," said Rini with a smile.

WHAM! Vik tackled his sister, slamming her to the floor. His fingers tightened around her neck, squeezing the life from her body.

Wendy snatched a potion from her bag—any potion!—and smashed it against his face. The bottle broke, and she dug the glass into his cheek.

Vik swung his arm backward, slamming his fist repeatedly into Wendy's stomach. She crumpled behind him.

But Jothi slammed her fist into her brother's throat. *Bam! Bam!* He fell off of her, gasping for air.

Wendy dug in her bag looking for a potion that could help—

But Vik grabbed her and threw her into the bedpost. Everything went blurry for Wendy. She fought to stay conscious.

"Vik! Please! Stop—I'm your little sister!" Jothi begged, climbing to feet, her voice hoarse while she fought for breath.

Vik spun and launched his fist into her face. Jothi flew back and hit the floor.

He climbed on top of Wendy. His hands wrapped around her neck and squeezed.

She pushed at his face, clawed it, but she was . . . *fading*. Wendy's resistance slowed. Jothi didn't get back up.

"Bless Vik and me with the ring, Paatti," pouted Rini, "won't you?"

Saraswathi's skin was burning. Every spot of aged skin that had touched ash was popping, swelling, burning with excruciating pain. She fell against the railing and sank to the floor. Her eyes fell on her granddaughter's limp body lying on the ground and her grandson strangling her granddaughter-in-law.

Saraswathi raised her trembling fist, opened it to reveal the ring, and slowly extended her arm to Rini, who sighed with a flustered grin, lowered her claw, and bent toward the ring when—

THWACK!

A heavy hit interrupted her from behind. She spun as—

Kesh stormed at her!

Like lightning he ran! And like thunder he slammed into her! Rini rocketed over the railing, her neck snapping by the shove alone —*crack!* And her body plummeted two stories—*flum-flum-flum* —till being impaled by the peacock fountain. *WHAM!*—bronze beaks skewered her body. Rini's skin began to sag, even tearing and swelling at the joints, bloody flakes peeling back as black mass protruded out.

"NOOOOOOOOOOOO!" Vik screamed. His nose was crooked and pouring blood from Kesh's massive kick to his face.

"Vik, Vik. Listen to me—" Kesh started.

"Rini! Rini! Rini!" Vik screamed like a madman as he ran toward Kesh.

Kesh reached out to him, but Vik charged past his brother toward the balcony and jumped. He hurtled to the lawn, and with a *SMACK*, both of his legs snapped on impact.

"Rinayy, Rinayyyy—My lahv—ma, ma, maaa Rinay . . ." Vik slurred. He crawled toward the fountain, dragging his limp, twisted legs, the bones protruding, with tears streaming down his face.

It was pandemonium on the patio: Relatives screamed in horror, some began dialing the police, and others crowded around the fountain. Kesh hung his hands and head over the balcony, watching his little brother inch his broken body toward the demoness. The fact that Kesh knew he would've done the same thing if he was still under the spell made the scene even more brutal and bewildering.

Wendy gradually caught her breath. She crawled over to Jothi, whose neck was already bruised and cheek bleeding from her brother's assault. Wendy dug in her bag for another medicinal potion, but there were none. Fortunately, Jothi began to groan awake.

"Jothi, Jothi," Wendy started.

Jothi's eyes fluttered open. Her awakening was sedate. Kesh carried Saraswathi to the bed, gently laying her down. Wendy turned to him, and their eyes caught each other; it was the first look in days that was real, and it said a thousand words—jumbled and passionate words, furious and tender words, spouse to spouse words. But Wendy ended that conversation by speaking.

"Is he dead?" she asked through tears.

"No—I don't know," Kesh cried. "His legs are broken."

"Maya could return any second."

Wendy helped Jothi to her feet.

"Paatti—" Kesh started, wiping tears.

"Paatti, did you summon it?" Jothi asked faster.

"No. Baby." Saraswathi's words were faint and flogging. "They come. No time."

"Paatti," Wendy pleaded. "Summon it now . . ."

Wendy's words, however pressing, slipped away as she drew closer to Saraswathi. The woman of power and prestige was now pitied—her face like a cold sore, a bruise, an infestation of disease. She could have been a hundred years old. She could have been a monster. But she was only Paatti right now.

"She may—say no—not yet—not always bless. I not know."

"She?" Jothi asked. "What do you mean?"

Saraswathi's left eye was barely visible, swallowed by an inflamed brow, but her right found Jothi quickly and tenderly, then swayed to Wendy.

"Ring shines—time you ask—only wait—see if she bless boon. I not know—ring shine, she hear you."

"We need to do this now," Wendy urged.

"Paatti, we need to try—summon her, call her, whatever," Kesh begged. "It's the only hope we have. We have to hope she'll bless us!"

"You need to ask her to save us! Heal yourself and Vik!" Jothi shouted.

Wendy, Jothi, and Kesh stood around the bed and watched Saraswathi drag her trembling hand up her chest, unlock her fixed fingers from which the chain dangled, and expose the ring. Once more, every light and eye glistened *at* the ring and *in* the ring. The morning's sun seemed to shine a beam straight from the heavens into the gem.

But a shadow grew over the ring, over Saraswathi, over the bed, obscuring the light, breaking the beam, and every head spun to the patio—toward the source of the shadow—toward MAYA.

She hovered.

In the air.

In the sky.

Bold.

Beautiful.

Bloody.

Madness in her eyes.

A grin upon her lips.

And she flew into the room.

A blur of black in a blink.

The blur grabbed Saraswathi's arm.

Snatched her like a doll.

And she screamed, her arm out of its socket.

She dangled from it, and Maya took her.

Out the patio, over the railing, down and away.

FIFTEEN

O h, *how she screamed*. It was this sound that echoed in chambers now. It vibrated through walls. It channeled chills and choice words. It was a mortifying melody that permeated the palace and property. The strings plucked were those of the heart, and the drums that were beaten were only heavy steps fleeing the scene—though many stayed, cowering and clutching one another at the sight of Maya and the matriarch descending, their world upending.

Maya plopped Saraswathi onto the ground beside the fountain. Vik had managed to climb into the base of water and blood, his hand gripping a saggy sack of Rini's skin. He was conscious but no longer spoke, wide-eyed and still as stone.

Maya popped the lid of a large jar. She walked in a circle, spreading ashes around herself, Saraswathi, and the fountain. About a dozen family members hid behind furniture with whispers—whispers of shock, whispers of prayers, whispers on the phone with the police. But Maya did not whisper. She spoke boldly and in Tamil, with dramatic gestures, and a practiced tone. Black symbols became embossed in the line of ashes.

Meena and Jack hid, crouched behind a bench—panting, petrified.

Wendy, Jothi, and Kesh came sprinting out of the palace as Maya rested her hands and voice from mystic labor. Maya shook her head at them, very disapproving yet still playful. Even beside a ruptured Rini, this seemed but a game to her. One she was determined to win. The way she bit her lip wasn't just cocky but competitive.

"Kesh, come here, baby," said Maya, pointing to the ground.

Kesh did not come. He didn't even look at her. Instead, he turned to Wendy with wet eyes. "I'm sorry," he said. "I'm so, so sorry."

"You have not been drinking your Tuborgs!" Maya shouted.

Kesh's hand crawled through the air toward his wife—but Wendy turned toward another crawler that caught the corner of her eye! Jack, on hands and knees, shuffled toward the ash boundary—and his mother. Fear was in his eyes but so was his mother. Like a good-hearted son, as he had always done, he rushed to Saraswathi's aid. Meena watched, anxiously biting her lip.

"JACK! NO—" Wendy called.

"DAD!" Jothi and Kesh screamed.

But he crossed the ash.

His hand stretched out and clutched Saraswathi but began to tremble. Blood seeped out his eyes, nose, and mouth—like he was a lemon being juiced by devils—and he plopped to the ground, twitching in torment.

"Amma—ma-ma—" dribbled out his lips in his last breath.

Maya turned to see Saraswathi's free hand searching her son's body for signs of life. "Baby, baby, no, baby, baby—" she moaned, tugging at the corpse. She shouted in Tamil, calling him an idiot—a fool—stupid!

Maya crouched. She wiped a glob of blood from Jack's chin and licked it.

"Tell me the name and give me the ring," she said.

Wendy pulled out the construction worker's phone from her pocket.

Maya began speaking to Saraswathi in Tamil now, threatening her while taking stabs at the name, prodding her to surrender. Through heavy breaths and big smiles she lavished her with every dark and dirty thing she would do to her and the family if she did not obey. Face scrunched and stubborn, the old woman clenched her ring and mouth even tighter in defiance.

Following the instructions on the phone, Wendy repeated the spell that she had performed at the construction site. Her hand mimicked the motions as best as she could remember. Her voice teetered between steady and shaky as she thought of the mouthless women tied up, and how each of them might face the same fate, or worse, if they didn't stop Maya.

Kesh and Jothi, to assist and distract, snatched up stones from the flowerbed and began chucking them at Maya.

Thunk! Thunk! Miss. Miss. *Thunk!*

Meena watched from behind the bench, her husband dead, her mother-in-law beneath a monster, and her children throwing stones like flies buzzing around a wild animal that could care less. The rocks that hit Maya landed hard, but she would not be distracted; her focus remained fixed on Saraswathi. Maya dug her fingernails into the old woman's face, causing her to bellow and bleed. Maya licked skin and blood from her fingertips.

Meanwhile, finishing the spell, Wendy blew.

The ash line scattered and dissolved into the grass.

Maya turned around with a grin, colored impressed by Wendy and colored red by Saraswathi. "You are full of surprises," said Maya. "*Soooo* sexy! Those sisters confessed to me you performed the spell—I was very impressed!—before I killed them." She almost laughed, then licked her lips dripping with blood and smeared her chin with a wipe from her hand.

"Do not tell her, Paatti!" Wendy shouted, her eyes swelling with tears for Real Maya and Real Rini. "She'll kill us all!" She stood boldly beside Kesh and Jothi, her eyes skittering across the scene looking for a sliver of a solution, a spark of a strategy, a next move.

"I will not!" Maya glanced at Kesh and pointed. "For sure— I'm keeping him. As my pet!" She turned back to Saraswathi. "I'll tell you what, I'll let you all live . . . *if* you tell me the name."

"We can all attack her at once!" Jothi shouted to her hiding relatives, some who were inching their way around the palace, out of view, to make an escape. "Maybe she can't take us all—"

Wisp! A rock came flying out of nowhere. So fast. So hard. A blink-and-you-miss-it moment. *Thwack!* It hit Jothi square in the face and sent her flying backward. "Yes, I can," said Maya, her hand still in the air from the throw. "I can take, and take, and take, and take, and take!" Maya snatched Saraswathi's hand, pulling the old fist, which was clenched tightly over the ring, toward her slowly— observing the resistance but unfazed by it. "I can take—whatever I want!"

Meena, still behind the bench, had her hand clasped over her mouth, over her raw and chewed-up lip. Her daughter lay flat in the grass, unresponsive. She wanted to run to her child—but what would that do!? She looked again, to the beast—the monster—to Maya. And to Saraswathi, who kept her hand enclosed over the ring. *That ring!* All this time, it had been something special! *But what was this name?* And why did it matter? Meena drew blood biting her lip while the memory of that night she'd seen Saraswathi speaking to the ring suddenly came upon her once again.

Maya released her tongue and widened her jaw, it stretched disturbingly wide, so much so that the edges of her mouth tore, showing every one of her teeth—more than any normal human—and the deep abyss of her throat.

"I just smashed your granddaughter's face in," she said. "I will slaughter every Muthu, take them as slaves or dinner. Tell me *the name*, Paatti."

Maya slid Saraswathi's full fist deep into her mouth and chomped down.

Saraswathi screamed, and screamed, and screamed!

Wendy dug in her bag. She pulled out potion after potion, throwing one after another at Maya's back. A few shattered, erupting boils and bubbles on Maya's skin. Wendy took steps closer with each throw, and Kesh ran after her.

It was a last attempt. Impulsive. Desperate. *Something*.

Maya continued to bite down, unconcerned. Even as her skin peeled and tore as black masses emerged from the glass potions breaking on her, she commanded Saraswathi, with a mouthful of her flesh: "Tell me."

Meena watched her son and daughter-in-law charge at Maya. Everyone else continued to cower and stare. Why wouldn't Saraswathi just buckle and tell Maya the name?! Stubborn, old hag! Meena recalled that night, so long ago, the vision as clear as the one before her. She saw Saraswathi, the blue ring dazzling in her hand, and her mother-in-law speaking to it. What had she been saying? Meena had heard something . . . It had been a word. *A name?*

Maybe—now that she thought about it. What was it? It wasn't a name she recognized—nor a word she had ever spoken before . . .

Something with a *Kuh* . . . *kam* . . . or *kolm* . . . or—

Kuh-min-ah! Was that it? Kuh-min-ah?!

Yes! It had to be it. That's what she heard—the word—the name that would save them! Saraswathi could not! Her children could not save themselves! All the other Muthus hid in terror, but Meena, she would save them, save them all—the hero, the future matriarch, the savior of the family!

Wendy lifted the last potion. She smashed it against Maya's neck. The skin ripped, revealing black scales of flesh, and Maya actually winced, as the liquid sunk under the suit of human skin, and onto the black of her real body. Yet Maya, her mouth enclosed over Saraswathi's hand—and *the ring!*—pulled back with her teeth tissue and tendons, blood and veins, shredding it from the bone!

Saraswathi howled! Kesh dove at Maya!

And Meena stood and shouted: "KUH-MIN-NAH!"

Maya's eyes jerked toward Meena—not at Kesh as he dove at her nor Wendy as she dug glass into her back—but toward the sound, the sound of *a name*. And Saraswathi, muscle and membrane being torn from her skeleton hand, agony like lightning shooting through her body, her life slipping from her, darkness swallowing all sight and all sound . . . she heard the name too, and in her breath, *maybe her last breath*, spoke what Meena had mistakenly heard, *almost heard*, the true name:

"*Kanmani.*"

It was a whisper. A slurred stutter of a dying woman. But the name somehow sounded clearer than the waves crashing down below, the screams of terrified relatives, and Kesh's tumbling over the unmovable Maya.

The syllables hung in the air.

Kannnnnnnnnnnnnnnnnnnnnnnnnnnnnnnnn.

Mahhhhhhhhhhhhhhhhhhhhhhhhhhhhhhhhhhhhh.

Neeeeeeeeeeeeeeeeeeeeeeeeeeeeeeeeeeeeeeeeeeeeeeeeeeeee.

"Kanmani?" repeated Maya, both in succession and question.

And then—AN EXPLOSION!

From Maya's mouth shot forth a burst of light, of power, of beauty, like she had swallowed a grenade of glory, like she was vomiting a star. The force of its fury flung her with supernatural might, and the ricochet of its reaction sent Wendy and Kesh soaring too. Saraswathi's head was whipped back, and the imprint of her body was forced into the earth a few inches.

It was as if the day had been night. The light of day was dark compared to the light of the ring. A blinding flash flickered and dazzled like the air was made of crystal, like the heavens were raining drops of diamonds. And the world turned blue, like the sea had swallowed them up or the sky had fallen upon them. It was blinding yet all that could be seen.

And it was only the aroma, the crumbs, the echo of *her.*

Of *Kanmani.*

She emerged from the ring like a ray reflected and refracted and released from the gem, shimmering forth both out of sapphire and as sapphire. Her form was of human shape yet twice the size. The earth beneath her steps seemed to carry her weight, the grass bent beneath her, yet she was *light* itself, a deep blue light, and a living, breathing gem—like colored glass, a crystal creature—and her shadows had deep and dark contours. The harsh contrast of her *being* blinded, making it impossible to look long or hard at her.

She was beauty, and she was bound—bound by chains of jewels around her wrists and neck. The prettiest prisoner.

All eyes were on her but could not remain on her. Wendy looked through a squint, but her eyes closed on themselves under the bright, and then forcing them open, she shifted around Kanmani's being, dodging beams of blinding light. She eventually found her eyes giving up—or giving *in*—and bowing to the grass, catching only Kanmani's feet—being caught only by Kanmani's feet.

Maya's eyes weren't as sensitive, but she squinted too. Her eyes also bounced on and off Kanmani. The ring, which had been in her mouth, now lay in her hand, glistening and pulsating among bits of Saraswathi's blood and tissue. Maya's cheeks were chubby. She turned over bits of flesh and bone with her tongue. She spit out a tiny bone or two and swallowed the rest.

Kanmani shifted, taking in her surroundings. She looked beneath her at Saraswathi, still and with her hand half torn off, at Rini and Vik by the fountain, at Kesh and Wendy in the grass, and finally, at Maya with the ring.

"I possess the ring," said Maya. She slid it onto her finger and wiggled her hand to show it off. "You see that *I* possess the ring?"

"Mmmmm . . . I see that the ring possesses you. As it has many." Kanmani's voice was harsh yet soft. She spoke in a whisper, but the whisper thundered in every ear, like her mouth was against each eardrum, banging it with her breath. Her words were slow and full.

"Will you grant me anything I wish?" asked Maya.

"She did not summon you here!" Wendy shouted, shielding her eyes as she looked upward. "It was Saraswathi—the woman at your feet!"

Kanmani held out her hand toward Saraswathi and made light dance upon her form in the grass like she was searching her with a fantastical flashlight—but then the light returned to Kanmani and left Saraswathi lying lifelessly.

"She no longer lives. It was her last breath which summoned me here."

Kesh rolled over and sat up, his eyes falling on his grandmother's beaten and bloody corpse. Through tears, he spoke: "We all know what blessing she summoned you for. She wished for you to save us—"

"I possess the ring!" interjected Maya. "Me! ME! She did not even have it in her possession when she spoke your name. It was in my mouth! What does it matter—Kanmani—Kanmani! I've said the name—I said it too—I've got the ring! You must grant my boon, right?"

"I actually shouted your name first!" Meena made her way around the bench, covering her eyes with her hand like she was talking to the sun. "I-I said it before Saraswathi, then she copied me. I believe I should get the boon—or even speak on her behalf—the dead woman's behalf."

"No, not you. You knew not the name, nor did you speak it. You did not summon me—"

"I did—I did! Just before, I stood and shouted—"

Kanmani waved her hand and a burst of light seemed to blind Meena. She began to wander with her hands outward, blinking in a panic. "What did you do? I can't see. I can't see anything. Somebody!—help—help!" She ran into the bench, smacking her knees and collapsing onto it. Meena, then, curled up like a ball and remained silent.

"This is a strange occurrence that the summoner should be deceased upon my arrival and that another now possesses the ring."

"I'm telling you—it was in my mouth when she said your name! She barely had it in her grasp! And I said it, too, just after."

"It was her flesh that felt the ring and her spirit that spoke first, even if her flesh was being torn apart in your mouth. It is the nature of my summoning."

"But she is dead." Maya stepped closer to Kanmani, her eyes in a squint so hard they were nearly closed. "Besides, I now possess the ring and summon you by your name."

"This is true."

"Please!" Wendy pleaded. "You cannot grant her this boon! She will use it to kill and destroy . . . even more than she already has. She is a demon disguised in human form!"

"I know what she is, but it is not I who determines the merit of a being or its boons. He chooses."

"He? Who is he?"

"The one who bound me and bid me here. The one whose power I bear and bestow. He knows the boon before you ask and has ordained whether or not I am to grant it."

"And what about my grandmother?" Kesh asked. "What about her boon? You said—she is the one who summoned you!"

"It is for this reason I reveal myself to you in this way now, unlike any boon before. It is a strange happening which we must resolve."

"Can someone speak on Saraswathi's behalf?" Kesh asked.

"You said *he knows.* He knows what boon we are going to ask, right?" Wendy added. "So you must know what boon Saraswathi was going to ask! You can grant it then!"

"He has not revealed this to me. Whether or not she knew what boon she was going to ask before her spirit left her body, I do not know. There is no guarantee I will grant a boon until it is asked, when he tells me his decree."

Maya chuckled. She picked a piece of flesh from her teeth. "You must grant my boon then. It is the only sensible solution."

"*What is the boon you request?*"

"Power beyond my present limitations," blurted Maya. "Power to restore my accomplice. Power to retain this body. Power to make my spells permanent, stronger." Her eyes rolled toward Kesh as that last line rolled off her tongue.

"*Is this a singular boon?*"

"Yes, yes! More power is what I desire. I wish to have more power than any other rakshasa."

"*Hmmmm. He bids me . . . grant you this boon.*"

Maya laughed and began to dance, throwing her hands into the air, her torn jaw hanging and bouncing, more visibly devilish than ever before.

Many of the Muthus, who remained silent out of fear in the shadows till now, began to moan and weep, even howl. Some passed out from trembling and imagining future torment. Others, seemingly gone mad, began to make a mixed laugh-cry emotion and claw at the earth—like digging their own graves might save them, like being buried alive was the greatest possible recourse. It may have been that they thought the cool of the earth and barrier of dirt might shield them from the warmth and loud of Kanmani, too.

Unlike Wendy, Kesh, or Meena, who had been eased into the supernatural realities before them, many of the Muthus had been wholly ignorant until moments ago. They were worse off than Meena in this moment. Not blind in the eyes but in human thinking and feeling—the sheer shock seemed to stupefy.

"*But first—*" Kanmani began, before being interrupted.

"Can you return life to Saraswathi's body? Even if just for a moment, for her to tell you her boon?" Wendy asked, retaining her reason, working for a way out, trying to be scrappy, scrappy, *scrappy.*

"*I am not permitted to do this—*"

"There must be a way—"

"*Hmmmm . . . I am not permitted to do this besides under one condition: that a willing person relinquish their spirit in exchange for Saraswathi's body to repossess her own. This spirit will leave this world and go to dwell with him.*"

"And what of my boon?!" Maya shouted.

"*He has permitted me to bless your boon, but Saraswathi's boon and its blessing remains unrevealed. If he bids me grant both, I will.*"

"But if Saraswathi returns, why must you grant the demon's?" Kesh shook his head. "Her boon is the inverse of what Saraswathi's will be! They cannot both be granted."

"*Saraswathi's boon is still a mystery, and he has already decreed I bestow the rakshasa's boon today. She now possesses the sapphire and would summon me back, once again, for another boon, should I not grant it now. I tell you all this: Today, he may bid me grant both boons, and he may not. If the Muthus choose to offer one of their own, willingly, in exchange, one spirit for one spirit, Saraswathi's life will be returned to her, and we will hear her boon.*"

"I've lost my father, my grandmother, and now you want us to give up another one of our own to *maybe* grant a boon?" Tears dashed Kesh's face. "Why would he grant a demon her boon and force us to lose everything—risk losing everything just to save a few of us? Is *he* a demon himself?! These are not blessings and boons— this is a curse! We're cursed!"

Kanmani spun toward Kesh. Be it wind or light or the sight of her glare, he was knocked backward and hit the ground.

"You demon child! You speak of things you do not know. Once more and there will be no second boon, no exchange of spirits. You will be left with the rakshasa, and you will know what it is to be cursed!"

Maya laughed while the Muthus—those still with coherent thinking—considered offering themselves to resurrect Saraswathi. Ironically, Meena, who had been so determined to be the family's savior, could not conceive of surrendering her own spirit. It simply did not make sense to her—seeing how she was the next mother in line, and all families need a mother. Not to mention Jack was now gone, and she couldn't just leave her children orphans! No, in her blindness, she thought of who, who, *who* would be best to suggest.

On the other hand, from the moment Kanmani had proposed the exchange, Wendy had resolved to do it. It wasn't that she wanted to be the one but that she was willing, and she felt it was the only way it would happen. Even so, she remained silent for some time. Maybe it was to see if anyone else *would* stand up. Maybe it was out of fear. Maybe it was just to take a moment and reflect—before dying and all.

For Kesh, it wasn't out of self-preservation that he didn't speak up. Rather, it was because of how furious he'd become at the ring, at Kanmani, and this whole paradoxical situation! It seemed to him only another nail in the coffin, another kick while they were down. Certainly, this being would not grant their boon *and* save them—not if it wanted to give Maya her boon as well! No! Everyone and everything was against him, and he couldn't see a way out, and this is why he remained silent. He wasn't going to play this game. This game with devils!

"Take Wendy—take her! It's all her fault anyway," Meena shouted from her curled-up position. "She's brought these monsters into our home, and this is how she can make it up to us.

Wendy! Wendy, you can do one good thing for this family, for once in your life, do us good! Make amends for what you've done!"

As absurd as it sounded, such a lie felt true to Meena in that moment. In her desperation to save herself, it could've been anyone's fault, but Wendy was the lowest-hanging fruit in their family tree. Fact or fiction—disposing of Wendy was already a part of the narrative Meena had begun to believe. Whether it was a flat-out lie or an exaggeration, if everyone could get behind it, maybe they could be saved at such little a cost!

"Oh, I like that," said Maya. She strutted toward Wendy. "You make amends! Come on, have a heart, you whore!"

Kesh jumped to his feet and rushed between Maya and Wendy.

"Amma, what the hell is wrong with you?! This isn't Wendy's fault! It's this psycho-bitch—this monster! Or mine—" He began crying now. "I'm the one who was under her spell and let her sink her claws into this family! Wendy is the only person who saw through their lies and has been trying to save us! Of all of us, she's the one person who deserves to live!"

"I'll do it," Wendy said. "You can take my spirit."

"No—NO!" Kesh spun toward his wife. "Take mine! Take me —I'll do it!"

Muthu relatives began to shout and whine now, some almost in unison—a horrifying harmony—each from their hiding places:

"Let her do it!"

"Take the girl!"

"She's a demon!"

"Send her away!"

"Take her—take her!"

Wendy and Kesh raised their voices to argue their case—but Kanmani's voice drowned out every other voice—so much so that

Wendy couldn't even hear her own voice when she spoke, not even in her own head, because Kanmani's was there, rumbling like wind and completely consuming.

"He has bid me take a woman's spirit, only a woman's, for he desires harmony in all things, even in an exchange such as this."

"Then someone—anyone—a woman, please offer yourself!" Kesh opened his arms, turning toward the Muthus, toward his family. "There's so many of you, old and with life already lived. This is my wife—*pleeeeeease!*"

But no one arose, no one stirred nor made a sound.

It was a suffocating silence.

He turned to Meena.

"Amma—I'm sorry, but please, will you? You-you-you have to understand, this is the love of my life—my everything. I can't live without her . . . I'm begging you!"

But Meena made no reply. She only curled deeper into herself.

"Then there's got to be another way!" Kesh forced his eyes upward at Kanmani, but they were forced shut. His words became slurred by his crying, slimed soggy with his tears. "Something—else, anything—else."

Wendy reached out her hand, sliding it upon his cheek, wet with tears, and pulled him toward herself. Eyes on eyes. She inhaled and exhaled, and said, "It's gotta be me, baby—"

"No, it doesn't—"

"It was always gonna be me. *She* knows it. I know it. *You* know it, too. It's okay. If there's a chance it'll bring Paatti back and save everyone, we gotta do it."

"I can't—"

"You can."

"Guh-bye, Wendy! Guh-bye!" Maya wiggled and waved her hand. "Have a nice death! Kesh and I will have so much fun while you're gone. Did I mention he put a baby in me? Soon we'll have little half-breed devils running round! Damn, you'll miss out."

But Wendy and Kesh seemed not to hear her. This was their moment, and it could not be taken from them. Their gazes remained fixed on each other, mourning magnets drawn together—a look that would not leave with death.

"Everything that's happened," Kesh said, through tears. "I'm so sorry. I love you more than anything. I can't *lose you*. I never, *never* wanted to hurt you, you have to know. I'm so sorry—"

"I know, baby. I know." Wendy pulled her fingers away from his cheek and slipped her hand into his. *He could hold her, one last time.* Then, Wendy closed her eyes and lifted her head up toward Kanmani. "You can take my spirit. I'm willing."

"Wendy, no—*no*," Kesh cried.

Kanmani extended her hand. Blue and white light flickered between the ring and her palm. Sparks became flames and flames became another explosion—an explosion of bold and blue, like the world was only glass and light and color. All eyes were forced shut, but eyelids could not block the bright. It was as if none had been closed. Wendy's spirit left her, her body became limp and fell, though Kesh never let go of her hand, only squeezed it tighter—as tight as a grip can be. Not even Maya could pry his fingers from her now. No, no, *nooooo*, he might never let go—even if her hand lay still for ages, even when it decomposed to the earth, he would sink into the dirt too, because he couldn't let go—how could he let go? Never again! He would hold her forever.

INTERLUDE

With godspeed, Wendy's spirit flew, traveling like light—by day, by night—with reason, with rhyme—by space, by time—a blur of all that is, was all and all a *whiz*.

It was an imperceptible whirlwind of the senses that made her completely senseless, making the nature of the matter, of time, of where she was, and where she was going impossible to understand—like shoving a camel into the eye of a needle, like being stepped on by a mountain, like swallowing the sea. Everything was everywhere, and Wendy was . . . was . . . was . . . *sitting*.

Suddenly, sitting.

Sitting for so long. *How long?* Forever. It seemed to be forever.

Maybe she had not been traveling. Maybe she had never traveled.

But could this be home? *It may be home.* But—

No, no, *no*. She was not always here. Not always. Only for a while.

Wendy felt like she had just awoken from a long nap—a nap to end all naps! A very restful nap, and she was groggy. *Groggy* was such an unusual word, a word Wendy had never said aloud before, though she seemed to forget if she could speak, if she had ever spoken, and she wondered what her voice might sound like.

"Grrrrrooooggggggyyyyy." The word crept off her tongue. But her voice was loud. It was very loud in this quiet place. Wendy wondered if anyone else had ever said the word *groggy*. Were there such things as other people? Of course there were! But where were they? Was she alone? Were *other people* only things of her imagination?

Keshhhhhhhhhhhhhhhhhhhhhh. He was a person—right? But he was a distant dream, a melting memory. Could it be that she had made him up? Wendy thought long and hard about him, but he seemed so far away, so faint and far. So dark and dim was any thought of him.

An image of his smile fluttered by. A laughing smile with spit and mint hanging from it. It sent flutters to her belly. And then she heard him laughing, like an ancient echo; laughter was bubbling up inside of her now. Wendy's tummy twitched, and she smiled, but the laugh subsided, and she sighed it.

"*Groggy?*" a low and calm voice asked.

Though Wendy saw no face, she couldn't help but sense that the mouth that spoke was smiling. Maybe the voice had seen the mouth with spit and mint, too! Maybe he knew Kesh—if Kesh was real!

It was so nice to hear another voice. It was nice to know she wasn't alone in this place. The voice sounded so familiar! Wendy figured whoever he was, he must be a friend. Someone she knew— or could get to know, especially if it was only them alone in this world.

"Do you know why I am *groggy*?"

"*It's because you are resting.*"

"Sleeping?"

"*No, resting.*"

"Oh, okay. I was resting?"

"You are still resting."

"I am?"

"Mhmmm."

"Are you?"

He chuckled, and it made Wendy rumble. She felt the vibrations of his voice, the warmth of his breath and joy. It made her smile and laugh too. That's a good start to a friendship—laughter—right? Wendy thought it must be.

"I am resting in a way. This is a restful place."

"Why are we resting?"

"It's good to rest before and after good work."

"Do *we* work together, then?"

"We have, in a way, and can work much closely together if you like."

"I think I'd like that, but I—do we know each other?"

"In a way."

"What is your name?"

"I have many names."

"What should I call you?—or what do I call you? If we've spoken before, sorry, I don't remember."

"You can call me . . . Saturn. How's that, Wendy?"

Wendy. That was her name. She knew it but had forgotten. It was nice to have a name—a sound, a word that belonged to her. Wendy, Wendy, *Wendyyyyyyyyyyyyyyyyyyy*. It was a good name; it was her name. She felt like she was hearing it for the first time.

"Wendy? That's my name?"

"It is."

Wendy tongued the name in her mouth and in her mind. No matter how many times she said it—or thought it—the name never became any less novel. She might've said it a thousand times. Even a million. Could that be possible? Could someone say a name—their own name—a million times and not grow bored?

Wendy didn't grow bored, but she did eventually begin studying her hand. She felt a warmth around it. Like it was being held—and there it was! That face again—and a sound, the sound of the same name . . .

Keshhhhhhhhhh.

But he slipped away. Again.

Wendy put one hand in the other. Slid each finger in between another. She felt tickles from her own touch, and she looked closely, scrutinizing her own skin. It was like a fabric of flesh, each crease and wrinkle sewn together to fit her. It was beautiful, this body. And it was hers? Did it belong to her? But then, where was his? Where was Saturn's body? Why did he not have one?

"Saturn?"

"Yes?"

"Are you being shy?"

"Am I being shy?"

Saturn laughed again. So full, so unrestrained, like he loved to laugh.

"Why can't I see you?"

"You can."

"I can?"

"In a way."

"What way is that?"

"I will show you."

"What are you thinking about, Wendy?"

She had been trying to see more of the picture . . . the picture of Kesh. She wanted to see beyond the mint and spit and smile. She was really trying, focusing all of her energy to try to see more of him, hear more of him, bring him closer somehow—but he was just so far!

"Trying—trying to remember things." Wendy closed her eyes and squinted hard. "But you're interrupting."

"Sorry."

"It's okay."

Wendy opened her eyes and felt cool rushing down her cheeks. She put her finger to her face and felt wetness upon her skin.

"I'm . . . *crying.*"

"Yes."

"I was thinking about where I was before I was here—at least I think it was before, and I think I was somewhere else—anyway . . . I just started crying. Can you see me crying, Saturn?"

"I can see. I have seen you cry many times since you arrived here."

"Really? That can't be—isn't this the first time?"

"Not all crying is with tears, Wendy."

"I don't understand."

"You are always crying in a way, just as you are always laughing in a way, but you put to rest one part of yourself to work out another. If you were to feel all the feelings at once, you would not feel them at all."

Wendy thought about Saturn's words. She wiped one tear after another. Each one felt colder, heavier, truer than the one before. Her tears were like streams that carried her closer to Kesh, toward another image, a clearer one—toward another sound, a louder one!

Soon—if it can be called *soon*—she recalled the scene from their honeymoon. She and Kesh had been cracking up, laughing hysterically, and he had accidentally spit out his drink on a stranger. This is why he had spit and mint hanging from his mouth. She had been laughing too. So hard. So very hard. She remembered that she and Kesh had laughed a lot together, and that they were married, married in another place, in another time, and that they loved each other—very, *very* much.

⁖

Wendy felt many feelings, and she remembered many memories. Only one at a time. Her memories washed over her, but it wasn't a showering—more like a bath. She soaked in the sights, the smells, the feelings of fights and hugs, worries and delights, screams and whispers, cries and laughs, being a child and being an adult. It was like each piece of the puzzle that was her life was being placed, one at a time.

And sometimes pieces didn't fit or didn't seem to fit. But whenever these questions arose, Wendy was happy to pause and partake in conversation with Saturn, for he was her puzzle partner.

"Saturn?"

"*Yes?*"

"How well do we know each other?"

Saturn hadn't spoken in some time. It was hard to tell how long, but Wendy felt that she was forgetting the sound of his voice. It was often like this when conversation paused, but as quickly as she spoke, he always spoke right back, and upon hearing him speak, she remembered the sound of his voice like he had never stopped speaking.

"We are growing in our knowing."

"I feel like we are old friends. Are we?"

"Yes . . . but we are new friends, too, in a way."

"You always say that. '*In a way.*'" She mocked him, the depth and slowness of his voice, when she said it.

"I do often repeat myself."

"It's like a riddle. You speak in riddles . . . sometimes."

"I like riddles."

"Why?"

"Because it's more fun finding a thing when you've had to search for it first."

Wendy searched Saturn's words. She did not understand how they could be old friends and new friends simultaneously, but somehow the paradox did *feel* true. Maybe because Saturn had said it. Maybe just because it was.

She could have been convinced that it really was only her and Saturn in the world, and that they had been together here, wherever here was, forever; and she also could've been convinced that this was the beginning of many things, of everything, of her and Saturn's friendship. Both truths seemed to be different sides of the same coin, one which she fingered in the palm of her heart.

⚬

"Can I ask you a question, Wendy?"

"Oh, of course!" Wendy wondered what he would ask.

"If you know a lot about a person, does that mean that you really know them?"

"I'm gonna say . . . no. Partly because I think that, partly because of the way you asked it."

Saturn laughed. A warm rumble.

"I think you're correct. Head knowledge is not knowing till the heart knows it too."

Buh-bmmm, buh-bmmm, buh-bmmm. Wendy could hear her own heart beating. She could feel it pumping blood, pumping life. The tune, the song of existence, it played rain or shine; it played against fear and love; it played through the day and through the night; it played with and without anyone listening. How long had Wendy's heart been beating? How many beats had it beaten in all? Though she seldom listened, it sang a song, an endless tune.

Wendy pressed her fingers against her chest. She listened to her heart's song for a while. She thought about how every person had a heart, including Kesh, that played its own tune. How beautiful!

"Sometimes it takes a while for the heart to catch up with the mind—and other times, the heart leads the way. With me, it seems that many, though they know much about me, haven't taken the time for their hearts to get to know me too."

The rhythm and rhyme of Wendy's beating heart began to sound, surprisingly, like Saturn's voice. Like one of his riddles. One of his laughs. The way it always beats—just like he's always there, ready to talk. Maybe this is how he spoke, *in a way*—even when he was silent—in the subtle melodies of life.

"I think my heart knows you, Saturn—or is beginning to, anyway."

"I think so too."

⚬⚬

As Wendy's friendship with Saturn grew, so did her knowledge, both in her mind and heart, of the past and all she'd been through.

Remembering was a tiring business, and she would rest from it by conversing with Saturn, which tired her in other ways. But both were good work, work she happily returned to whenever she felt rested.

"I've noticed something."

"Tell me."

"Everything is slow here. I don't know how or why I think it's slow, but everything *feels* slow . . . to me. Not that that's a bad thing. It's not bad. It's just not *fast*. I think I may have done things fast some other time, in some other place . . . before . . . and this is different."

"Yes, I know what you mean. It's a good thing you've noticed."

"Really? I was nervous to tell you."

"Oh, you don't need to be nervous, Wendy. We can talk about anything together. Anything you want."

"Thank you for saying that. So, why are things slow here? I'm just curious. I'm not saying I don't like it, but it does feel a bit . . . *weird*. It's like, like, like I'm chewing a piece of meat so long I forget if I'm supposed to swallow it, or if I'm still hungry—actually, wait a second, do we eat here? I've just realized I'm never really hungry, like, hungry like I've been before—wherever that was. Unless that is just an idea I thought up—eating, I mean. It's hard to remember what's an idea in my head and what's real sometimes. Sorry, what was I asking again?—Oh! Why is it slow here . . . if it is slow . . . here?"

Wendy could tell Saturn was almost laughing before he spoke.

"One thing can be more real than another—but all realities matter to me. What you see with your eyes, what you see with your mind, what you see with your heart is all seeing to me. . . . Do you see what I'm saying?"

Wendy was squinting, looking hard at what Saturn said.

"Your father, what's one of your favorite memories with him? Do you remember?"

Now, this question, Wendy could answer! It's always easier to find an answer that lies within than without. Wendy pictured her dad, his big belly, his stern voice, his scrappy nature, the way she could tell he was always working on something, even when he was sitting, even when he was still.

"I don't think I have many fond memories with him. I can remember only two."

"Tell me about the earlier one."

"Well, my dad likes to keep himself busy, one thing to the next —that's just how he's always been. So he didn't really ever hang around with us growing up because he always had something to do, somewhere to be, something to work on. The only thing, and I don't know why, that would cause him to just stop or slow down for a second was birds. He had this thing for birds—I really don't know why he did, but if you ever caught him not working, it was because he'd seen some species fly by or heard a tweet he recognized. He knew every bird and its sound. Anyway—"

"You never asked him why?"

"What?"

"You never asked him why birds were so dear to him?"

"No, no, I never did. I guess they just were."

"I can tell you if you like. He wouldn't have told you, even if you asked him. He's never told anyone before."

"Oh, yes, I'd like to know."

"His mother, your grandmother, died when he was young. He was too young to really remember anything about her—even her face, he can't really remember it. But what he can remember is this brooch

of a bird that she wore all the time. He remembers that bird. It was a robin. Since he doesn't have any memories to hold onto of his mother, he holds onto that bird. It makes him appreciate birds more than most people. He pays attention to how they fly and what they sound like—and that's what inspired his interest in them. He would never admit this to anyone, which is why I said he wouldn't have told you, but he believes that when he sees a robin, it's your grandmother. Her spirit in some way saying hello. He's very embarrassed of the belief and thinks it ridiculous, but believes it he does, indeed."

"Thank you for telling me, Saturn! I never knew—I could've never guessed that in a million years there was a story behind it. It sounds so unlike him. I guess that's why he never tells anyone."

"You're welcome—now, please, continue."

"Oh—right! So, as I was saying, I caught him sitting on the porch one day listening to the birds. I had wanted to spend time with him—and I thought I could steal his attention from the birds, which certainly I could not do—but I began picking up sticks and throwing them. I guess I wanted him to look at me while he listened to the birds—I don't really remember. I just remember wanting him to look at me, and he wasn't. Anyway, I began throwing sticks into this large tree in our front yard, watching them bounce from branch to branch and slip through the leaves, hitting the ground. It was fun, and I'd almost forgotten my dad—till he started yelling. He stomped on over to me and snatched the stick from my hand. I was afraid and started to cry, but he said, 'Don't you see! Look at the mother, Wendy! She's terrified for her babies!' My dad pointed my attention to a bird—maybe it was a robin, actually— that was hopping and flopping around, almost making a circle around us, chirping like crazy. It kind of freaked me out, and I cried again, but then my dad lifted me up onto his shoulders. He turned toward the branch that extended just above us, and I could see the nest. It was a little nest with little baby birds in it, like tiny, slimy, pink balls with beaks. They were so ugly, but I couldn't help but feel horrible that I had almost hurt them and that I had made their mother so mad. I was holding onto my dad's head, and as I peeked down, even from above him, I could see he was smiling while looking at the babies. 'Okay, let's let them be so the mother won't have to worry anymore.' My dad set me down, I wiped my tears, and we sat on the porch together for a while."

Wendy was crying while thinking back on it. It had been one of the only times she spent a quiet moment with her father. He had shown a gentle tenderness toward the birds—even toward her in his anger at this moment that was unlike him at all other times.

"It's a sweet memory, Wendy."

"Yes, it is."

"Do you know why I asked you about it?"

"Well, I've already learned something new about my dad—and it's made the memory even sweeter."

"I'm glad to hear that. You asked me why it's slow here—"

"Oh, right!"

"Yes, to answer your question, it's like how your father lifted you onto his shoulders to see what you could not, to see what he saw— through his eyes. If he would've lifted you even higher, into the heights of his heart, and told you what I've told you about your grandmother, you could've seen with his eyes even more clearly. Time is different here in many ways, but the slowness is to help you see with my eyes, to lift you up so you can see what you otherwise could not. You mentioned food; there is no urgency here to eat or earn money or sleep. For fear of losing those things, many have rushed through life and overlooked all that I have wanted them to see. There is a greater force than fear here

that drives our time, and it is unconcerned with twists and turns in the road, pit stops, and even turning around here and there to glimpse what we've missed. What many see as delays are life's greatest delights to me."

"I don't want to rush ever again."

"There will come a time when, even here, you will want to rush again, but I promise you: Moving quickly is not the answer. It is the journey that helps us find our ends."

"You put it so beautifully, Saturn—I love the slowness now, too. I'll never rush again."

⚬

Minutes, hours, days, months, years. Wendy and Saturn's time together could not be measured in Earth time. It could have been in the blink of an eye. It could have been a millennium. There were times of laughter, especially at the *beginning*—for lack of a better word—and there were times of seriousness, especially as their friendship deepened.

Saturn began peeling back the layers of her story, and together, they peered into the cavities of her character, though it seemed to be only at the pace at which Wendy felt most comfortable. A recollection was never forced, a feeling never contrived; it was the most organic expedition through her life. She dipped her toes into the waters of the wicked whirlwind that brought her here many times before plunging in. It takes a strong swimmer to wade in the pools of your own tears, and Wendy was taking it one stroke at a time.

As they turned each corner down the road of her life, Wendy began to anticipate the coming of the darkness, the culmination of the darkness that lay ahead. Like a swelling sound or a brewing storm, her past became clearer and so did her pains. And it wasn't merely a recollection of memories or unblurring of forgotten things —for Saturn, like her father with the birds, took her higher and deeper, to get a better, fuller look at even the darkness.

But it was not all dark.

There were cracks of light that seeped into every scene, and with Saturn's help, she began to remember much more than she had forgotten.

❖

"Hold out your hands. I'm going to craft something for you."

Wendy held out her hands. As she did so, she saw rock descend. Something invisible began chipping away at it—bits of mineral, dust, and rock were cut and carved away. The shavings fell and landed softly on the ground, but the core material became less gray, less rocky, and blue shone out. Invisible hands seemed to be washing the rock, then drying, and further sharpening.

A beak formed. Then a body. A large body. But it was not the normal size of a bird's body. Then, the big body was split into two bodies. *Ah . . .* and Wendy began to see the image forming. It was a peacock. And an old woman on it.

It was a sculpture of Paatti on a peacock.

Wendy laughed as the finishing touches were completed.

"You know what it is?"

"Yes, yes."

"This has cracked me up many times, Wendy. Not everyone makes me laugh, you know."

"I like to make you laugh."

"Some people think I am so serious, and I sure can be when it is time to be serious, but there are also times to laugh, and I enjoy those very much with you."

"I like to laugh too."

Wendy remembered Saraswathi. Every scoff and insult she sent Wendy's way since the day they met. Her peacock cane, her Amrut. The thought of her infuriated Wendy, but she couldn't hold onto that fury for long, for flashes followed closely behind: the sound of her screams, the sight of her blood and boils, her death.

"Humor can bring healing where there is much pain."

"Yeah . . . the peacock, it was the only way I could make it through sometimes."

"Humor can be a great escape—but you know what, Wendy?"

"I never know *what* when it comes to you."

"Humor—"

Saturn was cut off by his own laughter. He made the whole world rumble. An organic massage that tickled inside and out. It made Wendy laugh too. They were always laughing like this, one after the other. Like fire and smoke. Like thunder and lightning.

"Wendy, dear, you're too funny—how ironic! As I was saying . . ." Saturn seemed to catch his breath. *"Humor can be a great escape, but it can also be a great entrance into places that, otherwise, are closed off or, at least, are tricky to enter."*

"Do you mean conversations or, like, literal places?"

"Why can't it be both? The places of our hearts, our relationships, the physical space that your body operates in are so stitched together."

"Is that so?"

"You don't believe me, Wendy?"

"No—I do. I'm only playing devil's advocate."

"You crack me up, Wendy. Alright, alright, let's see if I can convince the devil out of you."

"I'm ready."

"The heart of humor is irony, the unexpected, the upside down. It isn't limited to shock and surprise, but it is certainly always accompanied by it. Humans are creatures of habit who live within patterns and anticipate consistent outcomes. Humor breaks the mold. It works backward, sideways; it tricks you and makes a fool out of you in the most lovely way, but only those who cannot take a joke become the butt of it. Laughter overpowers the senses and even reason. You have no control over it, and therefore, it is humbling. And this is one of my greatest reasons for it: Humans can be foolishly arrogant, prideful people, and it is this great reversal, this upside-down nature of humor that awakens them to true reason and sense of being. It is the upside down that often turns things right side up. This is true with homely humor and cosmic comedy. I do not wish to philosophize humor—because it is better enjoyed than talked about—but I do want you to see, with my eyes, the jokes that many do not understand."

"I can see that—that I've taken myself, taken *things* too seriously to get a joke. To understand life's jokes. But also, I feel like, there are things that aren't funny, you know? Even if it is ironic, that doesn't mean it's always right to laugh, right? There are some things that are too sad to laugh at."

"Of course. Just as every pleasure, if pressed too far, turns painful, the thread of humor that laces the world can be sewn too tightly and even snagged and torn."

"Mhmmm."

"Those that do such a thing do not get the last laugh, Wendy."

"It seems that Evil is always laughing."

"That is because Evil does not know—it does not know that it is the butt of the joke. Evil laughs today, but it will not be laughing tomorrow. You and I will laugh—you and I, Wendy."

"Yeah?"

"Yes, and we can laugh today, too, because we know we'll be laughing tomorrow. Do you see?"

"Sort of."

Saturn laughed lightly and Wendy thought she could feel his breath, like wind, brushing her hair back. But maybe it was just a feeling, an inner feeling and not an outward reality. It was hard to tell the difference here.

"That's enough cosmic comedy for now. Where were we?—right, Saraswathi on a peacock."

"Paatti on a peacock is ironic. It's also ironic how she dislikes the very people that want her love the most."

"Can I lift you higher?"

"Hmmm?"

"Into the branches—"

"Oh, right, yes, yes. I'm curious what you'll say . . ."

"It is ironic, too, how Paatti, who has treated you so horribly, has saved you so many times."

"Saved me?"

"Yes."

"How—when?"

"Many times. With the sapphire."

"I don't understand. What boons did she ask for me? I can't believe she would ever use a boon on me. She hates me."

"Saraswathi's love is clothed in judgment, condescension, disdain. Love should be naked and open to the eyes—but hers is buried, hidden, like the ring. She keeps it close to her chest and lets none see. You

must know, you are not alone in feeling rejection from her. Every Muthu longs for her embrace."

"Yeah, but it feels like she has a special disdain for me."

"She does."

"Great."

"But she has a special love for you too. She desires for you the same thing which you desire for yourself: a child. She has asked Kanmani many times for a blessing on your body to bear a child. In fact, what she has asked for, specifically, is healing for your body. Healing. Many times."

"And still, I remained unhealed."

"But you were healed. Many times. Why is it, do you think, that any time sickness has come upon you recently, it suddenly disappears? Might it be that Saraswathi was asking, almost daily, now, for your healing? And even when Maya and Rini plotted your silent demise by poisoning you, why is it that you were healed at the exact moment Saraswathi stroked the sapphire, summoned Kanmani, and asked once again in her bedroom for your healing?"

"They poisoned me? That's what that was . . . *With what?* Rini's wine? Vik's chai? How did Saraswathi even know I'd been poisoned? I don't understand . . ."

"She knew not what she was asking for, nor that you needed it at that very moment. It was simply part of her routine. She cut it quite close, honestly. You would've died within the hour."

"What!? Are you kidding me? That's giving me anxiety just thinking—wait, why was Saraswathi asking, like, every day? Did you tell her no and she just kept asking?"

"The ring bearer rarely knows if their boon is granted when they ask. Only in time is the answer revealed. Sometimes, yes. Sometimes, no. Sometimes, not yet. The sapphire shines, and you must wait. It is

only on this single occurrence—which was rather strange—where Saraswathi died at the summoning, that Kanmani appeared in bodily form outside the ring to settle the matter."

"Saraswathi had never seen Kanmani before then?"

"I wouldn't say that. She has, in a way—but not in that way."

"Why was no one else poisoned by the chai? Or was it Rini's wine?"

"Yours was only put in your portion—though Saraswathi was given a different mixture."

"Saraswathi was poisoned? Did she heal herself?"

"No, she never became aware of its effect, thinking it to be her arthritis."

"Hmmm . . . her fingers were swelling at dinner, and that's when she dropped the ring and started wearing it on her neck. Were the—the rakshasas were the ones causing her fingers to become inflamed, right? To make the ring more accessible and more likely to be passed on?"

Suddenly, Wendy's memories began to pelt her like heavy rain. What was once a bathing was now a flood—a flooding of so many questions and confusions, causes and concerns. Like a dam that Saturn had set up in this place finally broke and she was being carried away!

"Why all the subtleties? Why sneak and trick instead of just taking the ring? Oh! Because they needed to learn the name by which to summon it, right? But why not just torture Saraswathi to begin with? Was it just because it was a game to them? Did they have anyone else under any spells? And what of Maya's boon? Saraswathi's boon!? Saturn, what happens—"

"I know you have many questions, Wendy, but let us not attempt too many quests at once. The answers will not change, but your ques-

tions may. So let us take our time. There is no need to rush here. All that needs to be known will be revealed in time."

"Okay, okay. I'm sorry."

"What question lies heaviest on your heart?"

"I'm grateful that you blessed Kanmani to bless Saraswathi's boon to bless me with healing, but why did you not heal the one thing Saraswathi and I both *really* wanted you to heal?"

"Your womb?"

"Yes."

"Because your womb is not sick, Wendy. It is not sickness that keeps you from bearing a child."

"Then—what does?"

"It is a good thing you want, Wendy, but not every good is given to everyone. The world you call home is a broken home, and its brokenness spreads into each and every inhabitant's life. Like breaking glass, cracks grow and, when broken, shards scatter, some more visible than others, cutting and splintering the beauty of life. Some goods are stolen by this brokenness while others are withheld for the sake of a greater good—a good that can only come from cuts and cracks being mended, brokenness being made whole. It is Life laughing at Evil— one of my favorite jokes—that something broken, then mended, is somehow made more whole than it was to begin with. In such things, good is doubled by wonder."

"Do you laugh . . . at my pain?"

"I do not laugh at you in pain, Wendy. Nothing could be further from the truth. What I laugh at is Pain itself—this Evil—thinking it can keep you from the good I have for you."

Wendy burst into tears. Tears shed on the surface of her skin and beneath it—her heart crying its eyes out. The weeping overwhelmed her so much that she couldn't speak—not that she would've had any words to say. The hurt that flowed from her was too fast for words, too deep to be described. She only escaped this fit of woe when a large teardrop, larger than Wendy herself, fell from above and popped on her like a water balloon. This tear from heaven washed away her own, at least for the time being.

⚇

Saturn crafted many subsequent sculptures for Wendy—from object lessons to inside jokes to echoes of buried passions. This place —if it could be called *a place*—became saturated with blue and beautiful creations. Like an untouched island of wild and secluded life. Like a museum of Wendy's memories and muses. It was not, now, only the language and felt presence between Wendy and Saturn that inhabited the nuances of her story; it was the very world too. But this *world* was not any heavier or fuller than it was before. Rather, it was as if a very bloated Wendy had been unraveled, unpacked little by little; the weight of her worries was less and less in her and more and more held here.

Wendy and Saturn took their time tackling questions. And while Saturn didn't always tell her the answers she had been looking for, she did seem to be satisfied with their conversations. There was always food for thought. Food to be chewed on and turned over in the mouth of her mind. One question led to another, which led to an observation or introspection that Wendy had never thought to look for in the first place.

But as their journey into the caverns of her story deepened, the light nature of their talks darkened. Sights and sounds were no longer fleeting, and the grog that had once clouded her mind seemed to be dissipating. She was more awake than ever to the horrors that brought her here—and the horrors that she left behind.

Slowness was quickly slipping away. Each flash of Maya's sadistic, demonic face, and the Muthus helplessly hoping Saraswathi's boon might save them, and Kesh in tears holding her hand, and Jothi and Vik bloodied on the ground, and Jack, Real Maya, and Real Rini dead—these images burned into her mind like a fuse that was flying toward destruction.

It made Wendy want to rush—run, think, fight, scheme, beg, find some way out of here, an escape, a way back to them! She needed to know if they were okay, and if not, if there was some way to save them! What was Saraswathi's boon? Did Kanmani grant it? Whom would it save? How would it save them? What of Maya!? Would she kill them anyway?! What of Jothi?! Was she even alive?

Her eyes were not crying now, but her body was. The pressure of these pressing thoughts had her sweating, shaking, trembling! How could she be here talking with Saturn, making sapphire trinkets, recalling her childhood, when they were suffering—dying!

Death . . .

It was the one memory that hadn't fully registered till now. It had been hidden in the grog, but the grog gave out. Wendy recalled the exchange that had happened that day in full: *a spirit for a spirit.* Saraswathi's for Wendy's. That was the deal, right? But what did that mean exactly? Was Wendy . . . dead? *Was she dead!?*

"AM I DEAD?!"

⚛

"Would you like to see me?"

"I do not want a riddle, Saturn—not right now. I just want to know: Am I dead?"

"You are rushing to an answer when you must hold onto the question a little longer."

"I said no riddles!"

"I told you, Wendy, the more you remember, the more you will want to rush, but time works differently here. We have no need to rush."

"Saturn—please!"

"Wendy—"

"I want to know if I'm dead, and if they are okay—that's all!"

"Do you know what some say of me?"

"Don't you care?! Don't you care that I'm in pain!? My family, my husband, is with that demon! And I know *you know!* I thought we were friends. A friend would help a friend in pain! Just tell me! TELL ME!"

"You may want help, Wendy, but you do not want my help. I do see your pain—more vividly than you know—but what pains me more than your need for help is your rejection of the help I offer you. Have I shown you nothing since you came here? Tell me."

Wendy began to pace. She felt like she was on fire. There was a burning within her, and it was getting hot, hot, hotter with each passing second. Her hands clawed into her scalp like she was trying to pry out the answer from within herself—but she knew not the answer, not the answer she wanted to know.

Wendy started hyperventilating. The only thing faster than her pacing was her breathing. Picking up speed now—in, out, in out, in out, in out! And she groaned in between breaths. She was so angry! How could Saturn be so selfish! So nonchalant! He didn't care for her! He didn't care for anyone! This place—*THIS PLACE*—it was a prison! And she was his prisoner! If she was dead, this must be her hell—and how could she ever escape! Saturn and his slowness . . .

What was he up to this whole time? Had he divinely drugged her, like some slave, some plaything, a toy to treat so stupid. It was all a game to him! It was all a joke! That must be it. She had left one demon's grip to be snatched by another! He played nice and pretended to be some friendly philosopher, but it was all smoke and mirrors, just like Maya and Rini—God, just like them. He was never going to actually help her, was he? No, he just wanted to play pretend! He just wanted to slowly torture her with every terrible memory before locking her up for good. Well, she would not comply! Not Wendy—no! Wendy didn't give up, didn't give in, even if it was eternity. She would show him, show Saturn, that goddamn—

"Wendy."

Wendy's fists were clenched, and she looked up at the nothingness from where his voice boomed with a face of defiance, of defense, teeth grinding with eyes of fury. But for whatever reason, looking down on her like this—if only she could see herself like this, from Saturn's eyes—she looked like a child, a baby even, throwing a tantrum, hysterical, distraught, burning with a fire that bore no flame, impossible not to pity. Maybe damnable, if she wasn't so dear to him.

"Wendy, don't you see? Do you see yourself? I have told you to wait, and for this you hate me? Spurn me? Think me the Devil? Wish to torture me for all eternity? You turn each and every act of my love into an act of deceit and malice! Are we no longer friends because I will not tell you what you want to know when you want to know it? What friend are you! You wish to fill your mind while you empty your heart at the same time! You wish to know so much, but you do not wish to know me! Yet, I have known you since before you were born

. . . known your every cry and laugh, when you have been far off and when you have drawn near, when you have loved me and when you have hated me. But you . . . it seems you do not know me at all."

⋰

Wendy thought she knew loneliness.

Her parents' arms had been cold since infancy, and the Muthus dismissed her at every turn. Demons turned the one person who was close to her away, and she had left everyone and everything she knew to come to *this place*.

But such things did not seem lonely anymore. Does a drop in a bucket compare to a sea of seclusion that seems to go on forever? This quiet made her soul scream. This isolation made her ache in every way. She had thought she was in hell—*but no*, this was hell.

She was being sucked into the silence, sinking deeper and deeper. At first, she had felt Saturn's breath upon her, his presence here, all around her, like he was waiting for her to speak, to say something—anything. But the longer she bit her tongue, the further she drifted away at sea, and the further away he felt.

Till she was alone. Completely, wholly alone. Or so it felt.

She couldn't even hear him in her heart anymore. Each beat was out of tune, out of reach. It felt meaningless, silly even. It was only the sound of a heart—a very biological thing, like every other living thing. Nothing special. No song, no Saturn.

This . . . *loneliness*. The world felt empty, and so did she.

She scratched herself inside and out, but there was no itch to satisfy. Not in the crevices of her soul. She could not live without another song! Without a friend. Without him. Did she really think she could remain silent forever? Dupe the divine? Why had she wanted such a thing? How deeply did she long to hear his voice. Even if he were to scold her—to say the most horrible things.

Her anger, her silence, was eating away at her, and she felt nearly consumed. What happened when there was truly nothing left?

If she were to speak now, would he even answer?

Had he left her here forever? Alone?

She did not want to give up, to give in, but what was she fighting for? What good would staying silent do? Wendy felt she had been silent for too long, that maybe it was too late, but there was no alternative. There was talking with him, and there was silence. What would the silence tell her? How would the silence save her family—save Kesh? And what wrong did Saturn really do her?

He had told her to wait. And now, how much longer had her quest for an answer taken? How much more had this quest taken from her? Oh God, how she longed to hear his voice! Saturn, her dearest friend. The wicked thoughts she had, the hatred she had felt toward him—had he seen it all? How could he ever speak to her again? How could he ever love her? What reason was there to speak to him? It may only drive him farther away.

But then, Wendy *remembered . . .*

She remembered how Saturn prized slowness and waiting, and how nothing ever seemed long to him. Was it possible that this separation between them, though it felt like an eternity for Wendy, was only a mere moment for him? Or, even if it had been long for him, was it possible that he was still waiting for her? Waiting for her to turn back and speak?

There was only one way to find out . . .

"SATURN!?" Wendy screamed at the top of her lungs, hoping that however far away he was, an echo might reach him.

"There's no need to yell. I'm right here."

The resonance of his voice extinguished every ounce of loneliness almost instantaneously. Wendy could feel her heart, which had felt so empty, being filled back up—a song sounding from within! She opened her mouth to speak and tears overwhelmed her. Her voice trembled, and her knees gave out.

Wendy wept. "Saturn—oh. I-I am—so sorry—I—"

"Do you know what some say of me, Wendy?"

"I do not—please, tell me."

"They say I delay but do not deny."

Wendy continued to cry. "I thought you were gone—forever."

"I had not gone anywhere, dear. I was right here."

"I'm so sorry."

"Would you like to see me?"

"I do see you—I see you again! I am so glad to see you again!"

"Would you like to see me with your eyes? I would love to give you a hug, in person."

"You can do that?"

Saturn laughed. Oh, how she missed his laugh!

"Well, it won't be all of me . . . but yes, it will be me, in a way."

"Yes, yes!"

A shadow flickered like a candle's flame, multiplied into two, and took the shape of two wings beating the air, then stretched to the form of a bird, and the silhouette dissolved into a texture of feathers, becoming a living, flying crow. It was GIANT.

It landed at Wendy's feet and cocked its head.

Wendy looked at it, almost eye to eye due to its height. She opened her arms—

"I do like crows, but that's not me."

Wendy turned around.

Saturn had a big smile. It was the first thing she noticed. It was tender, wide, and held a massive mustache that curled on the ends. He was a large man with rich, blue skin that looked as deep as the sky and smooth as the sea. He wore varying blue robes, trimmed in gold and embroidered with such detail that, if you were to utilize a magnifying glass, each inch could tell a story, reveal a city of design, as if male and female artists of minuscule size had dedicated lifetimes to stitching its contents. And the robes were so long and wooly that it seemed to be the fur of some fantastical creature, either of ancient times or of another world entirely. The gold jewelry and gems that hung on him like ornaments on a tree were so countless and captivating that his entire presence sparkled, as if he was the ocean rippling under the sun. And even with such majesty, funny enough, Wendy felt that he looked like her father . . .

But he did not. *Not really.* He didn't look like anyone she'd ever seen before, yet he resembled so many faces. He looked so familiar. She hadn't seen Saturn in this way before, but it made sense —like this was how she was seeing him all along, just not with her eyes.

The fury and familiarity of his glory made Wendy cry again, but Saturn swallowed her up in his arms. If she had felt the epitome of loneliness, this was the antithesis of that. There had never been a place so warm, so welcoming, so right, as within his arms.

⸗

"I want to do things your way . . . the slow way."

"*Do you?*"

"I do."

Saturn smiled so that the curls of his mustache touched the edges of his eyes.

"*Right, then—where were we?*"

"Well, I was wondering, you know, if I'm dead, or whatever . . . but we can start wherever you like."

"*Ah, death. I suppose you are dead, in a way. However, it depends on your definition. If death is merely the separation of the spirit from the body, then you are certainly dead. The body you see now, which you look down at, touch hand against hand—there—it is not really your body. But let me tell you this, Wendy: While a human is, yes, both body and spirit, definitive death is not in the separation of these two but the separation of them from Life itself. You may think that life belongs to all living things, and it does, in a way, but all living things only have life because they belong to Life, the Giver of it, firstly, not the other way around.*"

"So, I'm sorta dead."

"*Yes.*"

"And will I stay *sorta dead*, forever? Not that I'm complaining, since I am here with you, but—"

"*Well, that depends.*"

"Okay."

"*Time works differently here, Wendy. You have heard me say it before, yes?*"

"Yes, of course."

"*But I do not mean only that it is slow. It really is different. We are not in the world you know, which is governed by the clock, though you certainly know this world, too, now. The Muthus are in imminent danger, but they also are not, from where we stand.*"

"So nothing has transpired since I left them so long ago?"

"It is not like that, Wendy. I know you are only familiar with time in one sense. Even here things appear to move forward, and they do, in a way, but for me—how's this—it is like I am a storyteller, and while I may put pen to paper, the story has always, ever been written in my mind, and my heart too. I have, in a way, brought you off the page, as I intend to do with all dear ones, one day. Are you following me, Wendy? I know it is a mysterious thing I am trying to tell you."

"I'm following—as closely as I can, I guess."

"Good, good. Look, Wendy, I have a special part I want you to play in the story I am telling, this particular one. You are already playing the role—you have been. But now, I must put pen to the page once again and even re-read what I already wrote long ago. I never spill ink, you must know. Every page is there for a reason, every word."

"I don't want to presume upon your kindness, but are you saying that you will write me back into this story? And if yes, how, if I am dead?"

"See! Wendy, you are following quite closely!"

"Oh, good. I'm glad you think so—because I am still quite confused."

Saturn laughed, and Wendy joined him.

"The letters I write are not merely words strung together. My words are living and breathing; they are alive, connected to Life, to me. Even the ink that is smeared, it thinks it can scramble the page and write its own stories, but it forgets that I hold the pen. The words think they can alter my story subtly, in the shadows, and that I will not notice or care, but the Devil is not in the details—though devils try to hide there—the details are mine too! What's waiting for them is worse than being erased or unwritten."

"They will not get the last laugh."

"Yes, Wendy! Exactly."

"So, you will save my family—save Kesh?"

"I will save them in the most ironic, upside-down way! It will be a joke, both cosmic and homely, and you, Wendy, you are not the butt of the joke. You are the punchline."

"Me? How?"

"I will show you. But Wendy . . . it is going to be the long way. I hope this is no surprise to you. It will require much waiting, much more than you have yet endured. But it is for this reason that you have had to wait much longer than others for many things, for this was always the plan, the story."

"Will you be with me?"

"Oh, Wendy, of course. I am always with you. Even when you knew it not. I will be with you down each twist and turn of the road, every pit stop, and every seemingly dead end till we get to where we're going and after. What do you say?"

"If you are with me, I will go anywhere, however long it takes."

"I will never leave you. I have never left you."

Wendy inhaled. Wendy exhaled. She looked into Saturn's sapphire eyes.

"What is it, Wendy?"

"Will Saraswathi keep her spirit if I return? I do not want to—"

"You will not be returning the way you left, Wendy. You made a great sacrifice that day, exchanging your spirit for Saraswathi's. Like we have said, it was a form of death. Now, you must pay the price for that sacrifice. You have called this place a prison, but where you are going will truly be. You will be reborn and renamed. You will be bound till your sentence is up—till it is time for you to be freed. There must be balance, harmony in all things. This is the cost to pay for the regeneration of your life and preservation of the Muthus' lives. With-

out knowing, they offered you up for this payment, and you offered up yourself, though you were most undeserving of it."

"Will it save those we have already lost? Jack, Real Maya, and Real Rini? The rakshasa killed them, didn't she?"

"No ink is spilled that I did not intend, Wendy. Just as you have a special part to play in this story, full of trial and triumph, so do they. But you must focus on your part, now, and trust the pen in my hand."

"I do . . ."

Saturn smiled again, his mustache curling practically into his eyeballs.

"Any other questions?"

"Maya said that Kesh got her pregnant."

"The rakshasas say many things, but there are bounds to their smearing."

"Is Jothi alive? Will I be able to save her? What about Vik—?"

"Part of the waiting is the not knowing, Wendy. You are going to have to trust me and the story that I'm writing. Any other questions?"

"I just have one more."

"Ask away."

"Will I get to be a mother one day?"

"Oh, Wendy. Don't you see, dear? Have I not lifted you into the branches? You have loved others before being loved. That is the most motherly thing. I will lift you higher still. If you are ready to begin your quest, you will find all the answers you need, in time."

"I'm ready when you are."

"I think we've waited long enough."

SIXTEEN

It wasn't any night because it was the night that he chose . . . the night that Saturn chose to send Wendy, shooting her from heaven's gun, flinging her upon the earth, where she spun, twisted, rolled—like light, like water—traveling and tumbling and finding her way into the hands of a Sri Lankan man as he stood knee-deep in the river, sifting and sorting, finally finding a beautiful, uncut sapphire gem.

Saturn cast Wendy into the gem, binding her to do his bidding, to bless the boons of strangers till her time came to be freed. The Sri Lankan man had hoped to find an earthly treasure but had been blessed with a heavenly one. The gem ignited with beauty and power, and at her sight, the man named her Kanmani, for it was the gem of his eye.

"You have called her Kanmani, and so she shall be. Hold her dear, and she will bless you according to my command and all those who call upon her name."

Saturn's voice rumbled from the sky; he spoke in Tamil, which Wendy now understood. However long she had been with Saturn, it had been long enough to learn a language. Maybe all languages. Though who knows what tongue they spoke in, if any? Could it be that their hearts were having conversations in a language too deep for human words?

Wendy—or Kanmani, for they are one and the same—was held dear by this Sri Lankan man, and he found great success and comfort from her beauty and blessing. Even so, he died a few years later, only ever passing on the knowledge of the sapphire and its name to his wife, who saw the gem, its beauty and power, to be a curse, to be "dealings with the demonic," as she had often called it, so she gave it to her brother, whom she hated, hoping it would appear as a gift but result in a curse. Only her brother did not understand the power of the sapphire or believe in it, so he did not hold it dear and broke it into seven pieces, hoping to make a profit, since he was a maritime trader, and while he kept a sliver of the gem for himself, only the last piece from which the gem was broken bound Kanmani, and this piece, he traded for spices to a Tamil-speaking man from Tamil Nadu, promising him blessings and telling him the name by which to call it.

This was the first time an ancestor of the Muthu family possessed the sapphire.

Kanmani was passed from hand to hand and from heart to heart. From pocket to wrist to neck to hidden holes and secret cubbies, she listened and watched a humble South Indian family rise from a lower caste to fortune, fame, and favor. She granted boons of lust and love, of wealth and worries, of little inconveniences and major milestones, of health and beauty . . . of fertility. She witnessed every ugly and pretty facet of this family, and while she watched them, they watched her. Her beauty and power were admired and desired, a holy heirloom that attracted the eyes of the body, mind, and heart.

Though the family lost knowledge of their history, generation by generation, Wendy retained it. She was present when life was conceived, born, raised up, matured, slowed, and taken away.

She sustained their success.

She nurtured their name.

She *mothered* them.

Kanmani did not understand it at first, but as time passed, her fondness for the Muthus grew, and she carried them along, as a mother carries a baby, lifting them when they fell, providing food and water, bestowing blessings. It was a long lesson, one of much waiting. She witnessed pain, poor choices, *people*—but it did not thwart her growing love for them, her tenderness toward them. Just as a mother who cannot hate her young, though they take and take and take, Wendy could not help but let the Muthu family become dear to her. It did not matter what they took of her in the present, nor what they would take of her in the future.

Minutes became hours, hours became days, days became weeks, weeks became months, months became years, years became decades, and decades became centuries. It was a long time during which she got to love them. As it is with parents who do not wish for their children to grow yet feel time slipping through their fingers, Kanmani felt things were moving too quickly and wished to pause time, if only it were possible.

She lived a private life. Her presence was acknowledged only in the lustful gazes of the sapphire's beauty and when a Muthu said her name to summon her powers for a boon. It would've been incredibly lonely, if it weren't for Saturn. She really did feel his presence wherever she was. She heard his voice in everything. She saw him, *always*. It was actually the same way that the Muthus only desired her for her beauty and power, which impressed upon her her own youthful ignorance: how she had done the very same thing all her life to Saturn.

Saturn's presence, his song, his handwriting, was everywhere. Even though she had never noticed it till now. Kanmani did not always understand the boons Saturn told her to grant nor the ones he didn't, but she did his bidding anyway. She learned to trust the pen in his hand. Though she seemed to become a mother in the most humorous, ironic, and upside-down way, Saturn became to her a father.

It wasn't just one thing about him but, rather, everything about him. He seemed to be the epitome of family. The thing she had always wanted yet never really known. It was in his laugh, his riddles, his presence, his calm, his answers and nonanswers, his storytelling, his patience—but it wasn't just these qualities that painted the picture of fatherhood or family. They were colors or strokes of the brush, maybe. What made her know that he was to her a father most evidently was that she knew that *he loved her*, that she was *dear to him*. Despite being trapped in the gem and forced to wait for ages, this truth came out in a myriad of ways, and it was the picture that hung firm in her heart.

This prison never felt like a prison to her. Every day—in the waiting, the pain, the confusion—Kanmani felt like she was a little girl, sitting on Saturn's shoulders, high up in the branches, and he was showing her things with his eyes. Wonderful, beautiful things that she had never known.

SEVENTEEN

The Muthus were bound and bowed. Dozens down on their knees, with ankles and hands tied by vines and branches that were chained to the earth. Some of their mouths were sewn shut by roots. Quite the family tree—watered by their tears alone.

After Saraswathi's spirit returned to her and Wendy's was taken away, the matriarch had asked Kanmani to send someone to save them. That was her boon. Kanmani did not reply but turned to Maya, lifted her hand, and granted the rakshasa what she had desired.

A surge of blue light illuminated Maya, and she was made *more*.

She began testing the limits of her new power. With simpler gestures and shorter incantations, she had tied up all the Muthus, including Kesh who wept on the earth, his hand still in Wendy's, her body lying lifeless. Then, with a squeal of an unintelligible slur of words that sounded more like an echo from hell, Maya stitched up the torn skin on her back and cheeks, and with a pulse of power, enhanced her beauty, like a shock wave that shed every hint of blood, dust, and dirt. Every ounce of ugly fell off her.

Maya squealed again.

ANOTHER PULSE. Her hair became tamed and styled. Her skin tightened. Her outfit dissolved into a two-piece of abstract color and design, enhancing her features.

Maya squealed again.

ANOTHER PULSE. Freckles and moles fell. Wrinkles were erased. Her cheekbones rose. Her skin tightened tighter. Another enhancement of beauty.

Maya squealed again.

ANOTHER PULSE! Her hair grew longer. Her waist shrunk. Her lips became fuller. Her skin shined, smooth like a doll. Another enhancement of beauty.

With every pulse, she became more beautiful, so much so that she didn't look human anymore. Her features became more symmetric. Her skin became more plastic. Her body became accentuated to the point of great disproportion.

Her beauty became disturbingly *perfect*, and in this perfection, she became so much more beautiful *than* anyone that she was no longer beautiful *to* anyone. Maya's madness was unmasked by her own making. Her enlarged eyes and smile no longer hid the truth of who she was but rather revealed it. She no longer looked human.

She was, if there was any doubt left, a rakshasa.

By the conjuring of her hands and tongue, Maya pulled Rini's body from the peacocks and made it levitate. She sewed shut each puncture and shoved inside each protruding bit of black mass, snapping bones and fixing flesh like a demonic doctor. Blood and breath returned to Rini's body, and she came alive.

"Should have listened to me, sis," said Maya.

"You have . . . the ring?" Rini was still getting oriented, her face flooding with life, jealousy, acceptance.

"Forever and always."

Maya flashed the ring like she was posing for an engagement photo. Then, she circled Kesh, who was bound on his knees. She grabbed him by the hair and sucked his mouth into hers—a long, wet, coerced kiss.

Rini looked down at Vik's crumpled, unconscious body.

"What happened to *my* guy?"

"We'll fix him." Maya winked.

"You look . . ." Rini took in Maya's new body.

"Sexy? Divine?"

Rini's eyes were pulled away from Maya by the piercing light of Kanmani who walked behind her—like sunlight hitting a piece of metal in the desert or a bright phone screen in the middle of the night. Rini squinted at the giant, magnificent blue being strolling across the lawn.

"That's—"

"Oh, yeah. Not sure when she's gonna pop back in." Maya gestured to the ring and shrugged. "But I am now the most powerful rakshasa to ever exist, so there's that. Only one boon for now, sorry, sis. But there'll be more. Plenty more."

Rini's eyes stayed on Kanmani, save for long blinks and eye bounces on and off because of the bright. She watched her make her way to the cliff's edge.

"You hungry?" asked Maya.

The Muthus squealed and squirmed. A meal having a meltdown.

"Kanmani! Kanmani!" Saraswathi shouted. She then yelled in Tamil to the blue being, pleading for her to grant her boon, too—to save her family.

Maya sent a root flying and sewed up her mouth.

"So . . . are we good to just do what we want with them, then?" asked Rini.

"I guess so. Apparently, he doesn't care for these creatures." Maya laughed and covered her mouth, like it was a secret.

"Maya," Kesh said, looking up at her, eyes forcing a smile through tears and heartbreak. "You have want you wanted. Why—why torment us anymore?"

"Because it's fun!" Maya perked up and smiled. "And I'm hungry!"

"What if you do with me what you want, and you spare them?"

"What if I do what I want with you *and* eat them?"

"All of them?" asked Rini. "We can't eat them all—"

"What do you mean we can't?!"

"A massacre will draw attention. It will upset him. This is already—"

"The rice is washed! He granted me the boon! He knew what that meant!" Maya began to laugh hysterically; spit stretched between her smile and twisted tears squeezed out the corners of her eyes. "We took the ring, fair and square! Now, let's use the power we've been given! He could've granted the old woman's boon, but he didn't. He doesn't care for them—these godless little shits— THEY'RE MINE!" Her jaw snapped shut and her teeth clenched.

"He denied Saraswathi's boon? What did she ask?"

Saraswathi squirmed and whined.

"Yes, yes! What do you mean?" Maya danced in a circle while she spoke, then paused. "She asked for them to be saved, and he—"

"That's not true!" Kesh shouted. "She gave no response! She could still save us—please, save us! Kanmani! KANMANI! My wife —she, she, she gave her life so that you might save us! Please, you said, you said this was the only way! Please ask him—ask him if he's willing to do anything, even to save just a few of us!"

"She gave no response?" Rini looked concerned. "So she still may—?"

"Wendy! No, Wendy!" Kesh screamed. "Don't take her!"

Maya and Rini turned toward Kesh, whose grip—his unbreakable grip—had been broken, and Wendy's dead body was . . .

GONE.

The spot was empty, with grass slowly rising from where the body *had* been seconds ago. A shadow of trampled lawn made a streak through the grass, and all eyes followed it toward Wendy's unconscious, limp body moving on its own, being dragged across the yard by nothing.

It was moving slowly but making its way toward Kanmani, who sat down on the cliff's edge, watching the ocean below.

Maya flew to the body! She fought to grab it—to stop it—but it swerved and evaded her; she caught Wendy's hand, and it slipped like butter from her grip. Maya hurried to Kanmani. Rini followed.

"Where's her body going?!" shouted Maya to Kanmani.

"It does not concern you."

"Why are you even still here?!"

Kanmani did not answer.

The blue being watched the blue sky and blue waters. The water rippled and rode into the waves, crashed on the sand, crawled up the beach, and then slipped away. Streaks of clouds smeared the sky, but it was mostly wide and open. A few seagulls flew between the heavens and the earth.

Maya and Rini planted their feet behind Kanmani, huffing and puffing. Maya used her hand to shade her face from the blinding proximity to Kanmani's light. And with her hand over her eyes, the sapphire ring gradually crawled off her finger and hovered in the air.

"What the hell!"

Maya swatted at the ring, but it slipped through her fingers.

Wendy's body was still dragging its way toward Kanmani. Almost there!

The ring rose higher in the air! Maya levitated to grab it—

But Wendy's limp body flung into the air and knocked Maya away!

Wendy's body and the ring continued ascending. Kanmani lifted off the ground. She began rising, too.

Maya and Rini flew in a dash at the ring!

But Kanmani, Wendy, and the ring met in the sky—

BLAST! A BURST OF BLUE!

The earth thundered! The sky was lightning!

Maya and Rini were flung backward by a pure force of fury—the fury of the sapphire. It was as if the sun had exploded. But the sun was dim in comparison to the sapphire. In fact, the sun was barely visible, as a brilliance of blue blocked its light.

The flames of this fire were jagged gems like ice.

The smoke was a blaring mist of magic.

Whir!—Whir!—Whir!—Whir!

She was a whirlwind. A spin and roar of light and power. The ring hovered like a spotlight, illuminating Kanmani's form of light and glass, which began to crack and shatter in the tornado; Wendy's body sunk into the blaring blades of beauty, and the color refracted around her frame, washing over her, like the light and jewel had become the sea, swallowing her up, and the light became so bright that everything became unseeable.

All eyes were forced shut, heads hung low, ears covered.

It could have been a second, but it felt like forever.

Until, eventually, the howl of the whirlwind dissolved into the heavy ebb and flow of beating wings. The light was lessened by a protective shadow. Eyes crawled open and found focus on a black form growing and drawing near.

It was . . .

A CROW. A massive crow, flying, hovering. The wind from its wings blew back the grass and the hair on heads. But it was only the steed, the beast of burden, the companion of its rider: SATURN.

He had blended in with the sky but slowly popped into the foreground, the blue of his skin separated from the blue of the sky, like he had always been there and only now wanted to be revealed. He donned the same royal robes, gems, and jewelry that Wendy had seen him wear, but he also wielded a golden bow with arrows that Wendy had never seen.

His mustache curled as he smiled at Wendy, at Kanmani. Their beauty had merged into one. The air held her as so many hands had before. The brightness settled on a sapphire glow that outlined her body. She was dressed in a gold sari, littered with sapphire gems and jewelry.

Sapphire light showered drops of diamonds from her like rain from a crystal cloud. She was like a goddess, a creature of glory and power, so holy and yet *human*.

Wendy returned Saturn's smile. It was an aged smile by long-awaited lips, an epochal and climactic grin that had finally grown.

"My dear Kanmani. My dear Wendy. My dear."

Saturn's voice came from him and the heavens. His words were heavy hail that hummed while being hurled into their eardrums.

"Is it really time?" Wendy asked.

"Yes."

Maya turned and fled, and Rini turned to follow, but *WHISP!* A golden arrow flew in a flash. It pierced Rini's foot to the earth.

WHISP! Another golden arrow sprung from Saturn's bow, catching Maya in the air and striking her foot too. It flew through her heel and yanked her to the ground, binding her, too, to the earth.

Rini and Maya fought the arrows with all their might, but they would not budge. The arrows were fixed in place and not going anywhere, thus neither were the rakshasas.

"Well, wait one more moment, if you don't mind . . ."
Wendy chuckled.

Saturn began walking away but looked back over his shoulder at her, and their eyes met, both laughing now and sharing a look, a laugh, a joke that only they got.

"Happy to wait." Wendy sighed as her laughing slowed to a peaceful stop.

Saturn's crow landed on the lawn while he walked over to Jothi. He rested his hand on her and she awoke. He did the same thing to Vik. He then lifted Jack's dead body, like it was a feather in his fingers, and laid him on the back of the crow.

Saturn ascended his beast, saddled up, and flew beside Wendy.

No doubt many of the Muthus had questions. But none spoke a word. It is this way with divine sightings. All words fall away. It was neither feet, nor hands, nor mouths that were tied up now. It was the spirits within the bodies that were held captive in his presence.

What comparisons could help you comprehend it?
A train wreck? A sunset? Taking your last breath?
What can words say to the one who wrote them?
How can ink look upon its spiller?

What a marvelous mystery that written words could gaze upon their writer, the book upon its author! The rakshasas epitomized fear. Kanmani epitomized wonder. But Saturn was wholly both. Maya and Rini wailed and shouted in Tamil, but the humans could do nothing except watch as he moved, listen as he spoke.

"The woman whom you know as Wendy has been with me since long ago—though even she did not know it till recently. You have sold her as you have sold your hearts, each of you, to your devils. Look within you and see! Every one of you, lusting for so many boons, so many blessings, that you have forgotten the Blesser! You curse one another— one of your very own. She carries the littlest of your blood and culture yet upholds it more than all of you! In her, I see your history—and your future! The sapphire has made your name great and given you many riches in the world's eyes, yes, but it has made you poorer than many in my eyes. See how two beasts have come and stolen so much with ease! Why is it your treasure can be taken so quickly? No, you do not treasure what I treasure. Now, Wendy—whom I revealed to you as Kanmani and whom I imprisoned long ago in the gem that I chose —will execute my decree upon you, and YOU—!"

Saturn turned to the rakshasas who flailed on the ground. The arrows seemed to be tied to the earth's core. Nothing could pull them free. They clawed at their own ankles, tearing at the skin to break free of their feet.

"Do you forget that it is my light which casts shadows? Do you think my eyes are not there?"

The rakshasas stopped clawing at their feet to cover their ears.

"Even in their failings, these humans do not belong to you! What fall is too great that I cannot catch? What depth is beyond my reach? You ask to become the most powerful rakshasa—oh! And this will make you a god? The greatest boons could not make you human. The

power which you possess now will not even be dispensed at your will. Yes, you are a god now! A god in a cage."

Saturn took Wendy's hand and looked at her.

"My dear. I will leave my power in your hands a little while longer, that you may be the executor of my mercy, and my wrath. You have seen with my eyes, and now, you will speak with my voice, be my hands, my feet. You may grant Saraswathi's boon, and in doing so, be freed from the sapphire, your sentence complete, and return to your family—to your husband."

"Will you . . . be with me still?"

"I am always with you, Wendy—just don't forget to see me, and to hear my voice."

"My lord, lord!"

Saturn turned to Kesh on his knees, head bowed, hands raised.

"You are right! I am guilty not only of dishonoring you but my family as well. I was the one, the one who called you a demon—blamed you for cursing us!" Kesh began to weep. "I am so, so sorry. I doubted your wisdom, your power. I allowed these monsters to infiltrate my family and take advantage of my lust. Yes, they deceived me with dark magic, but I know, in my heart, there was a well of darkness from which they pulled from. I could have left that night by the fire, when Maya arrived, to care for my sick wife upstairs, and I chose not to—making excuses in my mind—but part of me desired the monster, was attracted to her, and for that I deserve whatever punishment you see fit. I'm sorry, Wendy! I do not deserve you—but my-my-my lord, please, I understand if I am to be accursed, but please spare my family. Those who you deem worthy."

Saturn looked down upon Kesh, the man in tears. His love laid bare, so naked. Saturn spoke as if kneeling beside him, the way a father might to a boy.

"You sit beside demons, child, and call yourself one, and this itself proves you are not one of them. Yes, you bear guilt, but—see his example, Muthus—you, Kesh, confess your evil, though smaller than theirs, and because of this, find favor in my eyes, and no doubt Wendy's. Now hold your tongue, for I have heard your heart say much more than this and have already decreed what is to be."

Saturn removed two bell-shaped earrings fitted with sapphires from his ears, then handed them to Wendy. He smiled once more. His mustache—if it could be possible—curled higher and higher than ever.

"Do not forget from where all boons come."

He steered his crow around and flew into the blue, vanishing against the sky.

Wendy descended to the earth. It felt odd being back in her mortal body, being outside the cage of sapphire. *Buh-bmmm, buh-bmmm.* Her heart pounded life into her flesh. She felt her hair tickling the back of her neck. There was a light breeze swimming all around her. And the grass was soft and yet cool, nature snuggled against her feet. Wendy inhaled the breeze. The cool now ran into her lungs, and when she expelled it, she softly spoke a word in Tamil. At once every root and vine that had bound the Muthus fell and sunk into the earth.

Kesh climbed to his feet but kept his head down. Yes, Wendy was his wife, and she had returned to human form, but she was still glowing with blue light, a godly glitter sparkled around her. Her face seemed to have aged slightly yet only increased in beauty—a magnetic maturity.

"It's alright, Kesh. It's me—your wife. Come."

Kesh marched toward her, his chin slowly lifting as tears ran down it.

He paused just in front of her. Taking her in.

She slipped one hand into his, the other on his cheek.

Then, she pulled Kesh into a kiss. It was the kiss of ages past. It was wet, warm, and *real*—the smacking of lips, of sorrys, of souls. And everyone watched silently. Everyone except *Maya and Rini*. They cried and laughed simultaneously, hysterical as hyenas, still digging at their own skin, trying to rip free of Saturn's arrows.

"How . . ." Kesh brushed over, with his thumb, his wife's hand in his. "I don't understand what's happening . . . I—"

"I know," Wendy replied. "I'll help you see, in time, what Saturn has shown me. But all I want right now . . ." Wendy's voice cracked as tears swelled, "is for you to hold my hand and stand beside me while I carry out my last act as Kanmani."

Kesh squeezed his wife's hand and moved beside her. There was a warmth and light about her like he was standing beside a fire. The coziest, warmest, most wonderful fire.

Wendy raised her hand toward the Muthus and—

Every able man, woman, and child came charging at her!

What the hell!? Wendy was almost afraid, though she knew that, even together, they had no power over her right now. She just watched them to see what they'd do. Kesh squeezed his wife's hand even tighter now.

The stampede trampled Maya and Rini in the process, completely oblivious to their presence, though Maya managed to snatch one of Kesh's little cousins, a boy, by the ankle and pin him down. The rest of the Muthus ran at Wendy.

They *fell* at her feet. They *bowed* before her.

They all began to *beg* for her mercy:

"Forgive us, Wendy!"

"Hail Kanmani! Our Kanmani!"

"Spare the children! Punish us!"

"We are sorry, Wendy!"

There was sobbing and repenting, and Wendy was in quite a shock at the sight of them. Some began recounting various private wicked deeds, unrelated to the present matter, of which they had committed in their lives. Others repented of blaming Wendy and offering her as their sacrifice to save themselves.

There were too many words—too many people—and Wendy finally silenced them with a wave of her hand, shouting, "Please, listen!"

Everyone looked up at her with pitiful eyes.

"I'll rip out his throat!" wailed Maya, drawing Wendy's attention. "I'll bite off his head! SET US FREE NOW!"

Maya held the little boy tight in her arms, one hand around his neck. She began pulling him toward her mouth. Her lips and cheeks peeled back—this time, thick and yellow teeth like oily daggers emerged, two of them like tusks descended from the roof of her mouth.

Wendy whispered an incantation and wiggled her fingers. One by one, Maya's teeth were plucked from her mouth. Like notes played on a piano of pain. One after another. Almost like a song— *pop, pop, popping* like popcorn, kernels of consonance. The tusks were yanked out last.

Maya fell backward, howling, and the child managed to escape in the process, running to Wendy and falling at her feet too.

Rini waved her arms, shouting incantations at Wendy. But her powers seemed to have no effect. With a flick of Wendy's tongue and a snap of her finger, Rini's tongue tore from her mouth and flew to the grass—*flop, flop, flopping.*

Both rakshasas writhed on the ground, crying out with bloodied and slashed mouths, then returned to their previous strategy of clawing at their own feet to get Saturn's arrows out.

Wendy returned her attention to the people.

"Listen to me, now. I am not guiltless, but what evil you've done, Saturn has undone and turned for good. This family has been broken, but he intends to mend it, and it is this wonderful mystery that he has shown me: that what has been broken, then mended, can be made more whole than it was to begin with. I know you are afraid of me—but I love you. I have always loved you, and now, I have watched you for many years and grown to love you more deeply than you know. However long it takes, whatever imperfections we dig up and must find the beauty in, let us be whole once more—more than we ever were before. We do not need a ring and its boons to be blessed! See now, the greatest boon."

Wendy walked forward, Kesh following behind, their hands still clasped. The crowd split in two, forming a pathway for them. Wendy eyed Vik sunken into the fountain water, Jothi sitting up with blood pouring down her face, Meena crawling behind the crowd, still blind, and Saraswathi lying down, her eyes smiling at Wendy, even through the boils and burnt skin.

Wendy approached the rakshasas.

"Look away now. Soon these devils will be gone."

Maya and Rini began to plead for their lives, though their words were unintelligible. It is very difficult to speak—in Tamil or in English—without teeth or without tongue, with mouths torn open. Wendy watched their gestures, caught certain syllables. She could tell Rini was accusing Maya of being the instigator of violence, saying she deserved a greater punishment. Maya laughed and spit at Rini, then spit at Wendy, and began to throw a tantrum, flailing in the grass. They both begged to be killed—to be erased from existence. But Wendy remembered Saturn's words, that no ink is spilled by accident, and nothing can be erased or unwritten.

She lifted one sapphire earring in one hand and the second in the other. She had to let go of Kesh's hand to do this, and he stepped back.

"You look away too, Kesh."

He hid behind her and covered his eyes.

Wendy peeled at the air. Like she was opening an invisible book, an imperceivable curtain. She undressed the wind and Maya and Rini's flesh began to rip and roll. Their human suits were shed. The mortal masks removed completely.

They were naked.

Bulges of black broke free and sagged. Fat flaps of hairy scales littered their bodies. Like moles made of coals. Damn, they were big. Twice the size of humans that had been pressed and squeezed into a tiny outfit of flesh. Their heads were round yet long, with a muzzle like a donkey stretching from their cheeks, and wide mouths that displayed an array of teeth—though Maya's were now missing. Two horns poked through their scalps of skin, and the flesh slipped behind them like a jacket being pulled off their backs.

Wendy thought they looked like goats.

Goats with front-facing, bloodshot eyes.

Goats with the mouths of dragons.

Ghastly giant goats.

Maya and Rini hissed and screamed! They were mice caught by heaven's paw, birds snatched by heaven's claw, worms squirming between divine fingers. Wendy inhaled a deep breath. Sparks of blue began to flicker, and a bold, beautiful, and abounding light surrounded and swallowed up the rakshasas, then compressed them as if in the palms of her hands while they shrieked, and they were squeezed into beauty much more potent than the bodies they previously inhabited, bound and buried away in precious cages—in Saturn's sapphire earrings.

And then, Wendy exhaled.

EIGHTEEN

Some breaths feel final, and yet breathing continues. This is how that breath, the one that Wendy breathed after she bound the rakshasas in sapphire earrings, had felt. Like a story ending, a song fading out, a riding off into the sunset.

But the sun rose again. Time continued with tomorrow. Why?

Because every story's end is only the hinge, the coattails, and the crossroads of stories without number—each tale a thread of the most wonderful tapestry. Words are ever being written in the world, even if not all of them are recorded in this way. For those who know how to read in the language of living letters and ink that breathes, books are not closed and forgotten—no, they run like rivers, one into another, till the day they all meet in the ocean of the Narrative that connects all stories. *And even that is not the end.* A life so vast as the one Wendy had lived was still only a single river, one which ran, rather beautifully, into the next . . .

Her time with Saturn and as Kanmani became to her like an old dream, a dream in which you may have lived a lifetime—or a thousand lifetimes—and yet, when you awake, find yourself able to live again. Of course, this dream—and the nightmares within it—still made their way into reality, and Wendy was forever changed, but having rubbed shoulders with divinity didn't make doing the dishes or changing diapers or waiting for long, unmet desires hollow; it made them holy.

But this afterlife was not heaven—not yet. There were still delays, disappointment, and other devils to be destroyed. The difference was, Wendy knew how to find delight in such things. The weight of waiting, which had been so heavy, became so light to her. She did her best to share this load with her family too.

Some of the Muthus came around while others denied the divine encounter altogether. The ring, the rakshasas, Saturn—it was an unhealed wound they wrapped and hid, a truth they buried in the dark wells within. They scoffed and left the room when it was mentioned—when he was mentioned. And of course, those who denied the truth, denied Wendy, hated her even more than before.

Meena was of the sort. She never verbally blamed Wendy or Saturn for her blindness, but her heart stored up endless words against them, and her bitterness came out in a disdain for her daughter-in-law and all spiritual things. She became the fiercest materialist. Her vision never returned to her, but it was the blindness of her heart that kept her from seeing the truth. She began making up stories. How she fell and hit her head, causing her blindness, and how her cruel family played jokes on her about it! This is what the truth was to her: jokes. They teased her about gods and demons, claiming to have seen many things, and it was all a ruse to torment her in her condition.

It was a startling story the first time she said it. Did she, in truth, hit her head? Did she forget all that she *had* seen? How could she not remember the sound of his voice? The sound of the rakshasas screaming and Kanmani saving them?

And how did she explain her husband's death? *A heart attack,* conveniently the same day she hit her head. Meena held fast to her lies, and there was no use trying to convince her of the truth, for she knew the truth and chose not to believe it. How can the truth take root in a heart-soil tilled with lies?

Meena was given a cane and a dark pair of sunglasses that never came off. She cemented herself as the grump of the family, sitting in the corner chewing her lip, mumbling to herself endless complaints about her relatives. In time, her lip became so battered that it began to split and sag, and it appeared she had a forever frown—which was certainly true, in the deepest sense.

Vik was given a cane too—Saraswathi's peacock cane, in fact. It took nearly three months for his broken legs to heal, and even then, they did not heal fully. He rode in a wheelchair for those three months and took the next three learning to hobble with support. He retained a heavy limp all his days, a potent reminder of his first love. Yes—even before the potion had been ingested, Vik really did fall in love with Rini, the demoness. And because of this, his love life was never the same but not hopeless. The Muthus hired a full-time nurse to care for his recovery, assisting him with physical therapy and pushing him around in the wheelchair. She was thirty, a few years older than Vik, with a modest, girl-next-door smile. She was shy and sweet, and Vik's broken heart seemed to be getting stitched back together with every passing moment he spent with her. They were married within a year.

There were many attempts to help Saraswathi recover, but the injuries she sustained in her old age rendered her immobile. Ironically, having to be fed and bathed, pushed around in a wheelchair, softened her heart toward her family. She was forcibly made bare in this way, and it exposed her heart, making her tender. She was even gentle and generous toward Meena, giving her the thing she longed for most—too bad Meena had hardened her heart so that even her greatest desire, when met, greeted her cooly.

But Saraswathi was getting warmer and warmer by the day—even if she didn't have many left. She lived long enough to attend Vik's wedding, and she died while they were on their honeymoon. It was a sad day when Paatti passed on. But her final months had more of an impact on her and the Muthus than all the years before. The wheelchair in which she was pushed around had been custom-made in India and shipped over. The wheels were made of metals, but the rest was a smooth and handcrafted wood that intricately wove together to form the eyes, feathers, and—on the back—head of a peacock. So, in the end, Wendy's vision came to life: Paatti on a peacock.

The thread of humor really is sewn into the fabric of the world.

In one of Saraswathi's last moments with Wendy and Kesh, Wendy told her about the joke and how it had come true, and they had all shared a hard and heavy laugh.

Everyone in the family, especially the immediate family, became closer than ever, but the closest of all were Wendy and Jothi. Call it a big sister or a mother figure, Wendy was the person she called for advice, to chat, in heartbreak. They even vaped together occasionally—on *special* occasions. After these events, Jothi became heavily interested in ethics, and with a six-inch scar across her face from being knocked with a rock, she became—if there was any doubt before—a certifiable badass. She went on to earn multiple degrees in philosophy and authored a number of widely respected best-selling books. But like every brilliant mind whose heart still needs a home, Jothi found this in Wendy. It was often on holidays that they would get caught up in some ethical conundrum or psychological paradox, debating and discussing—amicably—for hours. It was no secret that Wendy was the reason Jothi never really left home but remained a loyal member and attended every future Kudumba Pandigai.

The rest of the Muthus were a mixed bag. And the bag was always getting shuffled around. There were the relatives that idolized Wendy, remembering her as Kanmani, and could never quite interact with her normally. There were the relatives that were profoundly impacted, socially and spiritually, by these events; these were the folks that bonded most closely with the immediate family.

There were also the materialist deniers—like Meena.

And lastly, there were the Muthus who found new gods to worship. They begged Wendy for her earrings and searched for them for years. Even though they had been ordered to close their eyes when Kanmani bound the rakshasas, many peeked. It was common for relatives to disappear on holidays for long stretches, and Wendy knew they were out hunting. Digging in drawers, peeking in vents—things were always missing and left out of place.

Soon enough, Saturn's arrows, which came free from the earth when the rakshasas were imprisoned, became new idols to them— objects of their affection and prayers. They rubbed them and whispered requests for boons. Wendy would've hidden the arrows somewhere far away, but Saturn had commanded her to leave them be.

It was not so with the earrings.

He did not speak of the earrings.

Wendy, many times, almost cast them into the ocean, but what if someone found them? What if they were plucked up by the wrong hands? *What if she needed them?* Wendy often wondered why Saturn had had her cast Maya and Rini into the gems. Why not destroy them? Why not take them away?

She never did understand.

They were a secret power that weighed heavily on her. She wore them a few times, and it felt like her ears were sagging. Her heart was sagging. She wondered how Saraswathi—and all those before her—had carried such weight. It was no wonder she had been hard-hearted. It takes a hard heart to carry such potent power.

Wendy did not like the way they made her feel. She buried them in the construction site of the Laguna Beach mansion once, where Real Maya and Real Rini had been buried. But when Saraswathi's life seemed to be fading, Wendy retrieved them. Thankfully the site had still not been finished yet. She dug them up and requested boons of healing for her grandmother-in-law. She took the earrings with her that day and hid them somewhere else. It was like this sometimes, when there seemed no other recourse, no way to save her from trouble or worry, that Wendy went and summoned one of the demons.

She would ask for a boon. Sometimes it seemed her request was blessed, others not. Wendy kept removing them and hiding them so much that one day, when she had wanted to find them, they were missing.

Maybe some relative had finally found them.

Maybe she had simply forgotten where she put them last.

Maybe Saturn himself, to keep her from temptation, had stolen them away.

Wendy did not know.

But it was better this way. It was a relief, actually. Deep down, she had longed for them to disappear—to vanish completely. It was always rushing that had led her to the gems, and because of this, it felt like betraying Saturn. No, he had never explicitly told her *not* to use them, but when she felt closest to him, in her heart, she knew . . . it was not the way he works.

She confessed this to him, eventually, and it only brought them closer. Maybe the earrings had been a test of sorts—and she had failed, multiple times. But even in her failings, she was brought closer to Saturn, and in turn, closer to her family.

How upside down!

How ironic!

What a joke.

Wendy and Saturn continued to talk often, to laugh often. It was much easier asking for his blessing, much lighter asking boons from him directly. Even if his answer was in delay, even if he spoke in whispers or in the wind, his favor was so much more beautiful than any sapphire had ever been. Every pain was full of promise, and every worry, a wonderful work. His way of waiting was the quickest way to the answers to the questions she should've been asking all along.

EPILOGUE

I t could've been any day when Wendy turned down the aisle, the wheels of the grocery cart squeak-squeak-squeaking, the floor sticky from some spilled liquid—stick-stick-sticking to the bottom of her shoe . . . and it was just some day, maybe Monday, maybe Sunday—didn't matter—because it was a day like any other, a day where her heart beat, singing its song, a day with events to cry and laugh at, touched by beauty and pain, a day where she had to wait—in line, in traffic, for unwanted emotions to dissipate—a day where she had to locate all the groceries on her list, including the jaggery . . . for the semiya payasam, which she had just made two days ago, and yet, they begged her to make again.

No one in the family could make it like Wendy. Nobody got close to making Saraswathi's recipe right. Only her. But it wasn't just at Muthu family gatherings that she had to make it, it was the requested dessert at home, too, and she was making it about once a week now.

Apparently twice a week, this week.

But she loved it. She loved to make it for them—Kesh and Jayakumar.

Here they came now, round the corner. Wendy heard them laughing before she saw them. The six-year-old boy came flying first, tripping over himself and falling onto his head and knees, and he slid right onto the sticky substance on the floor. But he didn't seem to care, this little one—little Jayakumar.

He just burst out laughing!

Wendy tossed the jaggery into the cart and watched him with a smile—her eldest son, the one they adopted from India. It was love at first sight, but even before they met him, they knew. When Wendy and Kesh had first read his name, they knew he was the one.

And here came Appa!

Kesh flew around the corner, chasing the boy, and completely wiped out! Such a harder fall than his son. But he rolled over and cracked up laughing, with spit and dust smeared on his cheek, and both boys looked up at Wendy, who was laughing with them.

And a kick—right on her bladder.

Could it be? Was the baby laughing too?

They were planning to name her Saraswathi, Sara for short. She was a complete surprise. Eight more years of trying with no luck, and suddenly, when they'd expected it least, Wendy became pregnant. Oh, she was going to be the most loved little girl! They could not wait to meet her, and it seemed, she could not wait to meet them . . . *to laugh with them.*

Wendy put her hand on her belly and felt another kick.

It was as if time slowed in this moment—in moments like these.

Wendy's eyes caught Kesh's eyes, while Jayakumar fell onto his father's chest, all of them with ear-to-ear smiles and residual laughs, looking like fools in the grocery store aisle, but she didn't mind any judgmental glances their way; she didn't even notice them. She was looking with heaven's eyes, now, high into the Branch of all branches. What she saw were hearts like magnets being drawn together by a divine force, souls being bonded to one another, smiles that would last forever, even in old and aching hearts, hearts that sang a song like a symphony—and laughs that got the joke, the cosmic joke in this homely aisle. She saw words being written, smeared ink painting a picture, the thread of all creation making its mark on this moment. She saw the Author, the Artist, her God laughing with them.

ACKNOWLEDGMENTS

Artists struggle to have their heads in the clouds, their feet on the ground, and their hearts somewhere in between. Without those who ground me, I'd have lost my head long ago—and surely wouldn't have had the heart to write a book.

Thank you to . . .

My wise and beautiful wife, who not only tolerates my obsessive passion to create but believes in me. We've gotten to live out every genre together, but life with you is better than fiction.

My son, Silas, you've made me want to write less. I've found something I'm more obsessed with now, and that's you.

My mom, who gave me a love for books and writing them. My dad, who gave me a world of culture and mythology to tell infinite stories from. My grandparents, who love me. And my friends, who have read my stories and prayed for them to come to life.

My editor, Molly Mills; my cover artist, Sober Scorps; my beta readers; and every YouTuber, Reddit user, or content creator that, unknowingly, assisted me with the publishing process. Every writer who writes even when nobody is reading. We write together.

My friend, my king, my savior Jesus Christ. If good artists steal, we must be stolen back by you first, for all the stories are yours. We must learn to read your writing before we can write our own. Show me how to write; let me trace your writing, your hand on mine. I'm only copying you because I want to be like you, Lord. My works are scribbles—I know that—but I scribble for you. Do you like it? I can do it again! Watch—

SCREENPLAYS & TV PILOTS
(By Merlin Senthil, still looking for a home)

CROWN JEWELS
Feature - fantasy, drama

Set in ancient India, a depressed, dying king becomes fascinated with a noble eunuch in his royal court while his heinous nephews fight for his favor to become the crown prince.

GRAND JESTERS
Animated TV Pilot - fantasy, dark comedy

A community of jesters harbor a terrible secret from the cruel creatures that enslave them while searching for the truth about their origins.

SHIFTING SHADOWS
TV Pilot - horror, thriller

A family of herdsmen—with an occult past—call upon uncanny forces when their village is attacked by raiders, only to unleash a greater evil upon themselves.

THE ELDER
TV Pilot - drama, comedy

The everyday struggles of a pastor trying to care for the people in his church after their senior pastor suddenly dies and the church starts falling apart.

POOR RICH

Feature - drama, comedy

An unlikely friendship forms between a wealthy entrepreneur and a homeless man, upending both their lives, for better and worse.

THE GRAND SCHEME

Feature - drama, comedy

After his daughter's marriage falls apart, a grumpy grandfather tries to help his teenage grandson pursue a high school crush, igniting a lost passion for romance in himself along the way.

LIVING ROOM

Feature - psychological thriller, drama

Five roommates, each combating loneliness in their own way, descend into madness while in search for community.

ABOUT THE AUTHOR

Merlin Senthil is a filmmaker and author known for his original fantasy stories, often inspired by Indian folklore, and for being a champion of raw and authentic Christian storytelling. He has penned the words behind countless viral videos and has multiple scripts in various stages of production. He lives in La Mirada, California, with his wife and son.

www.ingramcontent.com/pod-product-compliance
Lightning Source LLC
Chambersburg PA
CBHW031147160726
47991CB00004B/1577